# CRAVING

## MIA CASE FILES 3

KC BURN

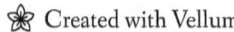 Created with Vellum

# ONE

*Wrong. So terribly wrong.*

Agent Oliver Cardoso scrambled up the hillside, unable to tell if the curses filling his mouth were silent or shouted. He couldn't hear fuck-all over the ringing in his ears. The concussive blast of the sonic charges had closed the portal—he hoped—but these new charges were a hell of a lot less subtle than the usual ones. Out here in the middle of nowhere, if agents didn't die at the hands of insane yeti, and their own tools didn't kill them, they could make allowances for the unexpected. But there was no way they could utilize these fucking devices anywhere near an urban center. Not if they wanted the Metaphysical Investigative Agency to remain a secret organization. These charges would crumble foundations and shatter glass. Change wasn't always progress.

Another glance over his shoulder verified his partner, Carmichael, clawing his way up the same hillside, blond hair as tufted and messy as the short cut could get. Streaks of dirt and blood colored his face, and he shook his head as though the simple movement would cause the stuffing in his ears to fall out.

If there were any chance Carmichael hadn't been deafened too,

Oliver would have told him not to bother. Only time could mitigate the concussive effects of these goddamned prototype charges. Maybe.

The blast reminded him with painful clarity of his biggest clusterfuck, over seven years ago, when he and his then partner were both relatively new to the agency. MIA had only existed for a few years prior to Oliver joining. Even now, there were so few concrete facts. Back when Oliver started, they knew even less.

A low rumble, felt in his feet rather than heard, sent an icy chill through his gut. He paused and glanced back at Carmichael again. Carmichael's widened blue eyes reflected horror, and as one, they both looked up at the distant, overhanging shelf of snow, high on the mountain's peak.

"Run," Oliver screamed, unable to resist the instinct.

They had mere minutes, if that, to crest the valley's ridge before the avalanche was upon them. If they could make it over the rise... well, they wouldn't be safe, but most of the crushing snow should funnel along the anciently carved glacier's path.

In desperation, they clawed their way toward the equivalent of high ground in a flood. If the portal had been any farther west, they'd have been in the direct path and wouldn't have a chance at all.

With their remaining strength, they clambered over the top and kept going along the ridge. The more distance they put between them and the flow site, the better.

The thunder of snow flowing past like crazed river rapids penetrated the auditory blankness caused by the sonic charges. As tempting as it was to look back at the furious spectacle, Oliver refrained. They only had a couple of hours of daylight left, and he was sure as shit not camping out again. Especially in this wilderness where they didn't do controlled avalanches and the power of this slide could easily set off another at any moment.

They kept pushing forward, the swirl of snow from the avalanche creating near white out conditions while ice pellets whipped at their cheeks but stopping wasn't an option. Oliver's breath came harsh and heavy, each exhale burning his lungs and each inhale freezing the hairs in his nostrils. Every step was a struggle in the knee-high drifts.

They'd prepared as best they could for the snow and cold, but much of their equipment had been lost escaping from a last ditch yeti ambush. The portal was closed, though, and the yeti infection solved. As long as they didn't die out here, the mission could be classed as success.

A COUPLE OF HOURS LATER, the tiny ski resort came into view. The setting sun lit it up in fiery orange hues and some of the tension keeping Oliver's shoulders knotted released. The slow return of his hearing as they trekked was also a relief, but he didn't have the energy to spare for conversation. He liked to assume Carmichael didn't either, but his partner was over ten years younger and fitter, despite Oliver's regular workouts.

Carmichael trailed him back to their room, silent, until they were alone.

Oliver turned and faced the man he'd brought into MIA almost three years earlier. Strangely, despite his taciturn and occasionally sullen demeanor, Carmichael made one of the best partners he'd ever had.

"Are you hurt? Can you hear okay?" Oliver let his gaze rove over Carmichael, checking for injuries and bleeding. If anything was wrong with Carmichael's ears, they were finding a hospital tonight. He wasn't risking another incident like his first near fatality in the field.

Their partnership had become even stronger after Carmichael settled into a serious relationship with Adam, whom they'd saved from a pack of Umbrae-infected werewolves.

Prior to Adam's appearance, Oliver had developed a tiny crush on his partner, despite not knowing if Carmichael swung his way. Fortunately, sanity had reasserted itself before he'd made a fool of himself, because he had firsthand, painful knowledge that working agency partnerships and sexual relationships didn't mix. At least, not for Oliver. Somehow, Carmichael and Adam made it work, and Oliver was happy for them, even when he envied what they'd found.

No one would ever know how Carmichael's expression—shy yet smug—when he spoke of Adam sent a shaft of envy through Oliver every time. He'd been keeping people at an emotional distance for so long, there was no one to know, no one to confide those feelings in. But he longed for a deep connection with someone. Maybe not a lover—he wasn't prepared for that level of vulnerability but he could admit he was fucking lonely sometimes. Carmichael was the closest he had to a friend these days, which made him dear in ways Oliver had never expected, and illustrated that Oliver needed to take more chances, open himself up more. Fear of getting hurt was a powerful force.

"What the fuck was that?" Carmichael's face flushed with his fury. But his volume was normal—for Carmichael—and even though he hadn't answered Oliver's question, at least Oliver knew his partner's hearing was fine. He continued to inspect Carmichael, sheer force of will keeping himself from lightly running his hands over the man's limbs, checking for further injury.

"Is *your* hearing okay?" Carmichael asked, his tone a mixture of unwilling concern and sarcasm. "Seriously, what the fuck was that?"

"Avalanche." Oliver peeled off his state-of-the-art ski jacket and threw it at the closed door. Carmichael raised an eyebrow but didn't say a word about the uncharacteristic emotional gesture. The jacket and ski pants worked perfectly fine, but fear had frozen Oliver down to the bone. Safe in his room, anger began to thaw him.

"Thanks, Cardoso. Gee, I never would have fucking figured that out for myself." Carmichael's eyes flashed, and his hands clenched into fists. "I know you're the expert, but do you think it was wise to bring the extra-noisy sonic charges with us? We set off a goddamned avalanche."

Oliver allowed himself a few calming breaths. Getting angry wouldn't change anything but his blood pressure, no matter how much he wanted to punch a fist through the wall. "I know. Believe me, I'm going to have words with the research and development department about this."

Carmichael began stripping off his outer layer, and instead of admiring the view like a lecherous old man, Oliver focused on getting out of his ski pants. For the most part, Oliver wasn't ashamed by his appreciation of the fine physical specimen that was Carmichael. After all, he'd never make a move on someone in a committed relationship. The only problem was his partner's resemblance to a former partner. And despite all the mistakes he'd made back then, sometimes Carmichael dredged up old feelings and made him wonder "what if?"

"That's all you have to say? Do we even know if we killed any innocents?"

Unlikely. Any dangerous overhang with innocents in the line of fire would have been subject to controlled slides. "I'll have the agency look into it. You know that's always a risk, but look at the bright side—the cleanup crew shouldn't have any psychotic yeti to worry about." Yeti weren't all that different from werewolves, aside from their penchant for cold, snow, and high altitude.

Carmichael grunted.

"Are you sure you're okay?" Oliver would do more than raise a stink with the head of R&D if Carmichael was injured beyond the shallow yeti claw marks they both sported.

"Bruised only. I got hit in the back by a couple of flying rocks."

"Broken ribs? Bruised kidneys? Should we get to a hospital?" Their extraction and cleanup crew would undoubtedly be delayed by both weather and the avalanche. If needed, he'd get Carmichael standard medical attention and lie through his teeth about the reason for the claw marks.

"Nah. Don't worry. Nothing to get Adam pissed at you for breaking me."

There it went. That fucking look. The one that told anyone with eyes how in love Carmichael was with Adam, gutting Oliver every time he saw it. Once upon a time, he thought he'd had the same thing.

"Good, good." Oliver stripped off the heavy black sweater he'd worn under the ski suit and hurled it at the door, too. Yes, they'd prevailed, but he was still fucking pissed at how close they'd come to getting killed. "Let me order something hot from room service."

Carmichael stepped over his pile of wet, snowy clothes and into the bathroom. Oliver reached for the phone, ignoring the muscle screaming in his back at the stretch, to order coffee and hot chocolate as well as a couple of burgers. Must have pulled something in their mad dash to escape the barrage of snow.

If he had his own Adam or Carmichael, he'd have someone to lovingly massage it. But he'd realized long ago there was no point in trying to find a relationship like that. Carmichael was the closest he'd come in a very long time, without the sexual element, of course. His friendship was important to Oliver. But a lover? Nope, not in the cards. There were too many lies he'd have to tell a civilian, and even if he reconsidered his stance on getting involved with another agency operative, trolling the office for dates sounded like the worst hell imaginable.

"Holy shit, Oliver!"

Oliver hung up the phone and turned back to Carmichael, who stood in the bathroom doorway. "What?"

The red flush of Carmichael's anger had completely vanished. "Get the fuck in here before you bleed all over everything," he commanded.

"Bleed?" Oliver shifted his shoulder experimentally, and the pain he'd assumed was a pulled muscle took on the characteristic of a fiery stripe along his back.

"Jesus, just get in here."

A wave of dizziness struck, and he became aware of the sluggish drip of warm blood down his back. How the hell hadn't he noticed this when he took off his coat and sweater? They had to be sliced to ribbons.

Carmichael ran hot water in the sink and opened up one of their first-aid kits. "Here, lean over. Rest your hands on the sink while I clean this."

Oliver obeyed, grateful for the support. "How bad is it?" For it to still be bleeding after a couple of hours... Shit, he might need stitches, and a lot of them.

"Not sure. Probably started to scab over on the way here and stuck to your sweater. Now hold still while I clean this out."

The gentle touches of Carmichael's work-calloused hands gave Oliver shivers. He hoped Carmichael would misattribute them to chills from blood loss and adrenaline withdrawal. Even though he no longer thought of Carmichael as a potential lover, it had been a long time since he'd been touched by anyone. A damn long time. Maybe he should make more of an effort to find a one-night stand.

He grunted and bit his lip as Carmichael proceeded to pour alcohol over his wound to sterilize it. That exquisite moment of burn when a cock pushed slowly in, stretching... well, it wasn't anything like the sting of alcohol in his wound, but the fact he was making comparisons to sex while trying to keep from screaming convinced him the injury wasn't that serious—and confirmed he'd been celibate too long.

Too many things about this mission brought the bittersweet memories of another blond from years ago to the surface, memories that he was normally able to keep suppressed as nothing more than a nagging ache over the relationship he'd fucked up royally.

A sharp knock on the door gave him a reprieve as Carmichael went to let room service in. Hanging his head, Oliver breathed deeply.

"Okay, let's finish this up. That burger looks awesome." Carmichael returned to the bathroom and gave his uninjured shoulder a little slap, the sound exactly like the slap of flesh against flesh during vigorous fuck-ing. Oliver valiantly held back a groan. Dammit. Been a long time since he'd had such unruly thoughts. But it had also been a long time since he'd had some unruly fucking. He'd have to hit a club when he got home.

"I don't know what did this, but the cut seems clean, and it's not jagged. I've done what I can but if we're not expecting back up soon, we need to get you stitched up somewhere."

The only thing Oliver could recall was a short moment when his forward movement, away from the tidal wave of ice and snow, had been halted.

"I'm not sure what happened. Perhaps a bit of stray barbed wire or the remnants of a yeti trap." Before the residents of the tiny mountain village had been turned into yeti by the infection of the Umbrae through the portal, they were experienced mountaineers and trackers. They were plenty capable of setting traps for unwary humans.

Carmichael gave him another slap—bastard—and washed his hands. "All done. Let's get some of that hot chocolate into you. You can use the sugar."

He must look worse than he felt, because Carmichael hadn't rolled his eyes when he mentioned hot chocolate.

Oliver dropped down on the toilet seat to rest a moment, craving the small slice of solitude.

Up on the mountainside, the eerie similarity between this mission and that first truly botched mission seven years ago—involving improperly set sonic charges—had caused him almost crippling doubt.

He was forty-three, one of the oldest agents still doing fieldwork. He was tired. Tired of the secrets, tired of training green agents, tired of switching partners. He'd already refused his superiors' request—twice—to take on a new recruit instead of Carmichael. The job was all he had in his empty fucking life, so what did it mean when he was too tired to do it?

But the longer he thought about it, his self-confidence slowly reasserted itself. He hadn't fucked up. This time the prototype charges were at fault. Those drones at research and development, all alike with their lab coats and their dismissiveness, were going to hear from him.

# TWO

A blue flicker at the bottom of Brandon Ellison's computer screen drew his attention and raised his heart rate. The notification of an incoming field report was the closest thing to an indulgence he allowed himself. Reading field reports shouldn't be a highlight of his day—he shouldn't even have access to them anymore—but those little blue alerts taunted him like waving candy in front of a toddler.

He let his cursor hover over the icon that would open up the most recent report. Each time, the anticipation curled in his belly, as good as speculating on presents before Christmas. Most current field agents he no longer knew. And for one... the rush of reading was tempered by pain. But he couldn't always stop himself. Those reports were like a drug he knew was bad for him, yet he flung himself into the addiction all the same. Humiliating as his secret was, he couldn't let an old flame sputter out.

A second before he allowed his finger to click, a flurry of email notifications appeared in quick succession, too fast to read the subject lines. Could they wait? Most of his emails these days were filled with bureaucratic minutiae and potluck invitations. An alarming number of potluck invitations. Someone needed to assign these jokers more work. One more thing on his list of changes he intended to make.

Hesitating over the icon, he swore. Instant gratification had fucked up his whole life—he liked to think he'd learned something from that debacle. Anything else could hold off until he'd dealt with his responsibilities. The responsibilities research and development paid him to shoulder.

Sighing, he moved his cursor away from the tempting blue icon, set his data to compile in the background, and pulled up his email program.

After wading past the garbage—the whole team could use a remedial class on informative subject lines—he found a flurry of messages about the prototype sonic charges the team was developing.

*Sonic charges.* He shuddered. Probably nothing more than clashing egos. Those messages could wait. Plenty of time to soothe ruffled feathers, although given the sheer number, especially from Parks and Kwan, he almost expected one or both of them to show up in his office. They'd better not. Nothing worse than being startled by unannounced, unplanned office drop-ins when he couldn't hear people approaching.

He was tempted to delete them all. Then one arrived from his immediate superior, Senior Director Joseph Wong, flagged as important, the subject line of prototype sonic charges preceded by the word URGENT in caps. Fuck. Which one of those high-strung ass kissers went over his head because they couldn't wait an hour or two for a reply?

He opened the message with an irritated click but didn't get a chance to read it before a hand grabbed his monitor and shook it.

Brandon slammed his chair back from his desk and looked up, heart pounding. A large, angry blond man snarled at him over the monitor, but Brandon didn't recognize him, nor could he understand the clipped words shot out through a clenched jaw. As he stared up at the intruder, he assessed further possible responses. Been a long time since he'd had any occasion to dust off his self-defense training. He wasn't even sure if he remembered enough to take such a large man down. He didn't want to summon security, either.

Without his hearing aids, and not expecting any visitors, it took him a bit to focus on listening. Now that he was paying attention, fortunately—or unfortunately—he didn't need any assistance hearing the ferocious man in front of him.

"What the fuck is the matter with you? Don't you fucking test anything around here? We could have fucking been killed!" Each swear word was punctuated by a fist pounding on Brandon's desk, making his office supplies dance.

Okay, he now *heard* the man, but he still needed help understanding him. Brandon stood and faced his accuser, although he had no idea what he was being accused of. If only he hadn't missed the beginning of the conversation, or in this case, harangue. Missing bits happened to him a lot.

The blond's face flushed with anger, and Brandon should have been afraid. But not much scared him anymore, and he wasn't exactly vulnerable, not here in his own office. The swirling hum of indistinct voices filled the room, interfering with the man's voice like a radio dial tuned a tiny bit off. They wouldn't be alone long, and the blond didn't appear to have a weapon—beyond his clenched fists.

"Out." Brandon wasn't going to have a long discussion without his hearing aids in. Reaching for them now would only make him appear vulnerable or as though he were conceding to the stranger's right to a fair hearing without an appointment. "Out, now."

Bright blue eyes widened. Sure, Brandon might not have the same amount of muscles, but he could hold his own. He crossed his arms, and when the guy's eyes narrowed and he loomed over the desk, Brandon figured he'd gotten his message across. Broadcasting his meaning with the fewest number of words was a skill he'd perfected over the years. Usually, though, it resulted in a cowed research attendant fleeing the room. This time it would likely end in security breaking up a brawl, because he wasn't backing down. Not on his own turf.

"I don't think so. Not until you tell me what that fuckup was all about."

What fuckup? Brandon didn't even know this guy.

"Carmichael!" came a roar from the door.

This was Carmichael? Who clearly recognized the reprimand, based on his surly yet sheepish expression.

Brandon trembled at the sound of a voice he'd never forgotten, and he clutched the edge of the desk as he forced himself to look at the door. Oliver flicked a glance his way before returning his attention to Carmichael. The attractive, brusque partner Oliver hadn't traded in once his training was complete. The first partner Oliver had kept for longer than a year, since Brandon. The one Oliver obviously liked.

Breath caught in Brandon's lungs like a fist had clamped around his throat, and he fell back into his office chair, ignored and apparently irrelevant for the time being.

With Carmichael turned away from Brandon, his words to Oliver were indistinct, like a buzzing insect had taken up residence in Brandon's ear, allowing him to only hear one or two words of each growled sentence. Oliver beckoned to Carmichael, and surprisingly, given his stiff, puffed-up presence, he obeyed.

With a few terse, understated gestures, Oliver proceeded to read Carmichael the riot act. Not for a second did Brandon need to hear Oliver to recognize his anger. He'd seen it once or twice before, and he'd never forgotten anything about Oliver.

He stared at the two men—well, one of them, really. Oliver was a little broader in the chest and shoulders than he remembered. Tiny flecks of gray lightened the dark hair at his temples, and minuscule crinkles at the corners of his eyes testified to the seven years' interval since Brandon had seen him last. Other than that, the man hadn't changed a goddamned bit. The dark suit made him look so official, almost menacing, but delicious in a way Brandon hadn't known Oliver was capable of.

One hand on his desk phone, poised to call security as he knew he should, Brandon rubbed the index finger of his other hand along his bottom lip. And stared at the bulge behind Oliver's fly. The memories the sight of that package induced were vivid and arousing. Just another minute. Just another moment to pretend that bulge was for him and not the sexy blond hulk of man beside Oliver. Then he'd call security.

The fly of those pressed navy trousers flexed a tiny bit. Or had he imagined it? Surely Oliver wasn't getting off on reprimanding Carmichael. Or had the tenor of their conversation changed while Brandon had been—oh God—ogling? His gaze flew up, and he caught Oliver staring at him, eyes almost black in their intensity. And Brandon suddenly realized how inviting his current pose must appear. As though he were deliberately enticing Oliver to... How fucking humiliating.

He yanked his finger away from his mouth, where he was practically sucking suggestively on it, and glared at Oliver. Oliver's lips thinned, and if warm, brown eyes could become wintery, then that's what his did as he deliberately turned his attention back to Carmichael. Damn him. Them.

Gritting his teeth, Brandon stabbed the number for security into his phone, annoyed that his shaking fingers made him fuck it up the first time. Before he had a chance to complete the second attempt, three uniformed guards barreled into the room. Their combined voices made it utterly impossible to understand any of them. A faint sheen of sweat broke out on his forehead, the phone's handset still clenched in his grip. Too many people. His breath became shallow and quick, his gaze locked on Oliver, who was trying to placate the guards by showing his identification.

God, not now. Not another goddamned panic attack. Not in front of Oliver and especially not in front of Carmichael, whom Oliver had stepped protectively in front of when the guards showed up. Brandon bit his lip and tried to breathe slowly and deeply.

Greg Wilson squeezed his narrow frame into Brandon's office, making it definitely too crowded, but despite the man's small frame and youthful appearance, he had a surprisingly penetrating voice, one that Brandon could easily hear.

Within moments Greg had quieted everyone, prevented a brawl between the guards and Carmichael, and given Brandon enough time to calm himself. Greg's ability to run interference with just about everyone was the main reason Brandon relied on the man to be his second-in-command.

In the now—presumably—silent room, Brandon stood, drawing all eyes. He licked his lips, concentrating on enunciating his words to ensure they were clear and distinct, giving no hint of his disability—he hoped. "This is unacceptable behavior. If you have concerns, there are appropriate channels. I expect you to use them."

He'd gotten pretty good at reading lips and thought Carmichael mouthed the word prick, but it wasn't loud enough for any response from the men facing him, aside from a sharp elbow jab from Oliver. Brandon frowned, and Carmichael glared back.

How did Oliver handle this surly, angry man all the time? Brandon had to concede the blond was built and gorgeous, but he didn't see Oliver compromising as much as he'd need to in order to keep a relationship on even footing. Nor could he see Oliver taking orders from an operative with so much less experience. Their partnership had to be one long, continuous battle. The Oliver he remembered was an adrenaline junkie, as were many MIA operatives, but he didn't like disharmony.

Oliver wasn't pleased with the dressing-down, but he nodded curtly and wrapped his fingers around Carmichael's bicep to usher him out of Brandon's office. Once the two men were gone, the guards smoothed their prickly plumage and filed out of the room, leaving Greg.

"Everything okay, Brandon?"

Brandon slumped back into his chair and nodded. He didn't trust his voice not to give away how shaken he truly was, and he sure as hell wasn't going to confide in Greg. Not that he had anyone else to confide in, but Greg was a colleague, not a friend or anything more, no matter the broad hints Greg had thrown out.

"Did you want—"

"Nothing. I have work to do." Too curt, perhaps, considering Greg had saved him from having a panic attack in front of his ex-lover, but he wanted to be alone. Even though limited symptom attacks, or LSAs, like this one, were easier to hide and deal with, they left him feeling vulnerable. Figured seeing Oliver would cause one, but it could have been so much worse. No way would Oliver—or anyone—have missed a full-fledged panic attack, adding that extra dose of humiliation to the encounter.

"Have you given any more thought to my request?"

"Having met Carmichael only convinces me he'll be disruptive in the lab. No, you'll have to make do with the few hours you've been granted each month."

Unbelievable. He'd only met Adam, Carmichael's boyfriend, a time or two, but he seemed like a nice young man. How he, or Oliver for that matter, put up with such a loose cannon was beyond Brandon. In fact, encountering Carmichael had shattered some assumptions Brandon had made. Carmichael wasn't Oliver's type. Especially not after he found himself a boyfriend. The Oliver he'd known would never muscle in on a committed relationship.

Over the years, Brandon had told himself he'd been the first in a line of bed partners Oliver had cultivated via agency partnerships. It had helped him justify his own poor decisions. But assuming Oliver had fucked every partner not only didn't jibe with the man who'd once been Brandon's everything, nor did it reflect well on Brandon to think the worst. The problem was that he still couldn't shake the conviction that Oliver hadn't seen him as anything more than a temporary diversion, and for that, he couldn't let Oliver or anyone know how much he still cared.

If he was wrong about all of it? No, he couldn't be. He couldn't deal with the ramifications of an error that colossal.

"But—"

"I'm not having this discussion again. Shut the door behind you." Brandon deliberately looked at his computer, pretending to be engrossed in the screen saver, waiting for Greg to leave. The man would not stop pestering about that damned portal-seeking project of his. Today was not the day.

Greg wasn't pleased at the casual dismissal, but despite a petulant glare, he did as bidden. For a change.

The slam of the heavy wooden door alerted Brandon to Greg's departure, and he scrambled out from behind his desk to lock the door. No way was he dealing with one more person today.

Back at his desk, he didn't even bother unlocking his computer. The emails and field report could wait; his working day was completely shot, and he needed to get out of there. He grabbed his hearing aids from the desk drawer, shed his lab coat, and left as unobtrusively as he could.

OLIVER SAT HEAVILY in the driver's seat and stared up at the fourth floor of the squat office building. He was literally shaking. Anger and shock had combined in some unholy mix, and he grabbed the steering wheel so Carmichael wouldn't notice. He hadn't seen Brandon Ellison for almost seven years, and it hurt every bit as bad as he'd expected.

His partner got into the passenger side and had the good sense not to say a word, but Oliver couldn't contain his fury.

"What the fuck were you thinking? You could have been arrested. Or shot."

Due to the specialized nature of their agency, agents didn't get fired, they got involuntarily separated, which usually meant jail or being institutionalized because secrecy was paramount. Quitting or retirement involved reams and reams of restrictions and paperwork that Oliver assumed he'd never live long enough to see. For most agents, the job was for life. But just because an agent didn't get fired didn't mean there weren't any repercussions for acting like an idiot.

"What the fuck was I thinking? I was thinking that those sonic charges could have killed us, and that's the man who authorized their use on our mission."

Oliver bit into the soft flesh of his cheek to keep from howling out in pain. He was well aware Brandon had authorized their use, and he didn't want to think what that meant. Surely Brandon didn't still hate him that much.

He breathed deeply, waiting until he could speak calmly—more or less.

"Be that as it may, there are official channels, and I've already logged the appropriate paperwork. Most of those R&D folks have no idea what it's like out in the field."

Although Brandon should know better. No matter how much he might not want to remember, it wasn't easy to deliberately forget.

"Shit, you've still got stitches in your back. How can you be so calm?"

"It's all part of the job, and I've had worse injuries." Although it hadn't been good. The bleeding hadn't stopped, and once their backup arrived, he'd ended up with fourteen stitches.

"I wanted to punch that guy."

"Be glad you didn't. Adam wouldn't be pleased with you if you got yourself in that much trouble."

In fact, Oliver wasn't sure how Adam hadn't noticed Carmichael getting ready to do something stupid, like threaten Brandon.

"No, I suppose not. But the bastard didn't seem to care at all." Carmichael slumped in his seat, looking for all the world like a six-foot-tall sulky boy.

"Enough." He wasn't going to talk about Brandon. He couldn't. Brandon was the last person he'd expected to see today. After being released from the hospital and rehab, Brandon had switched to R&D and moved to a satellite office on the other side of the country.

Avoiding him since he'd moved back to take the directorship a month ago had been tricky, but Oliver had managed successfully until today.

A few tense minutes later, Oliver pulled into the parking lot of their own office building. They walked in silence to their shared office, and Oliver was pleased to note his hands had stopped shaking. He still didn't think he could speak civilly to Carmichael, and the man seemed to sense it. Not that Carmichael was chatty anyway. His partner got to work right away, leaving Oliver to pretend he was working in peace.

He'd been right about one thing—Brandon's hair was almost exactly the same color as Carmichael's, even though it wasn't easy to tell with Carmichael's near-military cut. Brandon's, on the other hand, had been wild and ruffled and much longer than Oliver remembered. Looked good. Hot. Brandon's hair wasn't the only thing that was hot. Even the shapeless lab coat couldn't hide the lithe swimmer's build that had fit so well in Oliver's arms and in his bed. He hadn't changed a bit, although he'd been paler than Oliver recalled. The pallor might have been nothing more than the shock of Carmichael storming into his office like an avenging bull.

There'd been a moment when Oliver had caught the man staring at him, finger poised suggestively on that full bottom lip, blue-gray eyes slightly unfocused... Oliver had done a little time-traveling as his cock remembered that look. Maybe Brandon had been remembering the good times too, but it hadn't lasted. Within seconds his expression had become cold, remote, and Oliver's burgeoning erection had wilted under the disdain.

Oliver bit back a groan. It had been over for a long time. He was a fool to pine after someone he couldn't have. For a hot minute after they'd been initially partnered up, he'd thought maybe if Carmichael was gay, he could be interested. But Carmichael never outed himself to Oliver until Adam showed up, and by then, Oliver had long since moved on from potentially romantic to brotherly feelings for his partner. Today, he realized his romantic inklings had been rooted in Carmichael's superficial similarities in appearance to Brandon, and he hated that he'd not been able to root Brandon out of his heart. Stupid.

At his age, finding someone to stave off the loneliness for even a single night was hard enough without his perpetual self-sabotage. But he couldn't blame Brandon. Even if medical technology had advanced enough to reverse the disability they'd been told was permanent—and of which he'd seen no sign—Oliver had nearly killed the man and had rendered him unfit for fieldwork. It was no surprise Brandon still hated him. He hated himself. But he had to get over Brandon. Because that relationship was dead and buried.

Distraction came in the form of a slender, dark-haired man who barreled into their office after fifteen minutes of Oliver staring uselessly at his computer screen. Most times, seeing Adam and Carmichael interact gave Oliver a warm feeling, pleased that the two had found each other, despite the envy he buried deep down. Envy he now easily recognized as envy for what they had together, not any lingering attraction to Carmichael.

This time, though, there were no mixed feelings. No envy. Carmichael wasn't getting out of this altercation unscathed, and Oliver couldn't think of a better reprimand for Carmichael's idiocy. As easygoing as Adam was, most people never realized he had a fero-cious protective streak. Between Adam protecting Carmichael from himself and Oliver lodging a complaint in the approved manner, Carmichael would likely see no more than a few days' suspension, if that. Didn't mean Adam would tear a few well-deserved strips from Carmichael's hide. With Oliver cheering him on.

"Where have you been?" Adam phrased it as a question, but he'd obviously heard about Carmichael's misstep. Gossip traveled fast, even in a secret government agency.

Carmichael flushed, and his mouth opened, then closed. Was he seriously surprised Adam already knew? Unlike Carmichael, Adam talked to *everyone*.

Carmichael rose to his feet but Adam didn't back off one bit. His cheeks were flushed, his eyes narrowed, and Oliver suddenly realized they were going to have the biggest fight they'd maybe ever had in their almost two years together. Right in front of him. *Awkward.*

"See you later," he murmured as he escaped. Carmichael's bass growls and Adam's tenor sniping followed him into the hallway.

He headed to the break room for a cup of coffee, but the problem with being out of his office was that people kept expecting to talk to him. Oliver was hardly in a headspace to interact with them. He spied Cooper walking past, set his untouched coffee on the counter, and practically ran to see his friend.

"Hey, man, what's up?"

"Nothing. Why?"

Cooper shook his head. "C'mon. You look rattled. Surely it wasn't Carmichael's little gaffe, was it?"

Oliver lifted a brow. Rattled? His self-control should be better than that. "It was more than a little gaffe."

"Eh, not really. So, he yelled at the head of R&D. You guys were almost killed. I think you're lucky Carmichael didn't deck that son of a bitch."

Huh. Oliver had been upset at the cavalier attitude about using them as test subjects, sure, but he had good reason for his emotions to be all out of whack. Well, perhaps, not good reasons... pathetic reasons, as a matter of fact, but understandable ones. If Cooper thought Carmichael was in the right, maybe Carmichael hadn't over-reacted as much as he'd thought.

"Look, I know you're taking the matter through proper channels, but don't dismiss this. Keep your eyes open."

Keep his eyes open? What the fuck did Coop mean by that?

"I don't think, Br... I mean, Director..." Oliver faltered over the title. Not that Brandon wasn't smart and talented, but Oliver had never expected him to take that direction with his career. He'd loved the rush of fieldwork, the adrenaline, and the hero factor, even if no one knew what they did, how many lives they saved.

Oliver cleared his throat and continued. "I don't think Director Ellison will be so forgiving." Because of him.

"Oh please. R&D is so hot to get their hands on Carmichael, Ellison's not going to take a chance at pissing him off."

Under normal circumstances Oliver would have shut down any hint of the rivalry—estrangement, really—between the field team and the R&D team. It wasn't conducive to success, and Oliver wasn't sure how or when it had happened. It hadn't been like that when Oliver joined the agency. Maybe it was a natural progression of bureaucratic development. After all, the agency had still been so new when Oliver joined, it squeaked around the edges.

He didn't have the energy, the focus, to do this right now. Carmichael hated his time spent with R&D, but if he could help the agency shut down the ever-increasing menace from the Umbrae, it was worthwhile. "I... I..."

Coop gripped his shoulder. "Don't worry. It'll be fine. Hey, come out with me and Frazer, won't you? Dinner, drinks. Something casual at the bar."

"I, uh, thought Frazer was having exams."

Cooper flashed a white smile at him, and envy struck Oliver again. Huh. Definitely the contentment his friends had found that he was envious of, not the men themselves.

"Nope, exams are done, and he's wanting to let off a little steam. And he..." Coop broke off. Oliver wondered if he could take this break in the conversation to escape. He glanced around, but Cooper's fingers tightened almost to the point of pain.

Oliver met his gaze, not expecting the concern he saw in the depths of Coop's eyes.

"Oliver, please, you need to relax a little. Come out with us. Frazer's been asking about you."

"Uh, sure, fine. When?"

"Tomorrow night. Saturday's a great night to let off some steam. Okay?"

Oliver nodded. Anything to get out of here. Anything to distract him from thinking about Brandon. He checked his watch and groaned. Barely noon.

"Meet us at Bar None at six, okay?"

Oliver nodded again, and Coop's brow lifted, displaying his skepticism. "I'll come find you if you don't show. Because I'd rather not disappoint Frazer."

"I'll be there." Oliver pulled out of Coop's space. He needed to get out of there. Otherwise he'd never be able to meet up and be civil when faced with Coop and his boyfriend.

They were as bad as—or worse than—Adam and Carmichael, mostly because Frazer was so young, so sweet, and seemed to think the best of everyone. Considering all the shit he'd gone through at the hands of his brother, a man who'd embraced the infection of the Umbrae enough that he almost killed Frazer—and ended up dying at the hands of Cooper—Frazer's sunny personality was a miracle.

BRANDON SLAMMED INTO HIS APARTMENT, no less frazzled after the thirty-minute drive home. He wasn't quite sure how he'd explain his absence, but Greg would cover for him.

He'd always told himself he was too busy to meet Carmichael, but today's altercation had ripped away the self-deception. He understood Carmichael might be an asset in the fight against—or at least the detection of—the Umbrae. Adam, Carmichael's pleasant boyfriend, worked in the department on occasion, but Brandon didn't know the specifics of their relationship. All he knew for sure was that Carmichael meant something to Oliver, and that was enough to send Brandon running. Seeing them together today, seeing Carmichael's gorgeous brawn, he couldn't discount a more intimate relationship between them than simply partners, even if all signs pointed elsewhere. Which definitely made him a more cynical, less trusting man than he'd realized.

The phone rang, and he leaped for it, a welcome distraction. "Hello?"

"Brandon, dear, I was going to leave a message."

"Uh—" Brandon was interrupted by an uncomfortable screech. This was precisely why he rarely answered his phone. His hearing aids sometimes picked up weird interference. He readjusted his position and changed the volume.

"Really, surely there's something you can do about that."

His mother was another reason why he didn't like answering the phone. Then again, she often called when he was at work, leaving messages. He wasn't the only one practicing avoidance. "Mother. Enough."

"Never mind that. Why are you answering your phone? Don't you have enough work to keep you busy?"

"I'm not working. I'm at home."

"At this time of day? You didn't get fired, did you?"

"Fired? Why would you assume I got fired?" Because this was what he needed today. Exactly what he needed. "I could be sick."

There was a tiny pause. He almost snorted. He wasn't sure why his mother was so convinced he was such a total fuckup, but she always leaped to the worst possible conclusion, no matter what.

"Are you sick? You're almost never sick." Her voice was hesitant, quiet enough that he had to strain to hear her.

Calling in sick conjured up ghosts of his time in the hospital, fraught with the choking sensations of being weak and helpless. It had been years since he'd taken a sick day. Perhaps he couldn't fault his mother—for this. He caved.

"No, Mother. I just forgot something at home." Like his sanity. Or something.

"Oh, well, I was just calling to remind you about tomorrow night."

Right. Thirty-five, single, and the only thing in sight on his social calendar was spending Saturday night at some ridiculous political fundraiser thinly disguised as a celebration at his parents' country club. He had to give it to his mother—exasperation outweighed frazzled.

"I haven't forgotten." If only he could. Socializing with his parents, their friends, and their friends' families tested his patience like little else, and he hadn't grown more patient over the years. "Are you sure I need to be there?"

"Brandon. Of course. What would everyone say?"

Like he cared what anyone said. He'd stopped caring about other people's opinions a long time ago, but his mother... It mattered to her. Attending a small number of events was a small price to pay to be left alone the rest of the time. He'd long ago stopped hoping his parents were interested in him for more than bolstering their appearance as a family. He wasn't even sure if his family had ever been a functional unit in service of anything but his parents' social ambitions.

"I said I'll be there."

"Good. And do try to dress up a little, will you?"

He rolled his eyes. He never did anything right, and that had only gotten worse now that he was... even less perfect than he was before. "Bye, Mother."

He hung up and threw himself into his ratty old recliner. The chair looked like hell, but it cradled him like a lover and was more reliable than one. He rubbed at his ears, then yanked off his hearing aids and tossed them on the end table. The doctor assured him the chafing was psychosomatic, but he hated wearing them and rarely wore them at home.

The television remote sat beside his e-reader. Books, television, and movie streaming had become some of his closest, most alluring companions since his injury, as he had more control over the auditory input than with anything else. He'd started a book on the weekend and needed the escapism reading afforded him. Movies weren't going to cut it, not today. At least the book was a sexless fantasy, not a steamy romance, or he might lose his damned mind.

Sparing a moment's regret for the field report he wouldn't be able to read until the following week, he settled into a world where all problems could be solved by magic and tried to forget the work piling up and the fact that he might get his ass chewed out Monday for taking a last-minute long weekend.

# THREE

Oliver stood in the parking lot of Bar None, staring at the door. Was this a mistake? The suit might make him a little overdressed, but the protective camouflage of his job had spilled out into his personal life long ago. The casual fucks he picked up didn't care one way or the other, and aside from occasional visits with his family, he didn't have much of a life outside work.

Which meant not much to talk about, especially since most of the work conversation would need to be curtailed with Frazer present. That in itself amazed Oliver. Somehow Frazer accepted he'd never be able to know details of Cooper's career, and they still had a solid relationship. A cool breeze ruffled Oliver's hair, and he shook off his reservations. A beer and a burger. That's all. At most an hour, if he hated it.

As soon as he stepped over the threshold, the clatter of cutlery against dinnerware and the cacophony of voices assaulted him. A busy night at Bar None, but then, Saturday night was busy everywhere, as he had occasion to know. His job didn't often allow him the luxury of choosing his days off, and when they fell on a Saturday, he saw to his needs as necessary. Not tonight, however, or at least not here, not yet.

He caught sight of Frazer's light blond hair near the back of the bar and pushed his way through the room, wending around people and tables. Oliver was tall and broad enough that the press of bodies he had to squeeze through made him a little claustrophobic, and his decade working with MIA had fostered a deep mistrust of people. The ease with which Umbrae-infected humans could hide in plain sight, could disguise themselves, depending on which mythological species they developed into, unnerved him in crowds.

Frazer was the first to notice him, and his bright smile had a little more wattage than normal, even for Coop's cheery lover. For a change, though, his expression didn't include the faint whiff of pity—a relief until Oliver noticed the stranger. He glanced at Coop, who shrugged and went back to his beer, while Frazer's smile became a little strained, a little forced. Too late to turn away now.

*One beer, a burger.* The mantra kept him going forward despite his renewed reluctance to engage in socialization.

"You made it!" Even without all the clues he'd gathered so far, Frazer's overly eager and hearty greeting would have put him on alert. Frazer didn't have the guile of an undercover agent—he was up to something. Oliver guessed the stranger at the table was involved.

"Oliver, this is my friend Rob." Frazer confirmed his worst suspicions with words that sounded as though he were presenting a prize steer for auction.

Oliver nodded at Rob, who smiled sweetly. Shit, even Frazer was too young for Oliver, and Rob had to be at least a year or two younger still. What was Frazer thinking?

*One beer, a burger.* He almost snatched at a passing waitress with desperation, but he needed a beer—or three—if he was going to have to make polite conversation with some kid Frazer was trying to set him up with.

He settled into the seat next to Coop, across from Rob.

"Hi, Rob. How do you know Frazer?" Might as well make the best of it, even though getting involved with a friend of a friend wasn't a good idea. He glanced over at Frazer—was he a friend? Yeah, maybe he was. Sure, Oliver had family, but friends? He'd kept everyone at a distance for years, or so he'd thought. If Frazer was trying to set him up, maybe he wasn't as isolated and alone as he'd thought.

He gave Frazer a warm smile, hoping he made his appreciation of the gesture clear, even though there was no way he was getting involved with anyone, especially not this kid, no matter how much he looked like a cross between a farm hand and a surfer, with enough highlights in his light brown hair to fit Oliver's preference for blonds.

ONE BEER and a burger somehow became nachos, four beers, a burger, and shared chocolate flan that was almost as good as his mother's. Rob might be young, but he was witty and smart. Coop had long since lost the thread of the conversation and concentrated instead on teasing Frazer. To be fair, Oliver hadn't completely followed the whole discussion himself. Rob's interests lay mostly in research, neurology specifically, and once he got started, Oliver only understood a fraction of the terminology. He didn't have an advanced degree in anything scientific. All his educational background related to accounting, but he found Rob's enthusiasm fascinating and charming. The fact that Rob didn't seem to require much input from him was a relief.

Rob gave him a smile with a lot of heat as the waitress placed the check on the table. Although Rob seemed oddly shy of putting a specific invitation into words—considering how many he'd spoken all night—he was a sure thing. Oliver wouldn't have to detour past one of the dives he visited when he needed companionship of the dick-meets-dick sort. Rob might look like his usual pickup, but Oliver couldn't treat him like a nameless sex toy. Not one of Frazer's friends.

"It just feels good, you know, helping people, even if they don't know it." Rob picked up the thread of their conversation, the invitation in his eyes flashing like a neon sign.

His words were like a slap in the face and a punch in the gut all at once. The overhead lights took on a bright sparkle, and the noise of the restaurant rose in an indistinct swell as Oliver tried to breathe. "Excuse me," he muttered and fled toward the restrooms. He didn't go in but tucked himself in the cubby for ghosts of pay phones past.

Facing away from the bustle of the restaurant, he leaned against the wall and tried to regain his equilibrium. Tried not to remember Brandon uttering those same words the day they'd first met nine years ago.

The mission should have been easy. A single vampire shouldn't have caused them too much trouble, at least not in Oliver's limited experience at that time, and a great introduction for a brand new agent like Brandon Ellison.

But Oliver should have known better the moment he'd been struck speechless. Under normal circumstances, he didn't waste words, which probably explained why the director had continued with the mission briefing after introducing Oliver to Brandon, his new partner. Kyle Bennett, Oliver's partner before his promotion to director over the field agents, hadn't noticed Oliver couldn't speak, couldn't keep his eyes off the blond man. For all that Brandon's hair had been firmly controlled and he'd been dressed like a chairman of the board, Oliver couldn't help but imagine him on the beach in a pair of board shorts, surfboard tucked under an arm, sunlight glinting off tousled blond hair, sun-browned toes digging into the sand.

When the image morphed into coaxing that surfer boy onto his back on the sand and pulling the shorts down, easing the waistband over a cock hard and swollen for him, begging for Oliver's mouth, he coughed and tucked his chair farther under the conference table. Kyle continued to speak, unaware that Oliver had missed almost the entire briefing while imagining his new partner naked.

Kyle stood and gathered his folder. "You've got a couple of hours to get acquainted before you'll need to leave, but let's get this Umbrae taken care of before the situation gets worse."

Brandon turned his intent gaze to Oliver, a hint of fear lurking under the eagerness in his eyes. The fear, though, was enough to calm Oliver's lustful thoughts to a mere simmer. He didn't even know if Brandon was into guys, although a large number of agents were.

"It'll be okay, you know. We'll be fine." Oliver hoped to ease Brandon's nervousness, and not only because the fear would make it harder to complete their mission.

"I'm... It's a lot to take in, you know. And this..." Brandon fingered the weapon stowed in a holster so new Oliver could almost hear it mooing.

"It could save your life, you know. You'll get used to it, I promise." As uncomfortable as the weapon made Brandon, Oliver took comfort in the fact that the agency wouldn't have loosed him on the Umbrae without ensuring he could use it.

"I know. I've just never done anything like this before."

Who had? No one was supposed to know about the existence of the Umbrae or the activity of MIA. The current theory was that the portals opened in cycles, with decades or centuries between incursions. MIA had been created after a new upswing in portal activity just a few years ago.

"My parents won't understand."

Whoa. His parents? "Just how old are you?"

Brandon's face lit up in a blush. "Twenty-six."

Huh. Oliver had guessed right, and only eight years younger than he was, but the gap suddenly seemed a lot bigger.

"And your parents won't understand...what?"

"Just, well, keeping what I do a secret, dropping out of school, it'll be a lot for them to take in."

"Dropping out of school?"

"Yes. I'm supposed to be a surgeon, although my mother would have been okay if I'd picked lawyer. It's a lot of school, but Director Bennett said they'd arrange for me to finish out my classes, so I can go back or transfer the credits later if I want. My mother still won't understand."

"Tell her you're taking a sabbatical or something."

The rueful grin told Oliver that wouldn't go down well either.

"If there's anything I can help with, let me know." Oliver understood trying to please one's parents, but he was lucky that being happy with his own choices pleased his mother better than trying to mold himself into whatever he perceived her expectations to be.

Brandon laughed. "Can you make me not gay? That's already made me a disappointment. This will just be rubbing salt in the wound."

A tightness around those full pink lips stopped Oliver from replying. Brandon wasn't as okay with that as he pretended.

"Hey, most of us are family here. You'll get along fine."

Brandon nodded. A shadow fell over his face, and he touched his gun again, almost absently. "You ever have to kill anyone?"

Would telling the truth be the right move here? Oliver had been with the agency long enough that he'd started viewing the truth as a tool, to be used sparingly and only if he must. But lying to his partner and lying to civilians to keep everyone safe wasn't the same thing. It couldn't be.

"Yes, I have." He reached over and patted Brandon's shoulder, trying to ignore the temptation to caress.

Brandon glanced away. "Will I?"

Oliver breathed deeply. More truth.

"Yes. You will. But we don't kill unless we have to. Remember, none of these people chose to become possessed by the Umbrae. Becoming vampires and werewolves, committing atrocities—it's not a choice most would make. That doesn't change the fact that we can't let them kill other innocents or us, right?"

Nothing Oliver said would have any effect unless Brandon accepted the truth of his new circumstances. Without responding,

Brandon stood and began pacing. As distracting as his tight little ass was in those tailored, neatly pressed pants, Oliver had to find something else to say. He wanted Brandon to stay, he wanted Brandon to succeed, and he wanted to make this partnership work.

"We're helping people, you know." Oliver stood as well, but he didn't approach the smaller man.

"I could have stood up to her, I suppose. My mom told me I could go to med school or law school. Since I didn't have any idea what I wanted to do with my life, it didn't seem so bad to pick one of her choices." Brandon rubbed his head, mussing his perfectly styled hair, giving Oliver another quick flash of the surfer boy on the beach. But he didn't say a word to interrupt Brandon's musing.

"It's easier to go with what she wants, always has been. But I chose med school because it seemed to have more... potential for doing good."

Brandon looked at him, finally, a haunted expression on his face. "Did Director Bennett tell you how I got recruited?"

Oliver shook his head.

"One of my friends knew a guy who owned a farm just outside of the city who was having a field party. Which is basically where you drive out into this field and drink and fuck and smoke up."

Been a while since he'd been in school, but Oliver hadn't forgotten those types of parties. The appeal of such had faded long ago. Much easier and safer to get laid at a club where everyone was gay.

"Anyway, it was nearly dawn, and most everyone was fucked out, fucked up, or passed out cold."

"What about you?" Oliver wasn't sure which he wanted Brandon to be. Would it be hot or annoying to hear about Brandon hooking up with some faceless guy in a field, out in the open?

The tips of Brandon's ears went red. "Not that it matters, but I was apparently a little too nerdy for the guy I was interested in. There were... a lot of jocks at the party."

Too nerdy? No way. Brandon was smart, but that couldn't

possibly be a turnoff, not with that sleek body hiding under those pressed and starched clothes.

"So, you were fucked up?"

Brandon snorted. "No, not that either. I had a huge exam the next day and couldn't afford to be hungover. I should have driven myself, but my friend swore he'd go when I said. Then he hooked up, and I lost track of him for most of the night. I fell asleep in his car, waiting for him, and woke to screams."

"Oh, I thought you'd got bitten."

Although no one was sure how the first person, or alpha victim, became infected after a portal opened up, Umbrae-infected people, in their altered physiological state, were typically able to infect others through a bite. If the portal was closed within three days, a bitten person recovered fully. Otherwise the infected had about a one-third chance of surviving unscathed. The other two-thirds either died or went terrifyingly insane when their connection to the portal was severed.

For whatever reason, gay men had a better chance of surviving Umbrae infections, and once a person had recovered, they had some immunity to future infections. No guarantees, though.

Brandon frowned. "I did, actually. By the same guy who rejected me, except he was... transformed. Like a highly realistic version of a movie werewolf. It only took me a minute to figure out he'd torn apart half the people at the party. I was getting ready to run when he attacked me. Two men armed to the teeth descended and killed him while he was biting me. I helped them with the injured as best I could until their medical team came in. Director Bennett came with the medical team and explained things to me because I was the only one who hadn't indulged in the vodka they were going to claim had been spiked with psychotropics."

Oliver had had a few of those conversations since he'd joined the agency. They sucked but were necessary. If you couldn't convince the witnesses they'd imagined the whole thing, then you threatened them with ridicule, the specter of insanity, and prison. Most of them went along with the cover story, but Kyle must have seen something worthy in Brandon to actively recruit him.

"What about your friend?"

Sadness and grief didn't suit the surfer-boy illusion, and Oliver barely prevented himself from reaching out to hug Brandon. Touching him at all would be a bad idea.

"Danny? He didn't make it. Will killed him first. I found out later that the destruction of the portal sent Will insane and that the agents hadn't realized they were missing a werewolf from the den. An accident, mostly. This job, even though it's secret, lets me help people. It feels good, helping people, even if they don't know it."

Brandon shook off his melancholy and glanced at his watch. "Well, we still have ninety minutes. What did you do before you were recruited?"

"Nothing special." Oliver slid back into a chair, as did Brandon. "I was a CPA, and I occasionally did a bit of forensic accounting for a lawyer friend of mine."

The unfeigned interest in Brandon's blue-gray eyes made Oliver unwilling to mention that Tyson often thanked him with blowjobs, at least until the lawyer had finally settled down in a committed relationship.

"Methodical, then?"

"I like to think so." He'd been accused of such more than once, and not just in a professional capacity.

A soft, guttural grunt of assent came from Brandon's throat, and then he grinned, a mischievous sort of grin that made Oliver's cock revive, sudden and throbbing.

"This job is a lot more exciting, isn't it?" Brandon wiggled his eyebrows, and for a minute Oliver wondered if he could see through the table.

Oliver grinned back, ignoring the insistent thrum in his groin. Being an agent was more interesting and more fulfilling than he had ever expected. "Yes, it is."

"I thought it must be. It might be sort of... fun. I mean, I'm a secret agent!" This time the delighted laugh was untainted by bitterness, and if it weren't for the haze of lust coloring Oliver's perception, it might be a little terrifying going vampire hunting with someone who thought this job was fun.

Oliver cleared his throat. "Do you, uh, surf, by chance?"

Brandon's gaze became questioning and more knowing than it should be. "No, I don't. Why, are you willing to teach me?"

Oliver's breath faltered as the beach fantasy returned, stronger than ever. Perhaps it was for the best that it was only fantasy. This fascination with Brandon could only cause problems.

"No, I don't know how to surf." Disappointment welled up, strong and bitter, that he'd not have the chance to fulfill part of his fantasy.

"You don't?" Brandon's eyes narrowed as he assessed Oliver almost clinically.

Oliver's cheeks heated, and he wished there was a window to look out of, because he'd revealed far more than was wise. He shoved his chair back and stood, his back to Brandon. Hopefully his maneuver was quick enough to have hidden the still-throbbing bulge behind his fly. "We should maybe get ready to head out."

"We still have at least another hour." Brandon's voice was close, hot breath skating over Oliver's nape.

Dropping his head, he tried to reason with his cock, but with Brandon standing so near, his scent and body heat made the suggestion too tantalizing to resist. With a pained groan, Oliver turned and found Brandon in his arms like magic. Brandon was taller than he'd realized, and his slim form fit itself to Oliver's perfectly. There was no fumbling; their mouths met in a hot, wet kiss like they were destined to be fused at the lips. All of Oliver's objections melted away under the skill of Brandon's tongue, and his cock just got harder.

He spun Brandon and backed him up to the door, aggressively thrusting their groins together. A moment of rubbing against Brandon's hardness had the man moaning softly into Oliver's mouth. As

Oliver wormed his hand between them, aching to touch the hardness teasing his erection, the shrill ring of a telephone beyond the door made him pause. Lifting his head, he opened his eyes. Blue-gray eyes stared back at him, filled with heat. Moist, rosy lips remained slightly parted as Brandon gasped for breath.

"This isn't a good idea," Oliver whispered.

"Yes, it is. Do it," Brandon whispered back, hips thrusting against him, stealing Oliver's reason yet again.

Brandon licked his lips and yanked at Oliver's head. Oliver's objections were drowned by a cock he could almost hear throbbing in anticipation. He acceded to Brandon's insistent hands and dived back into the kiss while he opened their pants and pulled out their cocks so fast it was like he was competing in an Olympic sport. Helped that he usually went commando beneath his jeans, and Brandon's boxers were fairly loose.

The hot, hard flesh met in Oliver's grip, and as he stroked both cocks in his fist, Brandon's tongue thrust into his mouth, fucking it, a sensual parody Oliver would like nothing more than to enact in reality. But he didn't even have a chance to consider it. Brandon pulled his mouth away, and he grunted and shivered while his cock spilled over Oliver's dick and fist. The sudden addition of lubrication and the sight of Brandon's flushed face as he came tipped Oliver over the edge, and he pumped them both through their orgasm.

Oliver slumped against Brandon, forehead pressed against the cool door, without the energy to open his fingers to release their softening cocks. Tiny shivers shook Brandon's frame, and his heaving breaths fluttered Oliver's hair. God, what he wouldn't give for a bed right now.

A thump outside the door startled him, and he sprang away from Brandon. The lazy, sated smile on Brandon's face and the semihard cock, slick and glistening above his open, disheveled chinos made Oliver long to strip him naked and fuck him, but they were—*Jesus*—at work.

A knock at the door had Brandon jumping too, face flaming hotter than Oliver had ever seen anyone's.

"Helo's here early, guys. Get a move on!" a voice shouted through the door.

Panicked, and far too late, Brandon flipped the lock. They held their breath, waiting for the axe to fall, but miraculously no one tried to enter.

Shaking from more than just the aftereffects of a stupendous orgasm, Oliver reached for a box of tissues on the conference table. With a sheepish grin, Brandon joined him, and they cleaned up in silence.

This might have been the riskiest, most impetuous thing he'd ever done, even from someone who fought nightmare monsters for a living, but his brain had been totally melted by Brandon's hotness. If Brandon hadn't come so unexpectedly, Oliver might have taken the chance of fucking him over the table. Their careers might never have survived getting caught. Stupid, utterly stupid.

Once they were both tucked away, he had dared a glance at Brandon. And groaned. Although he'd been incapable of getting hard again so soon, orgasm hadn't lessened his desire a bit. The sweet, seductive smile on Brandon's face had told him they'd be doing that again—a lot.

He hadn't been able to find it in himself to be upset about it.

"Maybe we'll even learn to surf, together," Brandon said.

Maybe. If they could have managed to stop fucking long enough to get away for a vacation—and wasn't that fucked up? He'd known the man an hour and was already contemplating shared vacations.

But they'd never had the chance to learn to surf. Brandon had been serious about finishing his schooling, even though he changed his studies so he wouldn't have to do a residency. Between Brandon's school and his undeniably green status as an agent, they hadn't been sent on many missions and rarely saw each other in between. Oliver spent a lot of his time training other new agents.

Every mission they did share had been filled with fun and sex; most times, the mayhem of the Umbrae spawn didn't have a chance to cast a pall on their activities. Over two years, they'd spent whatever time they could together, getting closer. Brandon was the whole package, smart, sexy and they were incredibly compatible both at work and at play.

Until the day Oliver had fucked up. Irreparably. Brandon had been unable to forgive him. Hell, Oliver still couldn't forgive himself, so why should Brandon? His mistake had cost him the man he'd thought he'd spend the rest of his life with. Time had dulled the pain, but seeing Brandon the previous day had shaken him. Made him wonder if he'd ever be over Brandon. God knew, he'd never sought out another relationship and had even been wary of getting too close to anyone, especially his partners. But he tired of being fucking lonely.

"Hey, Oliver, are you okay?"

Oliver closed his eyes. Why did it have to be Frazer looking for him?

"I'm fine." Go away. Please.

But he didn't. When Oliver opened his eyes, Frazer stood directly in front of him.

"No, you're not." Frazer looked concerned, not judgmental.

"I... I..." What did he say? He wasn't even sure how long he'd hidden there in that dark corner, lost in his memories. Apologizing and leaving was likely the best course of action.

"I'm sorry. I shouldn't have surprised you with Rob. Coop told me it was a bad idea, but..." Frazer laid a hand on his forearm lightly, as though ready to snatch it back if Oliver barked at him. Had he really been so aloof that his closest friend's boyfriend was afraid of him? But not so afraid of him to avoid setting him up.

"Did you really think I'd go for Rob?" Oliver didn't even know why Frazer had bothered, but this was the first time he'd done more than mention the possibility of a setup. Oliver had shut down a few previous attempts, and no one had risked his wrath to do what Frazer had done. He should be angry; he should be yelling. But he was merely weary and confused. And feeling every one of his forty-three years.

"Well, yes. Coop told me you liked the brainy ones. And blond. Rob's a good guy, and he's almost blond. I like him. And he likes talking, so you wouldn't have to."

Oliver chuckled, a rusty sound he barely recognized.

Frazer smiled hesitantly. "You're not mad? I thought things were going well."

Oliver shrugged. Things had been going well, and Frazer had pegged his tastes pretty well, considering they'd come from nothing more than Coop's keen observation—because they sure as shit had never compared notes about what guys made their pants tight.

"Please, can I help? Is there something I can tell Rob?"

God, Coop had really lucked out with this sweet thing. Poor Rob. He must be cursing Frazer for subjecting him to such a crazy evening. "I should apologize."

Frazer shook his head. "He left already. He wanted to come check on you, but I convinced him that if you weren't feeling well, you wouldn't want him to see you at less than your best."

Another chuckle escaped. "You're a good man, Frazer."

"He's interested in seeing you again." This time Frazer's tone was hopeful.

The fact that Rob and the younger version of Brandon were getting tangled in his mind told him this decision shouldn't be made here and now. "I don't know."

"What happened? Was it the beer?"

If only. Oliver opened his mouth to lie about it, but something cracked the seal on his thoughts. "He said something that reminded me of someone else."

"That's it?"

"No. I mean, yes. He reminded me of... someone I loved."

"Loved? I'm so sorry." Frazer's eyes misted up. "What happened?"

"I hurt him, badly. We broke up."

Oliver's curt words clearly confused Frazer. "He's not dead?"

"Dead? No, of course not." It had been close. He'd thought, for several terrible moments, Brandon had died. They were the worst minutes of his life.

"How long ago was this?"

"About seven years or so." He'd forced himself to erase the exact date from his mind, the day Brandon had left the hospital and moved across the country to escape him, but he'd done nothing but bury it under a thin veil.

"Seven years? What the hell? He's not the reason you've never dated, is he?"

"How do you know I've never dated?" Amazingly, the teasing returned more easily than he expected. He'd not allowed himself this level of comfort with many people. Perhaps that had been a mistake. After all, no one could cut him like the loss of Brandon had.

Frazer flushed and became flustered. "Well, Coop said..."

Whether Coop knew the truth of it or not, Oliver hadn't dated. He'd gotten laid when he needed, but one-night stands obtained through bar pickups could hardly be called dating.

"Does this guy know how you feel?"

It still hurt—the sharp edges barely dulled over the years—the moment when Oliver realized Brandon had been serious. That he truly didn't want to see Oliver anymore.

"Yes. But he had a damn good reason for dumping me, and I understand. It's just that... I saw him again, yesterday. And then Rob reminded me of him, just for a moment."

Both of which had clearly rattled him, or he'd never have said so much about Brandon to anyone.

Frazer gave him a quick hug, a surprising comfort since no one besides his mom or his sister had hugged him in a very long time.

When Frazer stepped back, he tilted his head up to look Oliver in the face.

"And there's no way to resolve things?"

Not likely. Brandon still looked so much like the surfer boy he'd loved, maybe even more so with the wild, unkempt sandy-blond hair hanging to his shoulders. For a moment Oliver had thought he'd seen a spark in Brandon's eyes, a familiar spark of lust and longing. The accompanying hint of fear had been unexpected, and Oliver would have done anything to erase it, but seeing Brandon again had been like a body blow. He didn't even know what Brandon feared. Not after so long.

But soon a cold, angry mask had obliterated everything, out of place on that surfer boy's face. Oliver had no choice but to protect Carmichael from any repercussions, even though the shock of seeing Brandon again had made him want to throw up. He'd done the best he could and gotten Carmichael—and himself—the fuck out of Brandon's office.

"Seven years is a long time. Maybe it's time you moved on. Rob likes you, and I think you like him too. I can give you his number if you're interested."

Oliver sighed. Frazer was right. It was a long time to pine after someone, it was a long time to punish himself, and it was a long time to wall himself off from relationships. Problem was, could he change his ways now? Maybe Rob was the answer, although he had a hard time believing Rob would have the same goals and aspirations, being so much younger. Oliver needed to be sure he could give Rob a fair chance, and that meant doing some serious soul-searching. Did he still have feelings for Brandon, or had he merely slipped into a lonely and isolating habit? Until he knew the answer, stringing Rob along was not a good idea.

"Let me think about it."

"That's all I can ask. Are you okay to drive home?"

Seriously, Frazer was the sweetest thing.

"Yes, I'm fine." He wouldn't even stop by the strip, as he'd originally planned. The prospect of nameless sex didn't stir his groin one bit, a glaring signal he needed to get his head on straight.

Frazer squeezed his arm. "C'mon, let's get out of here."

Oliver let himself be led out to the parking lot. Coop gave him a weird look but didn't question his lackluster farewell. He'd better not get called in to work before Monday; his focus would be more fucked up than any other time since Brandon had ceased being his partner.

# FOUR

Brandon ran a finger under his collar. Each minute he wore it, the tie seemed to tighten further. It had been so long since he'd worn a three-piece suit, his only remaining one had practically moldered on the hanger. Somehow his mother had known, since she'd messengered over a brand-new Armani. Tempting though it had been to wear his rattiest jeans—the ones he'd purchased with more reverence than any other piece of clothing, bought for his first field mission as an MIA agent—it wasn't worth it. Tweaking his mother's nose with inappropriate clothing would piss her off more than almost anything. She never yelled, but she sure knew how to express her disappointment with a slight inflection and a twitch of her eyebrows. And the last thing he needed was more recriminations.

Speak of the devil... His mother materialized in front of him, and Brandon shrank back, the wall blocking any retreat. Not that his mother would have let him escape until she was good and ready. He grimaced. It was obvious the suit wasn't enough, because she still wasn't pleased.

"Honestly, Brandon. Couldn't you have cut your hair? You look like a vagrant." She plucked at a lock and tucked it behind his ear. "At least you're wearing your hearing aids. I expect you to mingle tonight, and don't embarrass your father."

Brandon's lip curled. She meant embarrass her. His dad hadn't paid any attention to him as soon as it became clear he had no interest in business or sports.

"Yes, Mother."

"And please don't..." She wiggled her fingers and pursed her lips in a moue that might have been attractive to some when she was twenty but now just made her look like a sour old woman.

"Don't what, Mother?"

She sniffed and turned away, but he knew what she meant: don't be gay. Never mind the fact that he'd slept with at least four guys in this very room, although she didn't know that.

Those previous teenage escapades might embarrass the guys in question, since they were now all stuck in financially or socially advantageous but miserable marriages. Poor bastards. They didn't embarrass him, beyond giving a clear demonstration of his atrocious taste in men either.

He pulled his hair back down over his ear. The one thing he didn't want to advertise to people was the one thing his mother didn't mind—much. The hearing aids were a visible reminder of his disability, which she wasn't thrilled about, but it was the lesser of two evils. God forbid he not hear every inane, self-aggrandizing syllable. She wouldn't want to know that the music provided enough competition to make any conversation difficult, which was exactly why he avoided situations like this. Not the only reason, but the most annoying.

For a heart-stopping second, the back of a tall, dark-haired guy made Brandon think Oliver had shown up. Ridiculous. Aside from the fact that there was zero reason for Oliver to be there, if Brandon was going to imagine Oliver anywhere, it wouldn't be at his parents' ridiculous country club, subjected to the casual prejudice of his parents and their social peers. No. What came to mind was one of his favorite memories, when he allowed himself to think of Oliver at all.

They'd been instantly attracted to each other and, perhaps foolishly, had screwed around in the conference room at MIA headquarters minutes after they'd been introduced. God, that memory was so hot, and it wasn't even the best memory. He had a whole vault to choose from, but his favorite was during his second-to-last mission in the field. Two years as an agent had been the best two years of his life. He loved the action, the sense of doing something useful, where he could quickly and easily see the positive results of his actions. Solving research problems thrilled him, too, but in a more muted way. Didn't sparkle in his blood like champagne.

His last mission had been one of the most difficult. It had taken so long before the agency began sending them on truly dangerous missions, which was mostly his fault. Continuing to go to school had kept his parents from kicking up a fuss about his change of specialty and, more specifically, kept his parents from finding out what extracurricular activities he'd been up to. The agency had been very supportive of his continued schooling and guided him toward courses that would put him into research and development after he ceased fieldwork, which had happened well before he'd anticipated. His schooling slowed his progress as a field agent, but Oliver hadn't given him grief about it. Going up against a nest of zombies, just the two of them, had been heady. Wild. Exciting.

As usual, they hadn't been able to keep their hands off each other.

The agency hadn't required them to share a room. If sufficient rooms were available, the agency would pick up the tab. But they didn't require agents to justify sharing a room either. After their first mission together, it had been obvious a second room would be a complete waste, as they'd slept together every night.

Brandon had never spent the entire night with anyone before Oliver, and waking up with their legs entangled, morning wood driving them to a sleepy replay of the previous night, comforted Brandon like nothing else. Sure, at the beginning his contentment with Oliver had been a little scary. As months wore into years, Oliver had become home, and Brandon had eagerly awaited each new mission. They'd never discussed the exact parameters of their relationship, but Brandon was gearing up to have that talk after his schooling was over for good.

Lying on his side, he'd watched Oliver sleep. The wide expanse of sleep-warmed bronze skin called to his fingers, and soon he'd be unable to resist the siren call. For now, though, he thought he should let Oliver rest. Hell, he shouldn't even be awake, not after their athletics the previous night. But they both knew this would be a short mission, and then he'd be back in classes for another four months.

Zombies didn't have the cunning other Umbrae-created monsters did. He and Oliver had been in town all of one day and by nightfall had identified—within a ninety-percent probability—the location of the portal. Unless they were under duress, agents didn't pull portals down at night. When severed from the portal energy, a third of the Umbrae infected became homicidally crazed—in a much more dangerous, less covert way than previously. Dealing with that fracas would be problematic enough, especially if they'd misidentified any of the infected, without having to do that shit at night. If things went well, they'd be cleared out by noon.

A lock of black hair fell across Oliver's forehead, making his nose twitch. Brandon reached out a hand to brush it away... and that was it. He wasn't able to stop himself. His hand traveled from face to shoulder to belly and then on to Oliver's burgeoning morning erection. Oliver began making the snuffly sounds that heralded his awakening.

Hand wrapped firmly around Oliver's cock, Brandon stroked him awake. God, he loved that moment when Oliver's eyes opened, filled with lust and happiness. Oliver grabbed his face with both hands and brought him in for a volcanic kiss that had Brandon stroking faster and cuddling closer. They fit together so damned well. Oliver had more muscle mass and was broader, but they were about the same height, which meant one could bend the other over just about anything and go to town. In bed like this, Brandon liked that their toes could play with each other as easily as their cocks or hands, no stretching required.

Oliver pulled out of the kiss but didn't let go of Brandon's face.

"Morning." Oliver smiled, and his hips began to move into Brandon's unfailing strokes. He wet his lips and looked over Brandon's shoulder for a moment before meeting Brandon's gaze. His brown eyes, so deep and warm, held an unusual seriousness. "You know you're the only one for me, right?"

The heartfelt words, the soft voice, the tender expression warmed Brandon inside and out, made him giddy, made him want to shout his love for Oliver to the whole world. Instead he tried to put everything he felt into his own eyes.

"For me too."

Oliver smiled back and took possession of his lips. Although very little had been said, Brandon thought their relationship had passed a significant milestone, and he'd never been happier.

The sex that followed was heart-of-the-sun hot, and they set sonic charges at the portal location in record time. Brandon wasn't able to wait, and he teased and taunted Oliver as they made their way to where they suspected the nest of zombies was. He wanted one more time with Oliver before they separated for his return to school again. He wanted to suggest moving in together, but he couldn't guarantee they'd see each other much more than they were, and he was a little afraid of losing himself in Oliver, heedless of any drop in his grades. Instead he made sure Oliver couldn't think of anything but him. Oliver was about to give in to his demands, despite the upcoming slaughter of crazed zombies, and turned to face him. But they were too close, or the charges hadn't been set properly.

The portal blew, Brandon thought his head exploded along with it, and he had no idea who dealt with the zombies or how he'd gotten to the hospital.

He wasn't perfect, never had been, but the resulting loss of hearing, and knowing it would never return, had struck a devastating blow to his sense of self. Waffling between blaming Oliver for his disability and believing he was only sticking around out of guilt and pity, egged on by his mother undermining his confidence under the guise of "comforting" him, Brandon made the disastrous decision to break things off with Oliver.

But the reminders of what might have been were too much. He'd transferred to the research and development department in a satellite office on the West Coast, and there he'd stayed.

It had all gone so badly, and yet he wasn't sure if he even remembered why he blamed Oliver in the first place. Especially since he'd been young, horny, and arrogant as hell. The years he'd spent alone, dwelling on that last mission, had convinced him that if anyone had been at fault, it had been him.

At the time, he'd told himself accidents happened and people got hurt, but that hadn't done anything to ease the seething tangle of emotions that threatened to overwhelm him. Running away hadn't done anything but ensure Oliver stayed out of his life, and destroyed any tenderness Oliver might have once had for him. Once again, his own failings were to blame and he didn't see any way to repair anything. Because seeing Oliver with his new partner told him there weren't any shreds of feeling left on Oliver's side to repair.

Living on the West Coast had at least gotten him out of these ostentatious social occasions his parents were determined to include him in. He sucked in a deep breath while locking those devastating memories back into the vault, then he pushed farther out of the way of the crowd and tucked himself beside one of the many life-sized toy soldiers. The Nutcracker-themed decorations were as lovely, luxurious, and as sterile as every Christmas had been growing up.

He unbuttoned the too-warm jacket and took another sip of wine. The excellent cabernet couldn't drown his bitterness, but perhaps he could he drink enough to make this evening palatable.

Mingle. His stomach roiled at the thought and he shrank back farther against the wall. Too many people here.

When his mother said she wanted him to socialize, she really wanted him to chat up some eligible women and do his best to pretend to be "normal" as she'd said more than once. She'd be thrilled if he could bamboozle some unsuspecting "suitable" woman for long enough to get married.

No matter how many times he told her it wasn't going to happen, she did have ample evidence amongst her peers to believe money could conquer all. She hadn't been able to grasp that he didn't care about the money, whether it be the fortune a wealthy wife would bring or his own promised inheritance. His salary and savings were more than adequate for his needs. An exalted social status held even less interest for him than wealth.

A presence at his shoulder startled him, and he spun, a drop of wine sloshing out of his glass and landing on his cuff.

"Oh, I'm so sorry."

Brandon smiled ruefully and inspected the damage while the stranger flagged down a server for some club soda. The wine had missed his ice-blue shirt entirely, and the damp spot was invisible against the deep black of his suit jacket.

Here he was, mingling against his will.

"It's fine. Don't worry about it." Besides, he'd never wear this damn outfit again if he could avoid it.

"No, no. That's a great suit, and I'd hate to be the one to ruin it." The stranger gave him a bright smile, filled with picture-perfect teeth, courtesy of an expensive orthodontist. The server returned with the club soda, and the stranger stood much closer than necessary to daub ineffectually at his sleeve with a tiny cocktail napkin.

"Because there are much better ways to ruin a good suit." The stranger's grin became predatory, and Brandon frowned.

Had he misunderstood? It happened with disturbing regularity since his accident, if he wasn't paying enough attention.

A thin, perfectly manicured black eyebrow rose as the man flicked his gaze more obviously at Brandon's crotch. Brandon's cheeks flamed as the man's lewd implications registered.

"Um."

"You don't remember me, do you?" The napkin dabbing became

nothing more than a cover for a not so subtle caress, although to the room at large, no one would be able to tell.

Brandon peered more closely at the black-haired man, who wasn't the same one who'd gotten him thinking about Oliver in the first place. This guy was too perfect. If Brandon's mother approved of him being gay, this was the man she'd want him to date. Someone who fit in their orderly, bland country-club existence. He was probably CEO or CFO at some Fortune 500 company, where his daddy was the chairman of the board, and he golfed like it was part of the workday.

But the black hair and the pale blue eyes triggered a faint memory. "Kevin? Kevin Waters?"

"Yes indeed. Been a long time, Brandon. You must be very proud of your father."

His lip curled. Proud? More like indifferent. Tit for tat.

Back when Kevin had bent him over his family's billiards table and taken his virginity, they'd been united in their rebellion against their parents' cold natures and continuous demands for academic excellence. Or so he'd thought. Kevin had been corrupted—or had at least accepted the relentless force of rich parents.

Expressing his disdain would not please his mother, so Brandon merely grunted, hoping the noncommittal noise would be taken for assent.

"How are you doing, Kevin?" Not that he much cared. He hadn't given another thought to Kevin the moment he'd left for college. There hadn't been any... feelings between them.

"Much better now that you're back. Maybe we could meet somewhere, catch up. You know."

Brandon didn't need to hear a word to comprehend he was being propositioned. But the diamond-studded platinum band on Kevin's left ring finger spoke volumes. The icy, anorexic blonde woman weaving through the crowd toward them, gaze tethered to Kevin's back, told even more of the story. Kevin wasn't interested in catching up but hoped Brandon would bend over for him as easy as he'd done back in high school.

"No, I don't think so. I don't—" Brandon broke off. He didn't owe Kevin's very married ass any explanation at all. "Maybe I'll see you around."

Brandon pulled his hand out of Kevin's grip and stalked out of the room. Socializing with a jealous wife was not what he'd signed up for, although he'd have to deal with his mother's wrath later. He couldn't stay here. He didn't belong here, never had. Not that there was anything for him to go home to either. Maybe he needed a pet.

He snagged a cab and gave the driver his office address. His work was the only thing that kept him getting up in the morning. The only place he belonged these days. And if he still longed for those action-filled days out in the field, battling Umbrae, so what? If R&D was the closest he could get, he'd take it.

# FIVE

Oliver strode through the office halls, barely a twinge in his back from his wound, or so he told himself. A simple infection wouldn't stop him. The doctor's visit and the trip to the pharmacy to pick up antibiotics had been executed with military precision, and he'd made it to work only an hour late.

The weekend hadn't been as restful as he'd hoped, what with the unexpected curveballs in the form of Brandon's return and Frazer's setup on his mind. Battling the Umbrae gave his life more than enough unexpected twists. His calm, predictable personal life wasn't exciting, but neither was it upsetting.

Coworkers edged out of his way, heads down as they passed.

Not one person said "Good morning," or looked him in the eye as he made his way to his office. Something wasn't right.

He frowned. Not that he expected everyone to greet him fervently—he'd been too aloof for too many years—but were people actively avoiding him? If there were any repercussions from Carmichael's temper tantrum last week, his bellows would have been audible as soon as Oliver stepped off the elevator. Maybe the Brandon/Rob conundrum had fucked with his mind more than he'd realized.

Oliver turned in to the office he shared with Carmichael and stopped dead. The large, dark-haired man seated behind Carmichael's desk was a stranger.

"Are you lost?" The man directed a vicious glare his way, sparking the recognition Oliver needed. "Detective Goodson? Luis?"

Still scowling, Luis nodded. "It's Agent Goodson now."

Of course, it was. Oliver quickly tabulated how long it had been since the messy vampire case where Goodson had suspected Frazer was a serial killer and attempted to charge him with multiple counts of murder. Goodson had experienced firsthand what an Umbrae-infected person was capable of, and Oliver had expected him to show up on MIA's doorstep sooner or later.

Oliver glanced at Goodson's throat, the scarring clearly visible from where the vampire had attempted to exsanguinate him.

"Good for you. Any complications?" He touched his own throat, and Goodson mimicked the move, scowl deepening.

"No, not really."

Goodson was alive, so he'd gotten off relatively lightly, all things considered.

"Congratulations on your new job." The last word rose in a tiny inflection. Not a question, precisely, but he and Goodson had spoken for no more than thirty minutes, and aside from letting the recruitment department know he was a potential candidate, Oliver had done nothing to prompt Goodson to show up unannounced. He hadn't even told Goodson where his office was, but the man *had* been a homicide detective.

More importantly, where the fuck was Carmichael? He hated people messing with his stuff, and Goodson had already been here long enough to alter Carmichael's desk configuration.

"Thanks."

The silence extended. Oliver shrugged, sat at his desk, and

booted up his computer. The man would be an asset to the agency. Having been a detective for several years, he'd be well used to the investigation, interrogation, and even undercover work most of them had to figure out along the way. Carmichael didn't need Oliver to protect his desk; he'd give Goodson shit when he arrived.

Goodson stared at him, but Oliver refused to look up. He paged through a couple of emails before the nagging curiosity made him look up.

"So... who's your partner?" More importantly, why the hell wasn't Goodson in *that* guy's office, harassing the poor bastard?

The incredulous, disparaging look that said Oliver was the biggest idiot in creation had his stomach twisting.

"No. No, it can't be."

"What the hell is the matter with you? They told me you always take the newbies."

Anger burned white-hot. Not again. Not now. "Who told you that? Never mind. Where's Carmichael?"

Goodson shrugged insolently, like a juvie accused of a crime he'd committed but didn't want to admit to. Yet how would a newbie have had any influence at all in partner assignment?

Oliver pointed a finger at Goodson. "Don't get comfortable."

Quickly skimming the rest of his unread email, he found the pertinent one, read it, then threw his stapler across the room. Kudos to Goodson for not flinching, because they were stuck together until Oliver could fix this mess.

After a few fruitless phone calls to his superiors, during which he studiously ignored Goodson, he concluded he had to bite the fucking bullet and contact his last resort. But what to say?

> *To: Ellison, Brandon <B_Ellison@autopartsandpastries.com>*
>
> *From: Cardoso, Oliver <O_Cardoso@autopartsandpastries.com>*

*Subject: Partner Reassignment*
*Director Ellison,*
*Please return Carmichael to active-duty fieldwork. I*
       *have no interest in breaking in a new partner.*
*Cardoso*

---

BRANDON'S HEAD hit the desk the moment he finished reading that blighted email. Oliver was not happy. Pissed off beyond all recognition might be a more appropriate description. Although they hadn't so much as texted each other since their breakup, Brandon hadn't expected the cold, curt email to slice through him like a sword to the heart. Oliver had signed the request Cardoso, like they were strangers. Brandon had never once called Oliver by his last name like that.

No matter how Oliver hated it, reassigning Carmichael was the only choice Brandon had. After escaping the obnoxious party at the country club, he'd slept in his office Saturday night. His mother would hate the wrinkles he'd put in his Armani.

The first thing he'd done in the eerie quiet of the office on Sunday morning was open the urgent email from Senior Director Wong. It hadn't been especially wise of him to ignore an urgent message from his boss, but there had been extenuating circumstances. Thankfully, the gist of the message had been "deal with your people; I don't want any more emails from them complaining about your lack of responsiveness," without any need for follow up.

The second thing he'd done was open the field report he'd received on Friday. To his horror, it was Oliver's report, detailing a sonic-charge malfunction—which induced a limited symptom attack so bad that Brandon had nearly thrown up. Nausea wasn't one of his usual symptoms, and he hoped this didn't herald a return to the more frequent, more debilitating panic attacks he'd had shortly after his injury. The memories of how sonic charges had changed his life were overwhelming, and he'd shut down the report without reading the rest of it.

All Sunday as he'd worked, the document lurked, pulsating with menace at the corner of his screen. More than once, his cursor had hovered over the file, but each time, his stomach twisted, and he'd moved on to be completely ineffectual at every other task he attempted. His reaction was out of proportion. Sure, he'd supported a number of research avenues providing possible ways to combat the Umbrae beyond the sonic charges. Any director with half a brain would have done the same thing; it didn't have anything to do with his sonic-charge-induced disability.

As the clock had ticked inexorably toward the hour where he'd have to decide if he was sleeping another night in his office, he'd sucked in a breath and clicked on the icon. Skimming the report, he homed in on the reference to the prototype sonic charges. Prototypes that had not been approved for field use. How the hell had Oliver gotten ahold of them?

Brandon had allowed himself a tiny grin. He'd faced down a field report about sonic-charge issues—written by Oliver, no less. Only one LSA. He'd call it a win. The alacrity with which he'd hit the Close button could be forgiven, considering.

As the document flickered out of sight, he'd glimpsed a reference to an injury Oliver had sustained as a result of the uncontrolled sonic discharge.

No sooner had the document closed than Brandon scrambled to open it again. Oliver—and Carmichael—had nearly died. Oliver sugarcoated it, but Brandon recognized his attempts to downplay the incident. Despite the cold, clammy sweat triggered by the vague descriptions, Brandon had forced himself to thoroughly read the entire report. The flurry of frantic emails about the sonic-charge prototypes made sudden, horrible sense, and the sheer number of stitches Oliver had required told more than Oliver's understated, emotionless report writing ever could. Knowing Oliver as he did, the man was probably getting ready to return to work Monday, telling everyone an enormous gash in his back was "tender but not enough to keep him from work." Ass.

After closing the report for good, Brandon approved Greg's request to have Carmichael temporarily reassigned to R&D. Before he left the office for the night, he'd also requested every bit of data on the prototype sonic charges. If he couldn't figure out what had gone wrong, he'd figure out how they'd come to accompany Oliver on his mission.

The email from Oliver hadn't been unexpected, but its brevity and abruptness were surprisingly painful. Brandon dithered over his reply for several moments, then returned an equally gruff and sparse message.

> *To: Cardoso, Oliver <O_Cardoso@autopartsandpastries.com>*
> *From: Ellison, Brandon <B_Ellison@autopartsandpastries.com>*
> *Subject: Re: Partner Reassignment*
> *Agent Cardoso,*
> *I regret to inform you that your request is not possible. Agent Carmichael's presence in my department is vital for our research at this time, or so I have been informed by my assistant. Senior Director Wong has approved the transfer, and the reassignment will continue for as long as I see fit. Do try to make the best of it.*
> *Sincerely,*
> *Director Ellison*

After all, it wouldn't do to let Oliver know he was trying to protect him from reinjury, when Brandon wasn't supposed to know about the injury at all. Sidelining his partner was an easy fix, well within Brandon's purview, and wouldn't raise any eyebrows. With Oliver refusing to switch partners, he'd be effectively out of the game.

Besides, if anyone figured out he still had a soft spot for Oliver, after his injury and the fights and the vicious words they'd exchanged, well, anyone would assume he was a brainless idiot. Or even worse, a pathetic fool incapable of moving on with his life.

The last line of Brandon's email was subtle, but if Oliver hadn't changed too much in the intervening years, it would keep his temper at a slow burn, give him something to stew over besides his enforced inactivity as a desk-bound agent, give him a chance to heal—because Oliver was one of those ridiculous "rub some dirt on it and walk it off" types who rarely wanted to admit to weakness of any sort. Brandon wasn't much better, but he'd learned a lot from the concessions he had to make for his hearing. Or, rather, his loss of hearing.

Parks ran into his office, a large stack of files partially obscuring her slender form. "Here's the last of the files you requested." Usually her tone fell in a register easy for him to hear, but her distress over the sonic charge debacle had her voice squeaking into a higher pitch.

Brandon pointed to another monstrous stack of files. "Leave them there."

"Sir, I'm sorry. I don't—"

He waved her off, uninterested in listening—or trying to listen—to her explanations. Not while she was acting like he was going to order her execution. "Is this the last of it?"

Parks nodded. "Yes, I'm—"

"That's fine. Thank you. Let Greg know I don't want to be disturbed."

She scuttled back out and shut the door behind her while Brandon surveyed the ridiculous number of files. Why the hell weren't these electronic? He'd become very good at sifting through data, but all this paper. What century was this department in? Just because the portals screwed up electronics in the field was no good reason to eschew them here at headquarters.

Presumably, his predecessor had objected to computerization.

Evidence suggested the man had been rather hidebound, and Brandon hoped to modernize some of his strategies and processes. If he could. For obvious reasons, he had to rely on his authority as director rather than gaining compliance from relationship building. Work, friends, lovers—he hadn't had a true relationship since the day he'd told Oliver to leave. Good thing this wasn't a democracy.

Sifting through the paper files wasn't optional. Despite the amount of electronic data related to the sonic charges, but he'd only be able to figure out the whole story with all the information, not just the electronic half. Brandon locked his door and sat at his desk, idly flipping and sorting through the dusty files before digging in deeply. This had the added benefit of enabling him to avoid seeing Oliver, should the man get it into his head to come tear a strip off him for the high-handed way he'd benched him and stolen Carmichael.

No matter what water had passed under their bridge, he didn't want Oliver to get hurt. Not a bit. And if that meant accepting—or avoiding—Oliver's wrath, so be it.

*BASTARD.* Brandon was punishing him. Still. Again. More. How many times could Oliver apologize? He'd apologized until his voice was hoarse. He'd pleaded. Cried, even. None of it had been enough, but with all the years gone by... Oliver's ire fizzled out. As much as he wished Brandon could forgive him, Oliver didn't blame him. Oliver had been the senior agent on that mission, and therefore responsible. Brandon's whole life had changed because of Oliver's carelessness, and if Brandon wanted to take that loss out of Oliver's hide for the rest of their lives, he wouldn't object.

An email popped up detailing warning signs of possible portal activity. He'd come to rely on Carmichael's intuition about which clusters of suspicious circumstances were most likely to be Umbrae related. Guess he'd have to go back to the old-fashioned way.

Oliver sighed and glanced over at Luis. The man glowered at a form in front of him, fingers white-knuckled around a pen. Oliver stifled a chuckle. Unbelievable that anyone could be pricklier and more antagonistic than Carmichael when he'd first been recruited, but somehow Luis managed.

"Take a look at your email. We've been sent a report listing suspicious activity. If we can narrow down some of them as portal related, we can determine where we need to send in a team to search for Umbrae-infected people."

Luis stared at him. "Suspicious activity? Could you *be* any more vague?"

"Just read it over. See if anything leaps out at you. You were a cop —you'll probably be pretty good at noticing which patterns fit normal criminal behavior and which ones might require our specialized attention."

With a barely suppressed eye roll, Luis did as Oliver told him. It wasn't a lie. The agency had customized algorithms to pull out suspicious data, but unless there were actual bodies or other hard evidence, they didn't have the resources to investigate every strange occurrence. Oliver found the computer-generated hot spots to be fairly reliable, especially as social media became more and more pervasive, but it wouldn't hurt Luis to open his perception to the slightly off-kilter world view that made agents successful and kept them alive. If Luis got a grip on what kind of activity could be related to a portal, it was less likely an Umbrae would catch him by surprise.

Oliver wouldn't admit it to anyone, but if he could postpone going out in the field for a couple of days, he'd be grateful. The infection in his back made his temperature fluctuate uncomfortably, and it ached something fierce. A few days where he didn't have to worry about someone inadvertently patting him on the back or risk getting it whacked in a fight was just fine with him. Being beholden to Brandon was something he could do without, but what Brandon didn't know wouldn't hurt him.

.   .   .

LATER THAT MORNING, Adam skidded into Oliver's office but came to an abrupt halt at the sight of Luis two-fingered typing at Carmichael's computer. "Oh. I guess you know already."

Oliver refrained from swearing. It wasn't Goodson's fault, and his transition to a new job would only be harder if Oliver couldn't contain his bitterness. "That I've got a new partner? Yes, I know that already."

Adam swiveled his head between Luis and Oliver, shock pulling his mouth slack.

"What... How could you?" Adam rounded on Oliver, a glare on his face the likes of which Oliver had never seen from him.

"How could I what?"

Luis lifted his gaze from the computer screen, fingers stilling over the keyboard as he observed them.

Adam became aware of the scrutiny at the same time. Instead of answering, he jerked his head toward the hallway. With a sigh, Oliver extricated himself from his chair, stitches pulling painfully, and followed Adam out of the office.

"What the hell is the matter with you?" The extra bite of pain in his back leaked out to an extra bite in his tone.

"Me? You're the one who ditched Carmichael. Where is he, anyway?" Adam did his best to get in Oliver's face, but he was a little too short. However, Adam was fully trained by the agency, and he could be dangerous if he wanted. Most times, his levelheadedness prevailed, but if Carmichael was involved... one couldn't always rely on Adam to remain calm and logical.

"I didn't ditch Carmichael. He was reassigned, temporarily, to R&D."

"Reassigned? Shit. He loves being your partner."

Oliver almost smiled. Trust Adam to tell him something Carmichael would never admit to in a million years.

"I thought it was at your request and the director took advantage to give me the newbie," Oliver said.

Adam spent a portion of his time in R&D, but Oliver didn't know the exact nature of his projects.

"My request? I didn't know anything about it. It must have happened this morning. He's going to hate that like poison. At least I know how to jolly him out of a bad mood." Adam wiggled his dark brows.

The last thing he wanted was to be reminded of a solid relationship, not when Brandon had popped up out of nowhere and stolen his partner, killing Oliver's attempts to remain blissfully ignorant of Brandon's reappearance in his city.

"What did you dash in to see me about?"

"Oh, uh, Goodson. I'd heard he'd joined the agency, and I was coming to congratulate you on picking out another one."

Oliver shrugged and bit back a wince. Picking out potential agents wasn't difficult. Showing an intelligent, reasonably curious person something as unexplainable as the Umbrae guaranteed they'd not quickly forget the experience. Add in a hint of adrenaline junkie and the opportunity for camaraderie with other people who understood what they'd gone through, what they'd seen...

The lure of the agency was more seductive than returning to a sane, boring life. With Goodson it was even easier. As a cop, he had a natural instinct to get the bad guy, along with the added impetus of revenge for his injuries. Based on the timing, Luis had come knocking at the agency doors the second his doctors cleared him for active duty.

"Yes, and here he is."

"This isn't right." Adam stared up at him, confusion and concern warring in his eyes.

Oliver was tempted to shrug again, but his back told him once was more than enough.

"I'm working on getting him reassigned."

Which wasn't a complete lie. Brandon could be made to see reason, maybe. Hell, after a few days of Carmichael's surly "cooperation", Brandon would probably beg Oliver to take him back.

"How can you be so calm about this? A partnership is an important relationship." Anger sparked in Adam's eyes, erasing the softer
emotions from moments ago.

Calm? Oliver wanted to wring Brandon's neck, a desire that had
tripled in intensity since his high-handed email. Once, Brandon
hadn't let his family's wealth and social status give him any airs of
entitlement, but that was clearly one more thing that had changed
since their breakup. Oliver's many years of keeping his emotions carefully under wraps made it second nature to hide everything, and
Adam's response showed how expert Oliver had become.

The problem was, every time he got pissy about Brandon, the
guilt—the sense that he deserved whatever Brandon wanted to dish
out—flooded back. Apparently, it looked an awful lot like calm.

Adam glanced both ways down the hallway, then leaned in to
whisper, "At least tell them you need a break to recuperate.
Carmichael told me about your stitches."

The muscles in Oliver's jaw tightened. He should be pleased
Adam cared enough to worry about him, but he couldn't quell the
irritation at being babied.

"I'm fine. If the agency needs me to seek out the Umbrae, I will
do so."

From Adam's compressed lips, Oliver hadn't managed to hide his
emotions this time. With a sharp nod, Adam turned on his heel and
walked away, his whole frame stiff.

"What's up with him?" Luis asked when Oliver came back in the
office.

"Nothing." Oliver sat, inadvertent contact of his wound against
the chair making him wince.

"You okay?"

"Fine. You find anything?" The last thing he needed was a near
stranger to start coddling him.

Luis cleared his throat and glanced at his screen. "Maybe. I don't
know. Give me some more time."

Oliver twisted his back. Nothing was particularly comfortable, but something about his office chair made everything ache. Or maybe it was the sight of his new partner. Not that there was anything wrong with Luis, but every time he noticed Luis in Carmichael's chair, he'd be reminded of Brandon. This week was going to be sheer hell.

# SIX

Brandon shuffled the stacks of files on his desk and tugged at a stray lock of hair. None of this made sense. In between his myriad other responsibilities, he'd read as many files as he could. He hadn't managed to get through them all yet, but he'd probably seen enough. As he'd believed, the prototype sonic charges were not ready for field use. There was no way he could be expected to know the finer details of all the projects under development, but he'd deliberately ignored this particular project. Someone had taken advantage of his aversion, but why?

Not that it mattered. He'd signed off on it, although he didn't remember doing so. Somehow, he'd allowed a number of dangerous, unstable charges out in the field... with Oliver. If his aversion to sonic charges had made him become careless, that was one thing. He'd resign immediately. But if anything, his personal history meant he'd be more likely to *block* use of sonic charges. Especially ones that hadn't been properly tested. It just didn't compute.

There had been a dark time during his recovery when he'd almost wanted Oliver to be injured as Brandon was, so he'd know. Embarrassing, shameful, and long since passed. But he still hadn't conquered the hurdle of feeling that he wasn't whole, and that short-coming made Brandon uncomfortable interacting with anyone, much less Oliver.

He rubbed his eyes and ran an assessing finger over the couple of days' worth of stubble. Hopefully he hadn't begun to stink yet; it had been a long time since he'd shown this kind of devotion to anything outside one of his own research projects. But his new responsibilities precluded him from doing independent research.

Although he hoped the incident arose as a result of his inatten-tion, he was for damn sure keeping his eyes open for any potential sabotage. Whatever the case, he couldn't—wouldn't—let this happen again.

When it came to Oliver's safety, or any field agent's safety, he had a responsibility to be sure he hadn't missed anything. He stacked the files and tapped out a request to Greg. He needed to take a more hands-on approach to the projects under his care. Getting used to his new role could no longer be an excuse, his hearing could no longer be an excuse. He was not the same man as his predecessor, and it was time the people reporting to him understood that.

BRANDON'S CALENDAR alert flashed on his screen. Tugging his hair firmly over his ears to ensure his hardware was well hidden, he looked up just in time to see Greg walk in his door.

"Director, here are the files you requested."

Greg slung paper folders across Brandon's desk. The messy sprawl hit the stack Brandon had neatened minutes ago, and teetered. Brandon slapped a hand atop the stack to prevent it from spilling to the floor. Greg glared at him, not even a hint of gratitude for providing Carmichael to assist him.

"Thank you, Greg."

Times like this, Brandon wondered why he'd even bothered

applying for this job, although he suspected his experience in the field had given him the edge over the other applicants. Not that he'd ever mentioned his fieldwork to his new subordinates. It had been a long time ago, and he wasn't about to justify his promotion to everyone who reported to him. Greg, and a couple others, resented being passed over, the other researchers hated conforming to the new policies Brandon had implemented, and he hadn't realized how useless he'd feel without having a hands-on presence in research. He spent more time acting as a babysitter than leading a team of prestigious scientists.

"You know I'm not your administrative assistant, right? I have my own duties?"

Brandon resisted the urge to apologize. He could hire an assistant, but there was no way he could hide his hearing loss from a person who spent so much time helping him. Greg might not have been his first choice, but the man did his job well and always enunciated clearly.

Better if Brandon ignored the man's petulance.

"How is your project coming along, now that you've got Carmichael?"

"It's been four whole *days*." The snide tone was impossible to miss, even for Brandon. Greg's nostrils flared, and his jaw tensed like he was biting back words that would get him fired.

Brandon shrugged. "Yes, well—"

Carmichael stomped into Brandon's office, completely dissolving Brandon's train of thought. He curled his fingers around his armrests to keep from standing. Carmichael seemed to take up a lot of real estate in the office, and the temptation to stand and draw his shoulders back was enormous. But if he intended to retain the power here, he couldn't let Carmichael's mere presence intimidate him.

"I don't recall having a meeting scheduled with you."

God, he sounded like a pompous prick, but considering how easy it was to sneak up on him, surprises of any sort were unwelcome. The fact that he had no desire to interact with Carmichael at all, despite the fact that both he and Greg were instrumental to the success of his own little brainchild, didn't—shouldn't—have anything to do with it.

Greg rolled his eyes. "Why don't you ask him how the project is going? Since he's standing right here."

A tiny bubble of mirth formed in Brandon's throat. Four days had been long enough for Greg to realize Carmichael wasn't inclined to be cooperative, no matter how instrumental the man's sensitivity to portal energy was to Greg's pet project. Brandon had figured that out after having had Carmichael in his office for all of four *minutes*, but this arrangement got Oliver out of field assignments until he'd recovered, and gave Brandon some leverage over Greg for having acceded to his request, however much the man might be regretting it now.

"Very well. Have a seat." Brandon gestured at the chairs that rarely got any use.

The glare from Carmichael didn't lessen a bit, and he sat down so hard the chair squeaked and rocked beneath him.

Brandon had never seen such contempt and borderline hatred in anyone's eyes before. He raised a brow, inviting Carmichael to say something. Greg sat too, but he didn't have a role in this particular battle.

"Send me back."

Had Brandon expected an eloquent argument? A scathing denunciation of his character? He could maybe work with those, but this sullen, stubborn unwillingness in a man as big as Oliver... Brandon had no idea how to convince Carmichael to cooperate. He'd not used people skills like that since his last mission in the field. Then again, Carmichael's cooperation—or lack thereof—was immaterial, as far as Brandon was concerned. Greg's data wasn't the answer to dangerous equipment and closing down portals. The sooner Greg realized that, the better.

"It's out of my hands, Carmichael."

And it was. He'd invested a lot of interoffice political capital in getting Carmichael reassigned before he and Oliver could be sent back out in the field. No way was the senior director going to let Brandon reverse course now.

Amazingly, Carmichael bit back the words "I don't fucking care," although they were easy enough to read in his blue eyes.

"I'm his fu— his partner. I'm supposed to be there watching his back. You're going to get him killed."

Brandon's mouth dried up as his stomach squeezed. Surely —*surely*—Carmichael didn't mean what Brandon inferred from that statement. But Carmichael's face held an awful lot of anguish for a man who was legendary in MIA for his stony-faced demeanor.

Brandon tapped a finger against his desk, unable to think about anything besides some asshole sending Oliver back out in the field while he still had stitches from the last field mission. And without his trusted partner.

Notification of a new email flashed on Brandon's computer screen, and he pounced on the distraction.

"Excuse me for a moment. I need to check this."

The email didn't look particularly important, but the delay would irritate Carmichael and Greg both. Any other time, Brandon would take no small amount of childish glee in that, but right now, he needed to use it as a distraction. He dug into the rosters as quickly as he could. He didn't have access to the full mission files and directives, but his position gave him more access to more information than any of his underlings in R&D.

Then he found the memo that must have sent Carmichael charging into his office unbidden.

Brandon clenched his trembling fingers into fists as he read the memo twice, then once more. How the hell could anyone believe Oliver was ready to go back in the field? Where had they found another agent to partner up with him so quickly? Brandon flicked a glance over at Carmichael.

"Get your gear together, and be ready to leave within two hours."

Both men stared at him, slack-jawed.

"Greg, you said your project was ready for field tests? Mine as well?"

There was only one project Brandon had managed to vaguely keep hands on, and that was the answer to dispensing with sonic charges.

"Um, yes." Confusion had replaced derision in Greg's eyes.

"Make sure you pack them up with Carmichael's equipment. We're doing field trials for both of them."

Both men spoke at once, which meant Brandon only heard bits and pieces of their arguments. If he thought about it too hard, he might recognize what a bad idea this was, but at the moment it didn't matter. He lifted a brow and waited until they needed to draw breath. He didn't care if Greg wanted to be present for field trials. Unlike Brandon, the man didn't have any experience in the field.

He gathered up the files Greg had brought, and stood. "You heard me. Get moving."


BRANDON STOOD in front of the scuffed, paint-chipped door and took a deep breath. Where had his impulsiveness gone? This wouldn't be the first time he'd done something he hadn't fully thought through, but this was the most impulsive he'd been since he was injured. Something about being out in the field invigorated him to the point of aggressive recklessness, none more so than what he was doing right now. And yet he couldn't seem to summon the almost manic burst of inspiration that had led him on the hours-long journey to this particular door. His limbs were rubbery, useless.

"What the fuck are you waiting for?" Carmichael reached over his shoulder and slammed his fist against the door. The wood shuddered under his knock. The blond lout might as well have just kicked the door down.

Brandon was parting his lips to berate his pseudo-partner when the door opened to reveal Oliver, wearing a black scowl, a towel around his waist, and not much else.

All the breath squeezed from Brandon's lungs, worse than when Oliver had shown up unexpectedly in his office. Faced with that muscled expanse of bronzed flesh, he found it difficult to focus on anything but keeping himself from licking.

"What the fuck are you doing here?" Oliver didn't seem nearly as distracted, but then, there was no reason for him to be captivated by Brandon. Only Brandon was stupid enough to still care. Oliver's gaze flicked up and to Brandon's left. "Carmichael? What's going on?"

Figured the sight of the blond behemoth smoothed down some of Oliver's bristles. What was going on between them? Brandon hadn't had the nerve to ask if Adam and Carmichael had an open relationship, and in his more rational moments, he didn't believe any of them would agree to that. Still didn't preclude the slim possibility that Oliver and Carmichael had slept together before Adam arrived on the scene. Hell, if it wasn't Carmichael, it had been someone. Oliver would not have been celibate for the past seven years. Not a chance. Even though Brandon had no right, the thought of Oliver and anyone besides him was still so fucking painful.

Carmichael grunted, and Oliver stepped back as though the man had asked to be let into the apartment. The wordless communication sent a pang through Brandon's midsection. Once, he and Oliver had been in sync. Of course, most of their wordless communication involved sneaking into dark corners and alcoves to get off. However improbable, the idea that Carmichael and Oliver's simpatico arose from a similar source made Brandon angry enough to scream, and he pushed his way past Carmichael into the room.

The room was almost unbearably grungy, with sad, threadbare furniture. Why had he insisted on doing this, again? Been a long time since he'd gone without the conveniences of his apartment. Trepidation threatened to have him turning around, tail tucked between his legs, but he refused to back down. This was too important.

A stranger with hard eyes and quietly controlled menace sat on one end of a faded orange couch. Good-looking in a rough, brusque sort of way, but dangerous, like a coiled snake. Possibly more dangerous than the other guys. The stranger caught Brandon's gaze, and the dispassionate assessment in his eyes sent a wary chill down Brandon's spine.

Returning the majority of his attention to Carmichael and Oliver, he stepped back against the closed door. Slightly farther away, he would be better able to follow the flow of the conversation visually and could concentrate on the speakers' lips. It hadn't taken him long to learn that if only one person spoke at a time, the combination of lipreading and hearing aids let him understand many conversations. In general, enunciation was a lost art, and a lot of people mumbled. Nervously he checked his hair fully covered his ears.

Oliver raised a brow and opened his mouth, but Carmichael spoke before he could say anything.

"Who is that?" Carmichael jutted his chin toward the stranger.

"Luis Goodson," the stranger replied. Even Brandon knew that wasn't a good enough explanation for the belligerent blond.

"My new partner." Oliver's words dropped into the tense silence.

Carmichael's eyes narrowed, and he turned his back deliberately on Luis.

"New partner?" Anger, obvious even to Brandon, pulsed in his tone.

Oliver shrugged, without any discomfort at being half-naked in a room full of men. Then again, if Oliver partnership with Brandon was anything to go by, Oliver could have fucked every man in this room. Despite Brandon's full awareness that his thoughts were more uncharitable than Oliver deserved, he couldn't stop his muscles from tensing, as though preparing for a fight. Goddamn Oliver. How could Brandon still care what—and whom—Oliver did after all this time?

"What the hell?" Carmichael rounded on Brandon, face mottled with rage. "This is your fault. I can do more good in the field than I can as a fucking lab rat, and now there's some asshole taking my place."

"We are in the field right now, and if a lab rat can stop the incursions of the Umbrae, shouldn't you be eager to help?"

Brandon didn't know where he got the nerve to upbraid Carmichael like that. He wasn't afraid of Carmichael—not exactly. They'd both had the same agency training, but it had been almost seven years since he'd last put his into practice, and even if he hadn't forgotten a single thing, Carmichael outweighed him by at least thirty pounds of muscle. Antagonizing him wasn't wise, but Brandon's impetuous streak had returned with a vengeance.

With a snarl marring his handsome face, Carmichael advanced, fists poised for a fight.

Oliver grabbed his shoulder. "Stop."

Amazingly, Carmichael obeyed.

"But you shouldn't even be out here. Not now."

"Luis noticed a few anomalies, I reported them, and we got our marching orders within the hour," Oliver said without any inflection in his tone.

"But what about—"

"Carmichael, it's okay. I'll fix this." Oliver's voice had softened while his hand dropped to Carmichael's forearm, and neither appeared to notice the intimate gesture for what it was.

Brandon blinked as a thought struck him. He didn't like the thought of Oliver sleeping with anyone else, but it was the bone-deep trust on display that truly made Brandon jealous. He hadn't trusted someone unreservedly like that since his accident, and he missed it, so fucking much. There was a deep hollow in his soul where Oliver had once resided, and the more he saw Oliver, the more he had to accept he'd acted recklessly all those years ago, and not just on that fateful mission. One stupid, ill-thought out statement, breaking up with Oliver, and his heart was still paying the price.

The sudden burn in his eyes told him he needed to concentrate on the mission, not his stupid feelings.

"You'll fix it?" Brandon cut in. "How will you do that? It's up to me when Carmichael is released from the R&D division. And is that any way to treat poor Goodson?"

All three men glared at him, but Oliver finally stopped touching Carmichael. "What are you doing here, Director?"

Brandon couldn't mistake the sneer in Oliver's voice, and all his carefully reasoned arguments for arriving unannounced crumbled under anger and hurt he wasn't sure he could control.

"Maybe I'm making sure you get the job done," Brandon snapped back.

"Are you implying I'm incapable of doing my job?" Oliver's black brows drew together in an expression that would have been more menacing from someone who didn't know what Brandon's O-face looked like.

Reason suggested he dial it back, interact like a civil colleague, but reason was crushed under a rancid tide of anger and regret. Brandon had done nothing but suppress his feelings since the day he'd been told his hearing would never fully return. Seeing Oliver again tapped a deep well of bitterness he hadn't known was festering in his soul, and words his brain tried desperately to abort spouted from his mouth.

"Can you? Without getting people hurt or killed?"

Anger added a rosy flush to Oliver's bronzed cheekbones.

"Injury is a risk. For all agents. Did you forget about that, hidden away in your safe little lab?" Every word gritted out like it was an effort to unclench his jaw to speak.

A slippage of the towel distracted them both as Oliver made a grab to keep the cloth from baring him completely. Which reminded Brandon of the sex he and Carmichael could have interrupted, and the slow-burning anger ignited.

Brandon raked a disapproving gaze down to Oliver's damp towel and willed himself not to remember exactly what was under it. "Are you and Luis enjoying yourselves here on the agency's dime? Or is it too much to expect you to be dressed during the workday?"

Oliver's eyes rounded briefly before he scowled at Brandon. Shit.

His words opened a conversational pitfall from which he'd likely not survive.

"Memory getting a little selective there, Director? Getting your hearing back made you forgetful?"

Oliver's lips twisted in a sneer, and there was no way Brandon could mistake the meaning of those words. Nor could he have forgotten their scorching sex, even if he'd had a full-frontal lobotomy.

A second later, Oliver snapped his mouth shut, a stunned look on his face.

Somehow, Brandon had fooled Oliver into thinking his hearing had returned, and the shock of that was enough to derail his anger. Tension still simmered between them, the knowledge that they'd both gone too far not quite enough to cool their tempers. But working together in close quarters like this would be a nightmare.

They stared at each other, panting slightly, another uncomfortable reminder of the good times he'd had as Oliver's partner, both in bed and in the field.

But they weren't alone. They were being observed by more junior agents, who probably hadn't been aware he and Oliver knew each other at all, let alone had a volatile enough history to devolve into a humiliating screaming match within minutes of being in the same room.

Oliver took a deep breath, hand firmly clutching the wrapped towel. "I'm going to get dressed, and then we can talk about this."

Brandon noticed they'd both sidestepped his ridiculous implication that Oliver couldn't shower while out in the field, especially at a time when most office workers would be home, fed, and couch surfing. The fact that it was full dark out already had done *nothing* to curb his runaway tongue. Peopling was an art he seemed to have lost.

"Good. This place is a two-bedroom, right? Which one aren't you using?"

"The one at the end of the hall." Oliver jerked his thumb behind him.

"I'll take it." Brandon grabbed his bag and edged around Oliver, trying not to be obvious about avoiding contact. "I'll get settled and meet you out here in ten minutes."

At that moment, he didn't actually care where Carmichael and Goodson slept. They could duke it out for the god-awful couch. Because no matter how dark his thoughts got, he didn't truly believe Oliver was sleeping with either man. Not now. Brandon could easily see Oliver and Carmichael hooking up before Adam, but he didn't see an inkling of sexual tension between Oliver and Goodson.

In the relative haven of the darkened bedroom, Brandon resisted the urge to slam the door shut, instead closing it carefully behind him.

What the fuck had possessed him out there? Wasn't the plan to be calm and cool... adult? He leaned against the door and dropped his head back with a muffled thunk. Even more pathetic was the semi-erection that pressed against his fly as soon as he'd spotted Oliver's chest with its mat of springy dark hair. Just like the first time he'd laid eyes on the man, an electric tingle lit up under his skin, sending blood to his groin. As much as he tried to convince himself it was nothing more than an old reflex, a conditioned response to the sight and scent of his ex-lover, Brandon feared the reality was rather more pathetic.

After a quick adjustment of his too slowly dwindling erection, Brandon peered about the room he'd claimed as his own for the next indefinite number of days. The place really was a rat hole. He'd slept in worse, but he was definitely more fastidious now than he'd been in his twenties. He sniffed.

Cabbage and old socks? Dirty diapers and mildew? The scent was indefinable but miserable all the same. His nose had better get accustomed to the stink real soon, or he'd be putting scented candles on the grocery list. He slung his bag onto the bed, prepared for any manner of vermin to be startled out of hiding, but nothing moved. A quick lift of the sheets confirmed a welcome lack of bedbugs. Gingerly he sat on the edge of the mattress. Nothing shifted or collapsed. Light from a nearby streetlight filtering around and through the moth-eaten curtains did little to cheer up the room. It did, however, illuminate a black duffel bag in the corner, heaped with crumpled T-shirts and cotton briefs.

Shit. He'd just appropriated Goodson's room—by having what probably looked like a bitchy queen-out. Even if Oliver was fucking Goodson, they weren't sharing a room. At least they weren't until Brandon showed up and gave them a good excuse to do so. He might be an idiot, but he was an idiot who wasn't giving up his privacy.

He had to stop thinking the worst about Oliver. All the bad thoughts sprang from his mother trying to "help" during his recovery, combined with a savage blow to his self-confidence. He was quickly coming to the realization that perhaps he'd also broken up with his therapist precipitously. She'd tried to tell him avoidance wasn't progress, but he'd convinced himself that isolation was the answer to all his problems. But isolation wasn't possible, not if he wanted to keep his job. Not if he wanted to keep Oliver safe. And he clearly had a horde of issues he'd suppressed instead of working through.

But suppression had to be the solution, at least until the end of this mission.

He yanked off his hearing aids, dropped them on the bedside table, and rubbed at his ears. Was it a good thing that Oliver thought he'd completely healed? He had no idea how he felt about it.

If he could turn around and go home, he would. It didn't matter that he'd burned even more political capital to come here in person. It didn't matter if Oliver found out he was still defective. It didn't matter if Oliver bruised his feelings on an hourly basis. Someone in the agency, possibly his own damned department, was up to no good, and if harming Oliver was either their purpose or merely a regrettable side effect, Brandon had to prevent it.

He pulled out his phone and fired off a quick text to his mother so she wouldn't worry if he didn't call for a bit. Not that she would, but it was the right thing to do. The tension of the day pulled at his muscles, and he twisted his neck, trying to loosen the knots at the base of his skull. He'd need a full-body massage once this mission was over.

His ten minutes were up, and he took a deep breath. Interactions with Oliver would be nothing short of calm and professional from here on out.

Frowning, he picked up the hated hearing aids and replaced them. Checking his reflection in the grimy mirror, he readjusted his hair. His hearing loss was not common knowledge, and it appeared that his subterfuge had worked more effectively than he'd ever imagined.

# SEVEN

In the living room, Brandon found Goodson sitting on the couch in the same spot he'd occupied all through the blowup with Oliver. Carmichael fingered the latch on the sliding door to the balcony. A pair of weather-beaten plastic chairs and a broken lantern stood on the balcony, the walls of which consisted of rusted bars and dented panels. There wasn't enough money in the world to convince Brandon to set foot out there.

"I told you, we've already inspected for security," Goodson drawled.

Carmichael studiously ignored him.

"It's laughable but the best a place like this has to offer," Goodson said.

"That's not particularly reassuring." Both men's heads swiveled toward Brandon. Carmichael took a careful step forward, hands slightly outstretched as though reassuring a wild animal. Brandon didn't blame Carmichael. He'd been acting like an irrational diva.

He was saved from an explanation by the arrival of Oliver. The neatly pressed pants and button-down shirt were attractive, a stark yet welcome contrast to the earthy, sensual man who'd greeted them while wrapped in a towel. But he'd look even sexier in a pair of form-fitting jeans and tight black T-shirt like Carmichael wore.

"Hey, you do remember Luis, don't you?"

Brandon started to shake his head before he realized Oliver's question had been directed to Carmichael.

"No, I don't." Carmichael wasn't ready to continue in a completely civilized manner, and given Brandon's own behavior, he could hardly judge.

"You sure?" Oliver wiggled his fingers in front of his throat. "Remember? When Coop met Frazer? The vamp he was hunting attacked Luis."

A flash of interest ignited in Carmichael's eyes. "Oh, the police detective that got vamp bit. Healed well. Didn't think you'd make it."

Brandon desperately wanted to ask what had happened, but he had no right. If he was still interested when he got back to the office, he could dig up the old field reports. But a vampire explained the shiny pink scar tissue stretched like a web across Goodson's Adam's apple. Most people assumed vampires left delicate little puncture wounds, but they were more likely to rip and tear with their enamel weaponry.

Goodson was less sanguine about his experiences, as evidenced by his flashing eyes, the most emotion Brandon had seen the man display. Was it the cop thing? Oliver could do it when he wanted, but for Goodson it had clearly been elevated to a way of life.

"Not to change the subject, but am I allowed to ask what the hell that was all about?" Goodson stabbed a finger at Brandon and Oliver like they were prime suspects and he wanted them to confess.

The impassive expression on Oliver's face was one he used to hide his thoughts. Rarely directed at Brandon—in the past—and he was disappointed to see it when Oliver looked at him, brow raised in question.

Brandon cleared his throat. Oliver might be close to his level, but as a director, Brandon was still nominally in charge. Which meant it was up to him to explain their heated argument.

Careful to moderate his voice, Brandon spoke. "I apologize. It won't happen again. Agent Cardoso and I are capable of working together in a calm, professional manner."

Goodson cocked his head as though he was assessing each word for veracity.

"That's right," Oliver added. "Earlier was just some spillover from the last time we saw each other... remnants of an unimportant argument."

*Unimportant.* Good to know where he stood. Yet he wasn't surprised.

"From Friday?" Carmichael asked.

Brandon didn't blame Carmichael for being confused. During that "reunion," he and Oliver had barely spoken.

Oliver glanced away, out the window. "No, we knew each other before he became director."

Surprisingly, Oliver left it there, without any catty commentary about their final parting. Perhaps he didn't want to share that pain any more than Brandon did.

The seating options were two lumpy, threadbare armchairs and the other half of the couch occupied by Goodson. Brandon wiggled one of the chairs around to give him the best possible options for viewing the others' mouths. The scent of mildew billowed up as he sat, and he wrinkled his nose.

"Why are you here instead of a hotel?" A good fire would improve the smell of the place tremendously. The landlord should be smacked.

If only he'd had access to the pre-mission data. Then he wouldn't have to rely on the dribs and drabs of information Oliver and Goodson chose to share. The adrenaline kick from being out on field-work was riding him hard. He wanted to get out there and do something. He didn't want to limit his activity to monitoring Carmichael's brainwaves and electromagnetic fluctuations.

"What's the plan? Do you know where the portal is? What type of creature are we after?" Brandon's words tumbled out.

"Whoa, whoa. Hold up there, Brain Trust." Goodson held up his hands, palms facing out.

Brandon stared at him. Brain Trust? Not precisely a respectful way for an agent to address his superior, but it was possible Brandon had misheard. Inquiring if he'd heard correctly would only trigger questions he had no intention of answering.

He had other questions he wanted answered too, but he settled for quirking a brow upward. Goodson just quirked a brow back at him, almost mocking, before settling back into the couch.

Carmichael moved behind Brandon, which was a terrible place for him to stand if he started talking from that position. He twisted around. "Sit down and stop looming, would you?"

Carmichael gave him a sulky look better suited to a teenager deprived of cell phone rights, but he complied and plunked down into the armchair to Brandon's left, facing Goodson. All the better to glare at the dark-haired man, apparently.

Brandon hoped his own jealousy wasn't as obvious as Carmichael's.

Goodson smiled back at Carmichael, smug and self-satisfied. What the hell was going on here? *Had* Oliver fucked each and every one of his partners? There were currents and eddies of emotion that didn't form a complete picture. History indicated Oliver's tolerance for partners—other than Carmichael—only lasted about a year, after Brandon's extended two-year tour as the man's partner.

Despite what his mother had insinuated in the hospital, he'd never believed Oliver had injured him deliberately, but the cool, remote Oliver who stood beside the couch like a marble sentry wasn't much like the man he'd known. Nor was the way he allowed his big, muscular, alpha-male boy toys to snap and snarl at each other for the right to put their heads in Oliver's lap. But again, the more he observed, the less sexual it all seemed. None of it was truly similar to his partnership with Oliver and electricity only seemed to spark when he and Oliver locked gazes.

But there was no denying Oliver had feelings, platonic or otherwise, for his long-time partner, and the vicious claws of envy still tore at Brandon.

For the time being, he and Carmichael were an unlikely team, facing off against this new pairing, two enemies joining forces to storm a common rival's defenses.

"Where's your equipment?" Dammit. He hadn't meant to ask any more questions until his previous ones had been answered.

"I'd like to know that too." Carmichael was all but growling. Shit, he might as well just pee on Oliver, considering how territorial and protective he was being.

Dammit. Seeing Oliver again, and reliving all those old-but-not-forgotten feelings had melted Brandon's logic circuits. He needed to take his cue from Oliver. Aloof. Unaffected. He could pretend for however long it took.

Oliver flicked a glance over his misbehaving puppies before he met Brandon's gaze head-on, with nary a bit of warmth in those dark brown eyes.

"To answer your first question," Oliver said, "the motels nearby were even worse than this. Hourly rates and regular police raids. Completely unacceptable for our purposes. This apartment is close to the portal's nexus, we believe, and it doesn't cost any more than a motel would. Besides, we might learn something. This was one of the apartments abandoned by mysteriously disappearing tenants."

"Abandoned apartment?" Carmichael asked before Brandon could, looking around with more interest than before.

"Yes. Luis discovered an unusual number of apartments have been abandoned in this area, in a fairly short time span."

The sound of Goodson's first name on Oliver's tongue cut like a razor. Weird, though. For all their apparent intimacy and the emailed request for the return of his partner, Oliver had yet to call Carmichael by his first name. Brandon didn't even know what it was. Somehow, Carmichael had wrangled personnel files to only list his first initial. Not that Brandon had looked. *Ahem.*

That didn't matter. They were here to do a job, if this truly was an Umbrae incursion.

Brandon snorted. "That's what brought you out here? People in this socioeconomic stratum disappear all the time."

The tide turned, and all of them stared at him, united against him.

"Your privilege is showing, Brain Trust."

No, he hadn't misheard the epithet this time. The contempt twisting Goodson's lips stilled whatever protest Brandon might have made.

"Folks around here are usually too poor to just up and leave whenever. There's no denying the slumlords make these places complete shit to live in, and if the tenants are lucky, they'll meet the minimum legislated standards, but most times they don't. Despite that, when apartments end up 'abandoned,' the tenants are either dead or homeless," Goodson said.

"There's a portal near here. I can feel it." Carmichael's tone wasn't any more conciliatory.

Oliver nodded. "The disappearances might not be related. Who knows? There might be a gang rivalry or garden-variety serial killer, or some other reason. But it's the best place to start for now."

Oh, Brandon so loved looking like an idiot. He pinched the bridge of his nose as a low-grade headache pulsed behind his eyes. He'd spent a lot of time over the past few days paying attention to a lot of people speaking, and he was feeling the strain. The hassle of flying hadn't helped any. In addition to the overwhelming noise, buffeting him from all sides, the changes in air pressure bothered him more than it used to.

Oliver's eyes softened a trifle. "We really don't have much, but I'm glad to get Carmichael's confirmation."

"And the equipment?" He'd forgotten what it was like in the field. Due to an almost complete lack of concrete information, most decisions were made by gut instinct and intuition. With the R&D department unable to come up with any solution to the portal's effect on electronics, very little had changed since he'd been doing fieldwork.

Oliver winced. "It was a bit of a long shot, and the agency thinks it's a reasonable way to get Luis's feet wet. There aren't any bodies yet. If these disappearances are attributable to a portal, the infection hasn't spread far. And the equipment would pose a great temptation for the criminal element in the area."

Luis huffed. "They'd murder us in our sleep for the stuff Oliver showed me."

Which wouldn't be difficult. This place was a far cry from Brandon's high-security apartment.

"Just because they're poor doesn't mean they're all thieves and murderers." Carmichael didn't much strike Brandon as politically correct, so he assumed Luis had struck a nerve with his assertion.

"No, but there is a documented gang presence, and they'd love to get their hands on some expensive weaponry."

The tension in the room grew palpable as Luis and Carmichael stared each other down. Brandon bit back an unexpected laugh, because he was pretty sure they were clashing over being on the same side of the argument.

Oliver cleared his throat, the sound enough to draw everyone's attention as he pointedly looked at Brandon.

"Your turn. What are you and Carmichael doing here?" Oliver didn't say anything about Brandon being unwanted, although he surely was thinking it.

"We're testing out some equipment that's ready for field trials."

"Sonic charges?" To anyone listening, Oliver's words were simple, only vaguely curious.

But the weight of them lay heavy on Brandon. "No, not sonic charges."

He wasn't going to apologize or explain how the prototypes had come to be in Oliver's possession. He still wasn't sure, and he wasn't prepared to discuss it in front of people he didn't know and wasn't

sure he could trust. Keeping his eyes open, assessing the situation—
that he could do.

"Care to elaborate?"

"Not really." His neck was tight from the stress of the day and
worry for Oliver. Oliver stared at him, and Brandon stared right back.

With a sigh, Oliver rose to his feet and walked into the kitchen.

The weight of Luis's and Carmichael's scrutiny increased
without the distraction of Oliver, and he didn't know if he could
stand it without blurting out something he shouldn't. Instead he
pasted on an unconcerned expression and stared at them, waiting for
one of them to break.

"I'll order some dinner. Might not be great, but they'll deliver."
Oliver brandished a handful of restaurant menus as he returned to
the living room.

The tension in the room eased with Oliver's reappearance, and
Brandon let his shoulders drop in relief. Eating was the last thing he
wanted to do. Tomorrow, after some sleep, he could make nice with
Oliver's acolytes, but for tonight he just wanted to be alone.

"I think I'll turn in, thanks."

Oliver frowned. "Are you sure? I know how pitiful the airline
offerings are."

"I'll be fine." And he would, even if he had to keep telling himself
that every day.

Goodson followed him down the hall and into the bedroom.

"Yes?" Which was far more polite than the words he wanted
to say.

Rolling his eyes, Goodson stepped around him and snagged the
duffel bag Brandon had forgotten about. "I need my bag. I'm guessing
as newbie, I'm stuck with the couch, and I'm not sleeping out there
stark naked."

Prickles of heat warmed his cheeks. "Right. Sorry."

"Night." Goodson didn't exactly slam the door behind him, but it
closed with an emphatic bang. Nevertheless, Brandon wasn't willing

to forego his privacy for the sake of a man who'd given him the epithet of Brain Trust.

Oliver had always admired his intelligence, but Brandon had learned in the intervening years how rare a commodity that admiration was. Maybe Oliver had been lying to him about that.

Brandon stripped and pulled on a pair of pajama bottoms. The hearing aids ended up on the bedside table again. He rarely slept with them in, but tonight he wanted to make extra sure he wasn't going to hear anything untoward from Oliver's room. If he wasn't mistaken, the two rooms shared a vent, and he'd rather not have definite knowledge if someone crawled into Oliver's bed tonight.

Picking up the paperback he'd bought for the plane ride, he turned it over with a frown. Why the hell had he bought this drivel? The fact that he'd managed to read nearly a third of it without having any idea about plot, setting, or characters was testament to the turmoil in his mind. He opened the book where he'd dog-eared the page and began reading. It didn't really matter if he knew what was going on, because the chance of him retaining any more information than he had earlier on the plane was slim at best.

Within a few minutes, his eyelids became heavy, and he let the book fall against his chest as he drifted off.

---

A RUSTLE AND a muffled clunk woke Oliver. The travel alarm clock told him it was just after midnight. He lay for a moment in the musty, lumpy bed to get his bearings. Each year, he missed his own bed that much more when he had to go out in the field. He really needed to figure out whether he was just having a bad few months or if he was losing his taste for the job.

He'd stayed up with his previous partner and his current partner while they watched TV and sniped at each other. By the time ten rolled around, he'd been as exhausted as if he'd been refereeing a soccer game. Luis's personality clashed with Carmichael's, who made things even worse by being extra curmudgeonly. Oliver hadn't told him he'd try to get them reassigned together. Mostly because he didn't know if he could. But he hoped Brandon might see fit to relent. Oliver snorted. Brandon would have to do so out of the goodness of his heart—he certainly wouldn't do it because of Carmichael's sunny disposition. All the sharp edges Adam had worked so diligently to smooth out had returned with a vengeance. And Brandon had no reason to grant Oliver any favors.

Seeing Brandon had done nothing but rake up buried inadequacies and guilt. And hard-ons that wouldn't quit. Even when Brandon was being arrogant and condescending, the urge existed to throw him down on the nearest surface and fuck him silly. Fortunately, no one had been looking at his crotch yesterday, because that towel hadn't done much to hide his burgeoning erection.

Properly dressed, it had been easier to hide his arousal, but he could have sat there for hours just watching Brandon. Stupid of him. Brandon had been more than clear that their relationship was over, and he didn't show any signs of wanting to revive it. He'd changed so much. As gorgeous as he was—that hadn't changed—he was so rigid. Not in a good way either. If he smiled, his face might crack. Laughing was unimaginable.

The Brandon he remembered—and unfavorably compared all potential lovers to—had been vibrant, excited and exciting, energized by helping people as much as from the adrenaline rush. Brandon had been broken by the accident, and neither of them had thought he'd ever fully recover. Yesterday proved that supposition false. Brandon had obviously regained his hearing, by nature or by surgery, and never once thought Oliver might like to know. Yet he was still bitter, angry, and as unattainable as the moon.

All those useless thoughts of Brandon highlighted that Oliver was losing his edge. He needed to concentrate on the portal and the deadly Umbrae, not what-might-have-beens, no matter how attractively wrapped.

Oliver grimaced at the stucco ceiling, illuminated by the obnoxious glow of a nearby streetlight spilling through the slats of the cheap Venetian blinds. As exhausted as he was—no surprise after only two hours' sleep—his whirling thoughts weren't going to ease up anytime soon. He groaned and swung out of bed, muscles stiff.

Coffee wouldn't be a good idea if he intended to get any rest at all, but he'd snuck some hot chocolate in with their supplies. Normally he didn't let his partners know about his sweet tooth; Brandon and Carmichael were the two exceptions, and he'd been partnered with Carmichael well over a year before he let it slip. Stupid thing to keep secret, but it felt too much like the comfort of a small boy rather than a grown man. Right now, he didn't give a rat's ass whether Luis found out.

When he flipped back the covers, the scent of laundry soap wafted up. Bringing his own sheets was another indulgence, but his job was difficult enough without having to worry about leftover bodily secretions from God only knew what source. His preference for sleeping nude made clean sheets even more imperative for his peace of mind. He pulled on a pair of sweatpants and padded quietly from the room.

The light from the fridge made him pause, heartbeat accelerating a tiny bit. A large lump on the sofa snored softly, so Luis didn't consider the midnight kitchen raider to be much of a threat.

Carmichael was a good-looking, well-built guy, but the firm, rounded ass peeking out behind the fridge door could only belong to one man, and Oliver's heart rate sped up even more, but for a different reason.

"Hey," Oliver whispered, but Brandon didn't respond. Speaking any louder would probably disturb Luis, and he didn't want to add more acrimony into the weirdly comforting silence of the witching hour.

Brandon stood and turned, a white take-out box in each hand. His eyes widened, and he stumbled back in shock, narrowly missing thwacking his head on the freezer-door handle. At least he didn't drop the food. "Uh."

Oliver smiled at the sleep-tousled hair and plaid flannel pajama bottoms.

"Hey," he said again. "I got you kung pao chicken. Thought you might be hungry later."

Definitely not the first time Brandon had grazed in the middle of the night, and without any dinner, he had to be starving.

The frown Oliver got in return wasn't what he'd expected.

"Can you grab me a plate?"

"Sure." Oliver turned away to pull out a plate. When he turned back, Brandon had placed the cartons on the counter and was fussing with his hair. Cute, really, considering it hadn't much helped—he still looked like he'd just rolled out of bed.

"What was that you said?" The frown was gone, and a sleepy, soft look returned to Brandon's face, the expression like a punch in Oliver's gut.

This was the first time since he'd interacted with the director where Brandon truly seemed like the man Oliver had fallen in love with.

"I, uh..." What had he said?

Brandon reached for a take-out box and opened it. "Kung pao chicken?"

Yes, that was what he'd been saying. "Yes."

"You remembered?"

The sweet smile made Oliver's smile widen. He hadn't forgotten anything about Brandon, no matter how willfully he tried.

"I knew you'd be hungry."

Maybe it wasn't wise to let Brandon know that, but then, he'd rarely made wise decisions when it came to Brandon. Something about this man made him toss out his better judgment as well as personal and professional pride. Which was a habit he needed to break. This mission was unusual enough without getting all hot and bothered over a great ass. He really wished he'd gotten laid last weekend. He could have too—Rob had been willing. But he wasn't sure Rob fit the bill for his normal fucks. Most times, he didn't even find out their names, much less have any sort of discussion with them beyond who was doing what. Then again, the real reason he hadn't gotten laid stood in front of him.

And Brandon was far more than just a great ass.

Brandon shrugged, eyelids still heavy with sleep. "Join me?"

"Sure, but I'm not hungry." Oliver poured water into the kettle and turned on the burner.

"Hot chocolate?"

Oliver pulled the package from the back of the cupboard while Brandon prepared a plate to go in the microwave. Oliver's eyes had finally fully adjusted to the low-level light, after having been dazzled by the much brighter fridge light. With Brandon's attention on his food preparation, Oliver took advantage of the time to admire his sleekly muscled back.

It would be so easy to close the distance between them, press his own chest against Brandon's sleep-warm body. He'd slide his hands down, hooking his fingers into the waistband of Brandon's pajama pants, inexorably moving them downward. Maybe they'd stall a bit, held up by the cock growing hard at Brandon's groin. A few adjustments later, the flannel would be pooled at Brandon's feet, Brandon bent over the counter, ass pushed out, waiting, asking for Oliver to drop his own pants and push inside. Fingers first, maybe tongue, then cock. He'd ride—

The microwave dinged at the same time as the kettle's whistle started. Oliver leaped to the stove to move the kettle while Brandon retrieved his food. They'd be lucky if they didn't wake the other men at this rate. Someone on this mission should have a decent night's sleep.

By the time Oliver had his drink prepared, Brandon was already seated at the rickety table. Oliver sat across from him and blew steam away from his chocolaty indulgence.

Brandon ate and Oliver drank, but the silence was comfortable, Brandon no longer prickly and disapproving. Whatever Oliver had imagined a few minutes before... A fantasy, nothing more. But he was confident they could work together.

"So, uh, how's your mom?"

Oliver tilted his head. Brandon's own mother was a cold, bigoted woman, as Oliver discovered at the hospital after Brandon's accident. It had been no surprise that Oliver had never met her prior to that, unlike Oliver's mom, who'd been one of the only people who knew the true nature of his and Brandon's relationship.

Oliver's mom had been warm and welcoming to Brandon, and he'd lapped it up like a starving man. Oliver had only had the opportunity to take Brandon home with him a couple of times, but it had been love at first sight. Mama had been as devastated as he was when Brandon left.

"She's good. Loves being a grandma."

Brandon's eyes widened, and he coughed. "You're an uncle? Little Mariela is a mom?"

Admitting it made him sound like a coward, but Oliver had been glad when Mama moved across the country to live near Mariela, her husband, and little Callie. The sympathetic looks and the hopeless questions from Mama about Brandon—and Oliver's pathetic love life —depressed him. Nevertheless, he couldn't suppress his smile. "Yep. Callie's three and a spoiled sweetheart."

"Oh yeah, your mom would be thrilled."

Definitely thrilled. Mama had dropped more than a few hints about his and Brandon's options regarding kids when they were together.

"Do you have pictures?"

"Not with me. Not on the job. But I'll email you some?" Was that a good idea? Maybe not, but Brandon's interest was genuine, and he didn't want to shut down the tentative truce they were developing.

"Thanks. I'd love to see them."

"Mama still asks about you."

Brandon stared down at his hands and shifted in his seat. Oliver shouldn't have said anything, but when he spoke to Mama next, she'd ask again, and this time he'd have to say yes, he'd seen the man who'd broken his heart.

Brandon lifted his head and stared into Oliver's eyes, composed. The composure was a mask—Brandon hadn't changed that much—but there was no point in calling him on it.

"Give her my best, will you?"

Oliver nodded. He cleared his throat, swallowed around the lump that had formed, blocking his breath.

They sat in silence for a few more moments before Oliver thought of something else to say. "Are you settling in okay?"

Brandon lifted his head and blinked at him. "Pardon?"

"Your move back to town. Are you settling in?"

"Oh. Yes. I found a decent apartment. Cozy." Brandon pushed food around with his fork. "You still in the same house?"

No, this topic of conversation wasn't any more comfortable. He'd have to get used to that if Brandon was sticking around. The majority of their relationship had taken place out on missions. When they were home, Brandon had been in school and claimed Oliver was too distracting. But sometimes he managed to convince Brandon to spend the weekend. Made him dream of living with Brandon forever, creating a life together in his small home.

"Yes, still." He thought about making an excuse about the sagging housing market, but he hated lying to Brandon.

The soft, sentimental expression made him wish he had. "That is a great place."

Silence filled the night again.

With half his plate empty, Brandon gave him a tentative smile. "So, I guess Carmichael won."

"Won what?" Had they started another conversation while Oliver had been gathering the courage to ask if Brandon was seeing anyone?

"Well, I saw Goodson on the couch."

"I'm not sure the futon in the den is winning. It's in even worse shape than the couch."

Brandon's forehead creased. "The den?"

Comprehension flooded Oliver's mind, closely followed by a spurt of anger.

"Oh my God. You really do think I've fucked every one of my partners, don't you?" His voice got louder with each word.

"Shush."

Oliver shoved back from the table, but more quietly and controlled than he would have liked. Being shushed was annoying as hell, even if Brandon was in the right—about that.

"For your information," Oliver continued in a low, menacing voice, "you're the only one of my partners that I fucked. That I loved. I've fucked many guys since, but never one of my partners. Not before you, not since you. And we both know what a goddamned mistake that was."

Brandon looked like Oliver had slapped him. As much as he might want to throttle the man right now, he'd never be able to bring himself to strike out at Brandon. No matter how poorly the man thought of him. The hot chocolate curdled in his belly.

"But what about—"

Oliver shook his head emphatically. "No. I'm not doing this now. We both need some damn sleep." If he had this discussion now, he'd not get another wink all night.

"But—"

"No. I'm going to bed. Alone." He dropped the mug in the sink, uncaring if the roaches got a little treat overnight, and practically ran back to his bedroom.

He sat down on the edge of his bed and rubbed his forehead. Goddamn. What the hell made Brandon think he'd turned into a complete asshole since their time together? Both asshole and slut might have some merit, but it wasn't like Brandon had been around to know for sure.

Had he thought it would be easy to close the gap between them? Work together as professionals? He was an idiot. Getting through this mission was going to be the hardest thing he ever did, even if they never ran into the vicious monsters created by the Umbrae.

The bedroom door slammed open, making him jump to his feet.

"What the hell was that?" Brandon was angry. Angry like Oliver had rarely seen him.

"You're going to wake up Luis and Carmichael." Oliver's own voice was loud enough to do that.

Brandon snarled and closed the door quietly with an exaggerated, mocking movement before whirling back. "What the hell was that all about?"

Apparently, they were going to do this now. Who needed sleep anyway? Oliver stared, anger boiling up inside.

"Are you going to answer me? You don't get to order me around or ignore me, Agent Cardoso."

Ignore him? If only. But it was the impersonal *Agent Cardoso* that made his anger erupt.

"Oh no, you don't, *Director*. You don't get to pretend we barely know each other. Not when you're acting like a jealous asshole."

"I'm not jealous of you." Brandon's words ratcheted up into a near shriek. "And we don't know each other, Agent Cardoso. Not anymore."

Waves of red-tinged anger rose up as Brandon continued to try to distance them emotionally even as he moved closer physically with every word.

"Director... I know what you look like when you sleep. The songs you sing in the shower. I know you like extra sugar atop sugary breakfast cereal, but you take your coffee strong and black. I know the shape and length of your dick. I remember the way your body feels between my legs, and the way your legs fit around my body. I know the taste of your jizz. I know what sounds you make when you come. The sounds you make when I've got my tongue up your ass. I know the heat of you stretching around my cock."

Oliver dared a glance down. Pajama bottoms and sweatpants weren't nearly enough to hide the effect their proximity and this conversation were having on them. He took a couple of steps toward Brandon, his straining erection close enough to feel the heat of Brandon's.

"But most of all, I haven't forgotten this."

Oliver grabbed Brandon's right arm, the one without a watch, and licked the inside of his wrist. A pained, guttural sound escaped Brandon's lips as his hand trembled. Then Brandon used Oliver's grip to yank them closer, pressing their bodies together, cocks rubbing just right, and Oliver groaned in concert with Brandon.

"Kiss me, you ass," Brandon whispered.

Oliver didn't bother answering. He covered Brandon's lips with his own and slid his hands down over the flannel-covered ass that still haunted his wet dreams.

The kiss quickly turned savage as they tried to devour each other's mouths, teeth clinking and tongues tangling. Oliver slipped one hand under Brandon's elasticized waistband while the other roved upward over the supple skin of Brandon's back.

Brandon pulled out of the kiss, panting in Oliver's ear. He leaned back slightly, allowing room for his hands to rub over Oliver's chest.

Squeezing Brandon's firm glute made him moan and thrust his hips harder against Oliver's.

"Naked," Oliver said, throat tight and dry with lust.

Lightning fast, Brandon flicked his hands into Oliver's sweatpants. Oliver copied his action, and a moment later, the bare, heated skin of his cock touched the wet-tipped head of Brandon's.

Brandon let out a throaty growl and pushed, following him down onto the bed. The full-body, skin-on-skin contact made the whole situation feel like a dream, and the aching pulse of the cut on his back took a firm backseat to the throbbing pulse at his groin. Brandon rolled his hips, rubbing their cocks together.

Oliver slid his hands up into Brandon's hair to pull him down for a kiss, but the hard plastic he encountered made him pause.

"Brandon?"

"Oh, for fuck's sake, don't stop." Brandon latched his lips against

Oliver's throat, jacked his hips faster, and Oliver forgot anything else in the damp glide of cock against cock and the sexy suction on his neck.

His balls pulled tight against his body, and he thrust up against Brandon as hard as Brandon pressed down. Fast and furious, he was going to come soon—too fucking soon. He flipped them over, barely disturbing their rhythm, slammed Brandon's arms down on the bed, and leaned over to suck on the pulse pounding under Brandon's wrist.

Brandon howled Oliver's name and shuddered as wet, hot cum erupted between them, a fraction of a second before Oliver spilled all over their bellies.

After he'd mostly caught his breath, he placed a gentle kiss on Brandon's lips and tucked himself into Brandon's side, barely able to feel the pinching stretch of his slow-healing wound. A half smile played about Brandon's mouth while his eyes closed. The memory of plastic under his fingertips prompted Oliver to lift a lock of Brandon's hair away from his ear. Like he'd flipped a switch, Brandon's sleepy, post-sex contentment disappeared as he batted Oliver's hand away and sat up.

"Brandon? What's going on?"

Oliver wasn't mistaken—those were hearing aids. His stomach twisted as Brandon grabbed tissues from the bedside table to clean up without looking at him. Oliver did the same and pulled on his sweatpants as Brandon donned his pajama bottoms, but more because he didn't want to have this conversation naked. And they were going to have a conversation, dammit. Not an argument.

"Brandon?" Oliver reached out for Brandon's shoulder and pulled him around. The cold, remote expression was back, as though daring Oliver to say anything. With the combined scent of their cum still hanging in the air, Oliver dared. "Sit down. We need to talk."

Brandon's nostrils flared, and for a second Oliver thought he might refuse, but he sat, reserved and imperial, like a marble statue.

"Hey, look at me." He grasped Brandon's chin and coaxed him

into turning his head. Reminded of a few recent incidents, he wasn't sure now whether Brandon had been ignoring him or merely hadn't heard him.

Guilt sluiced through him, as sharp and hot as that day seven years ago when Brandon had clutched his head and fallen to the ground, writhing, after Oliver had fucked up setting the sonic charges.

Brandon answered the question Oliver hadn't yet voiced. "Yes, they're hearing aids."

"Can we have a civil conversation about this?" Because the guilt and Brandon's sullenness were going to quickly spark Oliver's temper, and that was the last thing the situation needed.

Brandon shrugged, and Oliver took away his hand. Touching wouldn't make it any easier for Oliver to concentrate.

"I...I thought maybe you'd gotten better." Hoped, anyway, when it appeared as though Brandon had been able to hear.

"No. Not really. Better than when I got out of the hospital, but without these, I can't hear much." Brandon flicked a finger at his ear. "Even with them in, if it's too noisy, too low-pitched, too high-pitched —too anything—I might not be able to hear at all, or I might be able to get by with lipreading."

Lipreading? Oliver remembered the intent manner in which Brandon had followed some of their conversations and the way he'd seated himself earlier so that he had everyone in his line of sight. Shit. He should have picked up on that on his own. But then, he'd been hoping and praying he'd seen the signs of a full recovery, not the signs of a proud man trying to hide his limitations.

"What about implants? The technology has improved and—" The fierce scowl on Brandon's face made Oliver swallow his words.

"Not improved enough. The implants would destroy any chance of me hearing normally... if that can ever happen." Brandon touched his hair again, and another unwelcome realization kicked Oliver in the gut. The longer hair—which Oliver loved—and the constant fussing were a direct result of Brandon attempting to disguise his hearing aids.

The sounds of multiple sirens rose to a crescendo as they neared the building, then died off as they passed, reminding Oliver where they were and why they were here.

"Don't you realize how dangerous this is? If you can't hear, you could get hurt. How can I protect you?"

"Protect me? I didn't ask you to protect me." The acid in Brandon's voice had returned, like their sexy interlude had never happened, and his lip curled in distaste. "I know what I'm getting into. I'm not here to interfere with your precious mission. I should be able to get the data I need without getting kidnapped or killed. Besides, if it's anyone's job, Carmichael will be the one protecting me."

Oliver rubbed a hand over his face, getting another whiff of sex. Brandon had already proved to be a distraction, and this wasn't going to make it any easier.

"This was a mistake." He needed to be on his game. He couldn't live with himself if Brandon got hurt or killed because he'd been distracted by Brandon's body. "We can't do this."

"No, of course we can't." Brandon practically spit the words out. "You can't tell anyone."

"I don't think our sex life is anyone's business."

"Okay, one, we don't have a sex life. Tonight doesn't count as a sex life."

Brandon's air quotes around the words sex life infuriated Oliver like nothing else. "Whatever you want to call it."

"And that's not what I meant. I meant, uh, these." Brandon placed his palms briefly over his ears before letting his hands drop to his sides. Then his puffed-up exterior deflated, and he picked at a cuticle on his thumb. "I haven't told anyone here."

"Here? As in, this apartment?" God, this conversation was making Oliver crazy.

"No, at R&D. I mean, I think the senior director knows, and some of the people I worked with on the West Coast, but no one at the office... Well, if they know, it's not because I told them. Can you keep it quiet?"

Oliver was amazed Director Ellison hadn't made a reappearance to order him to silence. "I don't know. The potential for you getting into a dangerous situation—"

"It won't happen. I'm here with three agents, and I'm not going after the Umbrae myself." A flicker of disappointment darkened Brandon's face.

Good to know not a damned thing had changed in the intervening years. Brandon still destroyed Oliver's better judgment. This was a bad idea on so many levels, but he'd always had a hard time saying no to Brandon, even without the guilt all tied up in it.

"Fine. But I reserve the right to tell Luis and Carmichael if it's going to put the mission in jeopardy."

"Very well. Good night, Agent Cardoso." Brandon turned on his heel and left the bedroom much more quietly than he'd entered.

Oliver fell back on the bed. At least his return to Agent Cardoso hadn't been accompanied by the sneering contempt Brandon had given him before. An improvement of sorts, and it would make it easier to keep his distance. When they returned home, there would be plenty of time to figure out what their sexual interlude meant for the two of them, if it meant anything at all.

Stretching his arms pulled at his wound, and as though it were suddenly aware of his attention, the distant throb became a vicious ache. After digging in his toiletry bag, he dry-swallowed a couple of the painkillers the doctor had prescribed, then headed back to bed, hoping to sleep in. As much as he hated letting a portal fester any longer than it needed to, this mission was very much like the training missions he and Brandon had been sent on in the early days. Urgent, yes, but unlikely to be too problematic. Oliver didn't know if that was in deference to his injury or to Goodson's almost painful greenness, but for once, he was grateful. Sleeping in might put him in a better frame of mind. Or at least give him the ability to effectively reason with Brandon.

Swiping his hand across a couple of dark spots on the sheets didn't remove them. He flipped on the bedside lamp and peered closer. Blood. Dammit. He shouldn't have lain on his back with Brandon on top of him. But it had been so damned good. So right. Like he'd been living in a nightmare all these years and was suddenly awake and alive. He couldn't let himself get his hopes up. Brandon hadn't even looked interested in another orgasm, never mind trying to repair the relationship they'd had. If it could be repaired. Anytime Brandon looked at Oliver or touched his hearing aids or was reminded yet again that he couldn't hear the same as others, he'd recall how badly everything had ended. Impossible to imagine a reality where he and Brandon could forget the things that had been said and done.

He'd have to get Carmichael to clean and dress his wound again in the morning... later in the morning. Oliver lay back against the pillow. Once, he'd have teased Brandon about taking his virginity, but he didn't know how this unfamiliar, standoffish man would react to a joke like that.

The stress, his injury, and the soporific pull of post-orgasm lassitude combined to exhaust him, suddenly and unexpectedly. It would take more than the sirens blaring through the paper-thin walls to keep him awake.

---

BACK IN HIS ROOM, Brandon shut his door carefully. He'd been plenty loud already and didn't want any more noise to alert the other men in the apartment that he had completely lost his mind. He ripped the offending gadgets from his ears and hefted them in his hand. If he hadn't snatched his hearing aids off the bedside table before he'd gone rummaging in the kitchen, that whole interaction would have been a hell of a lot worse. Regardless, the temptation to hurl them at the wall almost overwhelmed him, but the momentary satisfaction wouldn't last beyond morning if he damaged them. Letting Brandon accompany the team was already troubling for Oliver without adding in defective hearing aids. If it weren't for Brandon outranking him, Oliver would have sent him packing as soon as he figured out Brandon no longer met field regulations.

He'd have to make sure he didn't do anything to make Oliver regret having him stay. That ship might have already sailed, though, after Brandon had rubbed all over him like a cat in heat. Problem was, Oliver flipped all his switches and had from the moment he'd seen the man. Time and distance hadn't changed that. Attraction, desire, and just plain love hadn't been the problem, hadn't been why he'd left. Oliver was as sexy as ever—maybe even sexier with that rugged, worldly-wise air and a chest and arms harder and more muscular than Brandon remembered.

Brandon fell back on the bed and rubbed a palm absently over his groin. The phantom sensation of Oliver's hot, hard dick rubbing against his remained. No matter what he'd told himself when he finally caved to the insistence of his throbbing erection, this didn't feel a damn thing like closure.

Maybe the sex—embarrassingly quick as it was—had been closure for Oliver. The subsequent rejection had been every bit as painful as he'd expected, blunted not one bit by the intervening years. But then, he'd known it would play out this way the moment he'd woken up in that hospital bed, the ringing sound in his ears drowning out everything else. How could a strong, healthy man like Oliver stick around, love him despite the changes his injuries would mean for their life? In his more rational moments, he knew he wasn't giving Oliver enough credit but his mother had managed to erode his self confidence in those critical few days after his diagnosis, enough that he'd allowed her to send Oliver away on his behalf. Possibly the stupidest thing he could have done, and he didn't see any way to change the past.

Oliver's words tonight, though, had been more painful than a werewolf trying to rip flesh from his bones. But Oliver had been right

—they couldn't do that again. Not if Brandon expected to remain professional and aloof. Aloof was necessary if he was going to keep his sanity and pride intact for the duration of this mission.

He glanced at the clock on the bedside table and made sure the alarm on his watch was set. He couldn't sleep with the hearing aids in, but he couldn't hear a regular alarm without them. His watch was designed to vibrate when the alarm went off. Although he rarely slept in, he suspected he'd need the alarm in the morning. No way did he want Oliver bursting into his room if he'd overslept. Dealing with Oliver was difficult enough; being sleep fogged would put him at an even greater disadvantage.

It was going to be a long fucking night if he didn't stop thinking about Oliver.

With a groan, he swung out of bed and grabbed the files from his bag. Might as well do something useful if he wasn't going to sleep.

TWO HOURS LATER, Brandon still hadn't made sense of what he'd read. An alarming number of active research projects contained irregularities in his name. Irregularities that could become deadly problems for field operatives scheduled to receive new equipment from R&D. Orders from inferior suppliers. Rushed testing. Incomplete testing. And he'd signed off on it all. Someone had been using his inexperience as director to put field operatives in danger. There wasn't enough of a pattern to determine if they'd been working up to targeting Oliver—the prototype sonic charges had resulted in the most danger so far—but the goal might be sabotage of all field operations. No matter how hard he looked, though, no single person was involved on all the projects.

Or was he being paranoid? He piled the stacks of paper on the dresser, turned the light off, and fell back onto the bed, staring up into the darkness. Could these be normal, procedural errors? Without files on computer, he couldn't run reports on average error rates or apply algorithms. And if the mistakes were deliberate, they didn't have time to digitize all the paper files first. Nevertheless, he had to keep his eyes open. Whether deliberate or accidental, such mistakes were unacceptable. At least none of the tainted equipment was present here, and there was nothing further he could do about the mistakes in the files until he returned to the office.

Among all the other questions he had, the one that loomed large was whether he ought to discuss this with Oliver. Despite their history, he was confident Oliver had no knowledge of the sabotage. But would he still trust Brandon enough to believe Brandon's misgivings? Would he help or would he report Brandon's irregular behavior? And was there any point in dragging Luis and Carmichael into this? They had no reason to trust or believe him, either.

Instead he forced his thoughts toward the next day and the new equipment he'd be testing out. He had no idea how reliable it would be, but he had high hopes. Greg had assured him the equipment was ready, confirmed by the documentation he'd reviewed on both projects. And again tonight, just to be sure.

He stretched and settled more into the bed as his eyelids grew heavy. His last thought before he fell asleep was disappointment that he wasn't feeling the sweet ache of having been fucked.

# EIGHT

Showered and dressed in a long-sleeved T-shirt and a pair of cargo pants, Brandon paced inside his room. Each time he reached for the doorknob, he pulled his hand away as though the metal would burn him. There was no reason to believe Oliver had mentioned their sexual escapade immediately upon awakening. Hell, the others might already know about it without anyone saying a word. Remembering his cry when he'd shot his load—God, it had been so good—his face flushed hot as his dick plumped. Damned blood didn't know whether to obey arousal or embarrassment and gave him a little of both. But he'd been loud, possibly loud enough to wake Goodson, if not Carmichael.

Knowing they couldn't have any more sex was a festering wound his mind kept poking at, keeping it from healing, and he wasn't too keen on seeing regret in Oliver's eyes over their loss of control last night. Why couldn't this be easy? He'd had years to get over Oliver, but the last few days had shown him clear as day that he'd not moved on. At all. Oliver obviously had, but shards of their relationship still lurked beneath the surface, hurting them both. They were so damned wrong for each other, but his heart and his cock had yet to be convinced.

He caught sight of himself in the mirror, looking a bit like a wild man. Must have been running his hands through his hair as he dithered, although he didn't recall doing so. He shook his head. He was a thirty-five-year-old man acting like a schoolkid with a crush. Not a good start to his new, professional relationship with his ex. Especially as he'd proven himself as impulsive as he'd ever been. And no matter how much he'd railed at Oliver in those early days, it had taken a long time to accept his own impulsiveness had been more to blame than anything else.

If only he'd learned his damned lesson.

A deep breath in reminded him of the breathing exercises he'd learned in the early days after the hospital. Closing his eyes, he took a few moments to center himself, paying attention to each breath. Once he was somewhat calmer, he opened his eyes, fixed his hair to cover his ears, and opened the door.

No more than a few feet of hallway to the kitchen, but far enough to have him reconsidering if he had what it took to face everyone. Cowering in his room wasn't a viable alternative, so he forced himself to move forward.

Carmichael stood in front of the stove, stirring a pan of scrambled eggs, while Goodson fiddled with an ancient, cracked coffeepot. They both looked up when Brandon walked in, but if they knew what he and Oliver had done, he didn't see a hint of it on their faces.

"Want some?" Carmichael pointed at the pan with the spatula.

Brandon shook his head. Eggs would be too heavy in his stomach, given the attack of nerves he'd had this morning. "I'll just have some toast. And coffee, please."

Carmichael tossed him the loaf of bread, which he thankfully caught, and Goodson pulled another mug out of the cupboard.

The scent of freshly brewed coffee tickled his nose while he waited for the toast in the toaster. He sat at the kitchen table, trying not to remember sitting across from Oliver in the middle of the night. Carmichael's precise movements drew his gaze. Relieved beyond what was reasonable, he was glad Oliver hadn't gotten together with Carmichael. Younger, stronger, great-looking, physically whole, and clearly competent. Brandon would have been a poor comparison. The only thing that came close was the blond hair, and Brandon's shoulder-length mane wasn't anything like Carmichael's close-cropped style.

Unaware—or uncaring—of Brandon's scrutiny, Carmichael dished eggs onto three plates. Brandon frowned. He hadn't wanted any. Carmichael stuck his head in the fridge, grabbed a jar of salsa, and scooped out a couple of spoonfuls onto one serving of eggs.

Brandon's breath caught in his throat as realization sank in. Oliver wasn't even in the kitchen, and Carmichael knew Oliver would want eggs and how he ate them. Not a surprise—or it shouldn't be. But he'd let himself believe no one knew Oliver the way he did. Proof of his mistaken assumption made his breath come faster, made his stomach twist. Even without sex, Carmichael had had a longer relationship with Oliver than Brandon had. If only Brandon had made better choices, that fact might not be a knife in the guts.

Carmichael picked up Oliver's plate and turned to hand it to the man—whom Brandon hadn't even realized had entered the kitchen. Like the times he'd been almost run over by a car or startled by a coworker, the surprise combined with his previous unease catapulted him into another LSA he was desperate to hide. How could they take him seriously in the field if eggs made him hyperventilate?

Unlike with a full-blown panic attack, which he'd never have been able to disguise, his experience with LSAs and the fact that no one seemed aware of his distress made it easier to talk himself down. As Brandon's heart rate slowed to merely racing, Oliver sat at the table across from him, those damned eggs mocking Brandon from the chipped plate.

"Good morning," Oliver said.

Brandon nodded, unable to detect a trace of sarcasm or condescension. Or warmth. "Morning."

"Sleep well?"

Brandon narrowed his eyes. Was that a dig? Commiseration? Or a shared joke? Once, he'd have known. Oliver had teased him a lot. Back when they'd been together, it would have been a joke and a sexy little reminder all in one, but he didn't know what it was now.

Oliver's lips twitched, and his gaze darted to the other men eating, butts resting against the counter, before he dropped an eyelid in a discreet wink.

Irrational relief flooded Brandon. A grin threatened to break free and he struggled to keep his expression neutral. Oliver wasn't a completely different person, but if they were trying to put their interactions on purely professional footing, the comment and wink were completely inappropriate.

Oliver didn't say another word, just started eating. Brandon nibbled on his toast, unable to stop watching the man across from him, drinking in the minuscule changes and committing them to memory. The dark hair had a few silver highlights, the eyes a few more creases. He'd already mapped new scars on Oliver's body last night, but he hadn't had a chance to prove he remembered just as much about Oliver's hot spots as Oliver had remembered about his. The base of Oliver's spine, the back of his neck, the inside of his elbow... Brandon hadn't forgotten any more than Oliver had.

He took a sip of coffee, but the movement didn't cause Oliver to raise his eyes. One time—God, he'd been so stupid, and Oliver had been stupid for letting him—they'd been surveilling a cave where they suspected a nest of werewolves had taken up residence. He and Oliver were holed up in a tiny copse of trees that had an open area inside. Perfect cover.

Brandon had shifted, trying to stave off numbness in his legs, and ended up behind Oliver. His T-shirt had ridden up, and his jeans had ridden low, revealing the area at the base of his spine covered in fine, downy hair. Brandon hadn't been able to resist. He'd opened his mouth and sucked. Oliver had shuddered as Brandon reached around, unbuttoned his fly, and stroked him to a fast, silent climax,

Oliver's arms shaking as he attempted to keep the binoculars trained on the cave entrance. So hot. Brandon would probably have fucked him too if a werewolf hadn't chosen that moment to make an appearance. Despite having had an orgasm, Oliver had been equally, if not more, ravenous than Brandon once they'd finally returned to their hotel room.

Brandon squirmed a bit in his seat before his focus returned to the Oliver in the here and now, not the Oliver who'd sprung on him like a sex-starved satyr.

For the first time, he noticed the biggest difference of all.

"Why are you wearing a suit?" Not that it wasn't fucking hot, but as had been proven over and over, it didn't matter what Oliver wore for Brandon to find him hot.

Carmichael sat in the chair beside Oliver, managing to loom even while seated. "He always wears suits."

"He does?" Brandon looked back at Oliver. "You do? In the field?"

Oliver gave him a nod and pushed away from the table to wash up his dishes.

"Director Ellison, you seem surprised." Carmichael's growling tone was surprisingly audible.

He rolled his eyes. A suit would be too suspicious and out of place while they were out gathering data. "Call me Brandon."

Carmichael relaxed a fraction, and Brandon opened his mouth to comment on Carmichael's not-quite question, but he sensed Oliver's glare boring into the side of his face. He had no idea what Oliver expected him to say, but didn't want to hear. Did Oliver actually wear them out on missions? He never had done so when they'd been partners.

Carmichael's blond brows rose in invitation—or challenge—and Brandon cleared his throat. "Perhaps we should get the equipment set up. Are you finished eating, Carmichael?"

He might have invited Carmichael to call him by his first name, but the man had better not forget who the director out here was.

Carmichael didn't miss the subtle rebuke. "Let me get your dishes for you, Director... I mean, *Brandon*. I'll meet you in your room when I'm done."

Brandon decided to accept the dismissal instead of running the risk of looking petty. It wasn't a battle worth fighting.

What did Goodson think of the charged atmosphere? He was getting quite the initiation to the agency.

He intended to give Oliver a wide berth as he strode out of the kitchen, but Oliver's intent gaze kept Brandon's eyes locked on him. He followed Oliver's finger as it tucked into his starched white collar and pulled it down long enough to show Brandon the purplish hickey he'd sucked up last night. Not an acceptable excuse for the suit, not when Carmichael thought it was normal, and not when he'd lugged the thing all the way here with, presumably, the intention of wearing it.

One thing Brandon knew for sure—he wasn't going to back down from the challenge that lit up Oliver's brown eyes. They weren't done until Brandon had gotten some sensual payback of his own.

Setting his shoulders back, he intentionally brushed against Oliver as he left the kitchen, reaching behind to squeeze Oliver's butt, assured neither Carmichael nor Goodson could see the swift motion with the bulk of Oliver's form in the way. He smiled at Oliver's soft gasp and continued to his room.

Just as well. He didn't really know how to act professionally around Oliver anyway. No point in starting now.

---

OLIVER CHECKED his holstered weapon and smoothed a hand down the front of his suit jacket.

"I thought we were supposed to be discreet." Luis rolled his eyes.

"We are."

Four strangers were hard to hide in plain sight, but in the projects, curiosity could get you killed. Even with his suit, he'd be taken for nothing more than a successful criminal. Wouldn't much matter if Brandon hadn't muscled his way in on this mission. Bad enough that he hadn't been out in the field in a really long time, but even worse that the mission was complicated by a completely green agent and Brandon's science experiment.

"Good fucking luck."

Oliver suddenly realized Luis wasn't commenting on his suit. He glanced over his shoulder and turned his head back so fast that pain sparked in his neck, and sucked in a deep breath. If Carmichael saw Oliver laughing, he was so dead.

"That getup's not exactly subtle, Brain Trust," Luis continued.

Biting the inside of his cheek to keep his mirth in control, Oliver turned back around. Brandon stood next to Carmichael, as pleased as if he were introducing them to his prom date. Although Oliver and Luis both got death glares, the majority of Carmichael's ire was reserved for the unsuspecting scientist standing beside him. No doubt Carmichael was thinking of all the ways he could murder Brandon with his bare hands in the next thirty seconds.

"What? It's not that bad." Brandon clearly believed his words, and Oliver bit his cheek harder as Carmichael's face flushed even more. The electrodes at the temple really were... obvious.

Luis snorted. "We'll look like we're escorting Hannibal Lecter to his shock therapy. Even in this neighborhood, that'll raise a few eyebrows."

"Oh please. You're exaggerating. And we can hide the transceiver with his collar." Brandon tweaked Carmichael's collar, making him look like a preppy '80s serial killer going to a frat party.

"Not that I don't enjoy seeing Carmichael like that," Luis waved his hand, and Carmichael shook from the effort not to lunge, "but what's our cover story? We only rented the one shit-hole apartment that we're now sharing with you two. If we're not looking for homeless to conduct experiments on or kids to steal for traffickers, who the hell are we?"

"Could we be going to college and need roommates to make ends meet?"

This time Oliver did laugh along with Luis. Brandon could be terribly naive sometimes.

Luis answered before Oliver got a chance. "None of us are young enough for anyone to buy that. Except maybe for you, Brain Trust. Maybe we could be your pimps. You're young enough for the johns, easy."

Brandon sputtered. "I'm thirty-five. I'm not even the youngest one here."

He did look like Carmichael's younger brother, though.

"Sure, whatever, kid." Luis waved a hand.

With the attention off him, Carmichael's face returned to a somewhat normal color. He snatched a blue hoodie off the couch and put it on, then pulled the hood up over his face. It effectively hid most of the hardware but didn't do a thing to disguise the disgusted look he threw at Brandon.

This was the most acrimonious mission Oliver had been on since Carmichael had met Adam, and infighting was only going to make them miss vital signs and clues to the portal's location and victims. Oliver strove for a conciliatory tone while making sure he faced Brandon and enunciated so he wouldn't miss anything.

"That's much better. I think, to account for the equipment and all, we ought to be looking for a place to set up a meth lab—if anyone has the temerity to ask. That should keep any nosy questions to a minimum, and I'll see if I can get headquarters to monitor the local police communications to try and keep them off our backs."

By rights, he ought to get Brandon the fuck out of the field. Portals were dangerous, even though this held all the signs of being a 'beginner' one. But with Brandon outranking him, aside from being stubborn as a goat, the only feasible way he could do so would be to report his hearing issues to the upper ranks, and he couldn't bring himself to do that. He didn't know what was going to happen between them, but going behind Brandon's back would make him livid, and that wasn't going to improve relations between them. Not one bit. He'd just have to be extra careful to make sure Brandon didn't get hurt. Whether or not Brandon wanted his protection or not, he was getting it.

Luis nodded and grabbed his own jacket. "I'm guessing the cops don't spend a lot of time here anyway. Maybe come in a bit and roust a few vagrants, but that's it. In places like this, we're—they're—it's hard to police."

"And you're our mob boss, are you?" Brandon raked a glance down Oliver's suit, pausing at his neck.

Oliver's cheeks heated slightly. He didn't know what he'd been thinking, taunting Brandon earlier. The last thing he wanted to do was explain how the suits made him feel safe, reminded him constantly that he was on the job and needed to be aware at all times. A reminder of the walls he needed to protect his heart and mind, to not let his guard down. Rattling Brandon had been a joyful bonus, or so he'd thought. Instead he'd just egged Brandon on, encouraged him to grab Oliver's ass, for God's sake. Oliver had been the one rattled after those brief moments in the kitchen. He'd been the one with an unwelcome erection that he hoped neither Carmichael nor Luis noticed.

Still, he hadn't been an agent for over ten years for nothing. He shrugged. "If the shoe fits..." He held out a hand and frowned at it. "Too bad I don't have a ring you can kiss."

Carmichael smothered a snort, Luis stared at him, and Brandon glared. No matter that Oliver might have started it, their middle-of-the-night agreement to act professional with each other had vaporized the second Brandon's hand had touched his ass. He was no longer interested in fighting with Brandon. Oh no. He had tussling of a different sort in mind.

His imagination was all too happy to supply him with ideas, and he grabbed his trench coat and held it protectively in front of his groin.

A smile flickered over Brandon's mouth for a half second. Oliver didn't know if it was in appreciation for going along with the joke or because he knew why Oliver needed a shield, but he didn't care. This Brandon was the closest to the man he remembered, and he was grateful. The four-foot-thick concrete and steel-reinforced emotional walls between Brandon and the rest of the world had thinned.

Luis frowned. "We're not going to wander around the neighborhood like an aging posse, are we?"

This time it was Brandon who smothered laughter, but Oliver was careful not to single him out. If they were relaxed enough to laugh, maybe the tension between Brandon and the two other agents would smooth out.

Brandon really had thrown a wrench in things. If it were just Oliver and Luis, Oliver would have suggested wandering around, checking out areas in the neighborhood that warranted further investigation, either as portal locations or potential nests of Umbrae, which had been getting wilier of late. Two of them would be less inconspicuous than four of them.

"One of us should talk to the guy who rented you this apartment. He should be able to tell you something about the people who lived here and when they disappeared. He might know about others," Brandon said.

"Good idea. Why don't you and Carmichael go talk to him while Luis and I take a look around the neighborhood?" Better to piss off the super than have to worry all day about Brandon getting into trouble. Not that he didn't trust Carmichael to keep him safe, but with Brandon's wholesome, surfer-boy looks and the length of time since he'd been a field agent, it seemed too much like throwing a tasty morsel of fresh meat into a pen of starving lions.

Besides, he'd been good at putting people at ease, back in the day. Surely, he'd not forgotten all of that, not with him making it to director.

Oh shit. He definitely hadn't forgotten Brandon's mulish expression, the one Brandon got when he was ready to dig his heels in about something.

"No way. I'm going to look for the portal. That's what I'm here for. That's what Carmichael is here for."

The sharp reminder that Carmichael was no longer his partner, at Brandon's behest, made Oliver scowl. Brandon drew his shoulders back and took a deep breath. They hadn't fought often, but this had all the earmarks of a wild one.

"For fuck's sake. You're both being idiots." Luis's words broke the tension brewing between him and Brandon as they both turned to stare. Not many people dared to talk to their superiors like that, although Oliver had always been secretly amused when Carmichael did. Perhaps that was one of the reasons he got along so well with both Carmichael and Brandon—he respected people who'd speak their minds when it was needed. Signs pointed to him liking Luis, too.

Luis gestured at Carmichael's temple. "Does that thing need you to be there to monitor it, or does it record whatever it's supposed to pick up?"

Brandon's brows pulled together as he considered Luis's words. Had Luis enunciated enough for Brandon to understand? Should Oliver repeat them? This was going to get even more complicated— yet another reason why he didn't want Brandon out without his supervision.

Then Brandon shook his head. "No, I guess I don't need to be there."

"Fine. I'll go with Carmichael, check out the neighborhood," Luis said. "You two go interview the super. We'll compare notes later."

It wasn't a bad plan, although Oliver thought perhaps he should have suggested it. Spending the day alone in Brandon's company came with a whole different set of complications, but in spite of that, he'd much rather be the one looking out Brandon.

Brandon stepped close to Carmichael and took hold of his hand. The sight almost made Oliver growl. Brandon directed Carmichael's fingers to a tiny button on the transceiver.

"Press that when you notice anything out of the ordinary. It will mark the recording, and I'll be able to take you back to hot spots to get more readings tomorrow. It's supposed to take a GPS reading also, but considering the effect portals have on electronics, we definitely can't rely on it being accurate. So hit the button, and also make note of the time and your location, please. Also, make sure you track your route, just in case I see something when I analyze the readings that you didn't notice."

Luis slid a map and a small notebook into his pocket and patted it. "Let's go."

Fortunately, the discussion had taken care of Oliver's overeager libido, so he slid into his coat and gestured for the others to precede him out the door.

The portal's presence hung like an oppressive pall in the air, making the squalor that much more squalid. They all felt it, but pinpointing its location wasn't a simple task, even for Carmichael. Not when it could be hiding behind any one of hundreds of doors, in any one of several buildings.

THE FOUR OF them took the elevator down to the first floor together. Oliver and Brandon didn't immediately search out the super's apartment but waited in the foyer as Luis and Carmichael exited the building. There were a few people wandering around the entryway, but the two of them didn't garner any extra attention. A blast of chill air swept into the building as the door closed. It wasn't freezing out yet, but winter was almost there.

"You know, these buildings all look quite similar. Are you sure they have different superintendents?"

"No, I'm not sure." A thought struck Oliver. He turned to Brandon and tapped him on the shoulder.

"Yes?"

"Were you able to hear that?"

Brandon's lip curled. He clearly didn't like to talk about his hearing, but Oliver needed to gather as much information about what

Brandon could hear and when. It might make a difference if they came across the Umbrae, although Oliver was going to do everything in his power to make sure Brandon didn't get anywhere near danger.

"You speaking, you mean?" Brandon's distaste wasn't hidden at all.

"Look, I need to know..." Shit. They shouldn't be having this discussion out here. "The super can wait. Let's go back to the apartment for a minute."

The mulish expression threatened to make a return, but Oliver gestured at the older woman who emerged from the elevator with a bundle buggy.

"Fine, let's go." Brandon sprinted for the elevator doors and stuck his foot in, halting their closing.

Oliver followed him in, and after they'd gone up a couple of floors, Brandon stabbed the red button. The elevator shuddered to a stop.

"So...talk."

"I don't think that's a good idea." Oliver flicked a glance to the camera overhead.

"Oh, the camera? Even if the thing is working—which in this dump I doubt—no one's going to be paying attention. And they sure as hell won't be listening. Sound isn't exactly standard issue in elevator security."

Oliver bit his cheek to keep from laughing; he probably shouldn't encourage Brandon. But then he remembered the reason they were in the elevator in the first place.

"Brandon, whatever our respective ranks are back at headquarters, there can only be one team leader out in the field. And that has to be me. You've been out of the field too long."

Brandon gave him a tight nod and didn't argue.

"I also need to know what you can hear. If it comes down to a life-or-death situation, I'll need to know if you can hear my instructions."

Twitching his hair nervously, Brandon looked everywhere but at Oliver.

"Well?" He hated this, pushing Brandon, making himself sound like a disapproving father. God knew he didn't feel at all fatherly toward his surfer boy.

"I'm not going to be in danger. I have no intention of interfering with your investigation." Brandon shifted the strap of the messenger bag he wore, still avoiding Oliver's eyes.

Could he not just answer the damned question? "You are already interfering."

"I have a job to do, same as you. I won't get in the way. I won't tangle with the Umbrae. What more do you want? I know I'm no good as an agent anymore."

Still refusing to meet Oliver's eyes, the man seemed to fold in on himself, looking almost as morose and remote as he had in those dark days in the hospital. Oliver's anger faded away under the almost over-whelming urge to pull Brandon into his arms and tell him it would be okay. But as that hadn't worked back then, there was even less reason to think his comfort would be accepted now, much less be helpful.

He couldn't ignore Brandon's pain. With a light touch under Brandon's chin, Oliver forced him to look up. "This has nothing to do with your abilities as an agent. It's nothing more than needing to know what precautions I need to take."

Not entirely true, as he worried more than he ever had before, but a lot of that was fear of history repeating itself and Brandon getting hurt because of Oliver.

Brandon stared deep into his eyes as though trying to catch Oliver in a lie. "Yes, I could hear you. I wasn't lying last night."

"And you'll take my direction?"

Brandon glared at him and puffed up again. "Of course, I will. You're the leader. I'm just a useless desk jockey. But you're going to have to trust me, trust that I'm not lying to you."

The biting words hurt, and he didn't know exactly why Brandon felt Oliver's concern was out of line. He didn't know how to explain it had nothing to do with mistrusting Brandon, but more about knowing Brandon's limitations.

"I know my limitations, Agent Cardoso." Dammit, it was like he'd plucked the thought right out of Oliver's head. How did he do that?

Oliver gritted his teeth and tried to ignore that he was back to Agent Cardoso again. In the intervening years, Brandon had learned the fine art of putting someone in their place. But Oliver wasn't going to be put anywhere so easily.

Oliver glanced at the camera again. Was it working? Did it matter? The fight had done nothing but heat his blood, and all he could think about was writhing in the dark with Brandon and the firm squeeze on his butt earlier that morning. He wanted Brandon's hands on him again. Like last night, they moved closer, as though a gravitational field pulled them together.

"Are we done fighting?" Oliver's voice sounded plaintive, even to his ears.

"I don't know. Are we? Are you going to trust me?"

"Yes." He didn't have a choice. Brandon's arguments were... mostly sound. But more importantly, trusting Brandon was the only way to avoid these arguments every thirty seconds. With Brandon under his damned nose, he hated being at odds, and the last thing he want to do right now was argue.

"Can we..." Get out of this elevator. Go back to the apartment. His hands twitched, itching to feel Brandon's hair sliding between his fingers. The throb in his groin became insistent, and he tried to discreetly adjust himself. But Brandon saw.

"Why, Mr. Mob Man... do you have an offer I can't refuse?" Brandon sank to his knees on the grubby carpet, and the air left Oliver's lungs in a strangled whoosh.

He darted another glance at the camera. Would the lengthy pause in the elevator's function mean they'd soon be interrupted by a well-meaning "rescue" from the fire department? Then Brandon unbuttoned Oliver's suit jacket, slid his fly down, pulled his dick out into the open, and licked. Oliver no longer cared about anything but the sensation of Brandon's tongue against him. He groaned and leaned against the wall, his head lolling to the side.

He'd always been a little weirded out by mirrors in elevators, but the scene showing in the mirror was better than any porn. Eyes closed in sensual pleasure, Brandon opened his mouth and enveloped the head of Oliver's cock. An odd disconnect in sensation made him jump, as the visual was so intense he almost wasn't expecting the wet heat. Even better was watching Brandon fumble to bring his own dick out. Oliver groaned and let Brandon's incredible skill bring him to the brink within a few minutes. He shuddered, wanting to prolong the experience because it was so damn good, but this time quick was better. Best, even.

Thrusting his hips gently, he gave in to his earlier temptation and threaded his fingers through Brandon's corn-silk hair. A wicked little curl of the tongue and an increase in suction almost put him over the edge, but it was the finger that wormed its way under his balls to press on the soft skin behind that had him pouring spunk down Brandon's throat. Brandon swallowed and groaned around Oliver's cock as he came, the vibration almost too much sensation. In the mirror, Oliver watched Brandon spurt. Fucking gorgeous.

Somehow Brandon managed to get them both tucked away while Oliver tried to get his breath back. Brandon stood, bouncing with energy, and rebuttoned Oliver's jacket for him.

He scrubbed his foot over the spillage, grinding it into the stained industrial nap. Oliver grimaced.

"What? What else am I supposed to do? Hell, I should probably burn these pants just from kneeling on this carpet. No one's going to notice another cum stain."

"Another? How can you tell?"

Brandon laughed, the sound easing something inside Oliver. "You're crazy. Odds are good at least one of them is."

Oliver considered that for a moment. Frankly, cum stains were probably the least of all possible evil biohazards lurking in the industrial weave.

"Ready?" Brandon asked.

"Ready for what?" Oliver's muscles were still rubbery, like wet noodles. Orgasms were always outstanding with Brandon.

Another laugh answered him as Brandon started the elevator again. The door opened on the sixteenth floor. Instead of getting out, Brandon hit the Lobby button and they waited as the doors wheezed shut again.

"Are you going to let me do the talking?"

Talking. Interrogation. What the fuck had he been thinking? Oliver's brain was complete mush after that stunning blowjob. Too bad it had happened so damned fast. Next time they were going to have to take it much, much slower.

"Sure. You can talk to the super." Look at him, trusting Brandon.

The doors shuddered opened, and Oliver followed that tight ass out of the elevator and down the hall. Brandon flung a knowing look over his shoulder. "Just like old times, eh?"

Yeah, just like old times. The beginning of a smile curled Oliver's lip. The recklessness that had plagued their previous partnership wasn't nearly as one-sided as he'd tried to make himself believe. But having Brandon here just made things better. More colorful. Sparking with electricity. As long as no one got hurt, Oliver doubted he'd regret any of it.

---

BRANDON PRACTICALLY RAN down the hall. Interviewing people wasn't the most interesting part of being a field agent, but he loved the adrenaline rush of being in the field. Loved it. Being able to pretend he and Oliver were still partners made it much more exciting.

Once again, he hadn't been able to resist Oliver's dark good looks. He'd missed the sex and knowing his rebellious Oliver was still buried on under those suits, had been hot as hell. But even more, Oliver mere presence filled the empty place in his heart, and it was going to be hell to let him go again. But this feeling of rightness, of utter completion, wasn't something he wanted to give up any sooner than he had to.

But he had a job to do, and if he didn't get his mind out of Oliver's pants, or daydreaming about rekindling what they'd had, he'd never be able to prove he had what it took to help with this mission. That despite all the marks against him, he was responsible enough to pull his weight. He'd managed to push the sabotage out of his mind for a short while, but he couldn't let himself forget that the mission was under threat from someone other than an Umbrae-possessed monster.

Fidgeting, he waited for Oliver to catch up with him before he knocked on the super's door. His parents had trained him early on how to make small talk, which was one of the reasons Oliver had often let him interview people, but it had been a long time since he'd bothered to try. Since his injury, he'd done his best to avoid human contact. Until this week, anyway. His retreat into solitude hadn't done him any favors, as his ex-therapist had told him more than once. After this was all over, he was going to look into finding someone on this coast to help him out.

A tall, gaunt man with a scraggly beard opened the door. If Oliver lost about a hundred pounds and tried to grow a beard, he'd probably look a lot like this guy. An acrid scent wafted out, and Brandon barely kept from wrinkling his nose. The man had apparently stopped showering as well.

"Hello, Mr. Moore. My friend here just moved in, and I was wondering if you have any other vacancies?"

Moore grunted and handed him an application from a small table beside the door. "A few. Bring this back. I'll call you."

The door started to close, but Brandon got a foot in to block it. "Is that just for this building?"

"No, I've got openings in all three buildings on the street. I gotta go. I was just getting ready to eat."

Brandon shuddered delicately. Moore's apartment smelled ghastly, and it turned Brandon's stomach to even think about eating.

"Thank you for your time." The words had barely left his mouth when Moore slammed the door shut in their faces. Oliver didn't seem fazed by it, so perhaps Moore had been as uncooperative and uncaring when they'd rented the apartment.

Brandon wanted to suggest going back to the apartment, taking advantage of some alone time, but so far sex had been preceded by an argument. When they were both in a fully rational state of mind, he wasn't sure he could convince this new version of Oliver to shirk their responsibilities. Once upon a time, he'd considered it a worthy skill and practiced it at every possible opportunity—but once upon a time, Oliver had been predisposed to indulge him. Besides, he could take this as an exercise in practicing restraint. He'd already indulged in risky behavior once today, no sense in pushing his luck. With Oliver as the temptation, it was still more adult and responsible than he'd ever been on a mission.

Instead, they walked out to the main street and wandered past the depressing selection of stores, as well as the three buildings that appeared to be under the same management. If it could be called that. The weather was chilly enough that the leaves had all fallen, but Brandon wasn't sure the bushes and trees would survive for another season.

Trash filled gaps at the base of the bushes, and scraps of paper blew haphazardly across patchy brown lawns that were as scraggly as Moore's beard.

No, he'd never again complain about his boring apartment. He shivered and wrapped his arms around himself. The thought of being obliged to live here—and have the situation get bad enough that he'd have to abandon everything—horrified him. Moore clearly didn't care whether the people had left on their own or become victims, as long as he was getting rent money on behalf of whatever slumlord was responsible for this dump.

At the far end of the street, where it stopped in a dead end, was a fourth apartment building, which backed onto the highway. Without any further discussion, they both walked to the building and stood on the cracked sidewalk, staring at it in silence. The building fairly pulsed with menace, but the grim exterior would have done that even without a portal in the area.

"I think it's here," Oliver said.

"I think you're right," Brandon agreed. He squinted at the faded sign on the door. If he got closer, he'd be able to read it clearly, but he didn't much want to. "Does that say the building is condemned?"

He turned to face Oliver, the white-noise hum of the speeding vehicles on the nearby highway creating enough interference that he might not be able to hear what Oliver said.

Oliver's expression changed a fraction of a second before a hand landed on Brandon's shoulder, and he whirled about in a defensive stance. Carmichael backed off, hands spread wide.

"Easy there, Brain Trust," Luis said.

"Sorry. I didn't hear you." His cheeks got warm, and he checked that his hair wasn't revealing anything it shouldn't. He glanced back at Oliver, who stared at him, speculation in his eyes.

Carmichael mumbled something, and Brandon took a few steps back to try to get everyone in his sight line. Why oh why did the portal have to be here?

Oliver frowned at him, and Brandon widened his eyes, trying to appear innocent. He wanted to help, but this depressing-as-fuck cul-de-sac magnified the nearby highway noises.

"Hell, even I can tell there's something wrong with this place," Luis said. Brandon's fingers itched to rip the electrodes off Carmichael's head to start sifting through data, but there would be plenty of time for that later.

"You been inside yet?" Oliver glanced back at the squat little structure.

"We took a break to grab a coffee, see if anyone knew anything about the building."

"And?" Oliver prompted.

Luis shrugged. "Been condemned for a couple of years."

"A couple of years?" Brandon couldn't believe it. Who let a building sit like that for years? "Why hasn't it been torn down?"

"Costs money to tear down buildings," Luis replied. "In this economy, well, it's just not going to happen. Normally I'd expect a spot of arson, but it's too close to the moneymakers over there."

Brandon whirled, but all he saw was the apartment complex they were staying in, with the three decrepit buildings obscuring the sun. "What moneymakers?"

Luis pointed over his shoulder at the buildings, standing close enough to his ear that Brandon didn't miss a word. "We're living in them. When you're taking in rent and not doing any upkeep or maintenance aside from bribing the occasional city inspector, those places are almost pure profit."

Brandon shuddered. Disgusting. They were lucky their apartment wasn't worse than it was. He turned back to the group. "Arson, you said?"

Luis nodded. "Sure. Look at that place. The amount of capital required to get this place even close to code would be astronomical, and clean demolitions aren't cheap either. Arson is a cheap way to clear the land with the added bonus of insurance fraud. In this case, it's likely that setting this one on fire would take out the viable ones. So, it's a good bet the same slumlord owns all four buildings."

"Do we think he could be the alpha victim?"

Luis looked blank, and Brandon remembered his knowledge had come from being a cop. Once they'd moved to the specialized knowledge of MIA, Goodson was still a very green rookie.

This time Carmichael spoke. "No, probably not. The owners almost never show their faces down here in the projects. Don't want to take a chance of dirtying their hands."

Brandon wished the hoodie wasn't obscuring Carmichael's face, because his tone had become vicious and bitter, more so than Brandon had heard before, like the big man had a personal reason to hate slumlords. Maybe he did. Prior to joining MIA, he'd been in the military—Brandon had found out that much about him when he'd believed Carmichael had replaced him in Oliver's affections—and he wouldn't be the first kid to escape shitty circumstances by doing so.

Oliver nodded. "Probably the alpha victim is a homeless guy who'd taken refuge inside."

Yeah, that sounded more likely.

"Let's find a way in." Brandon didn't want to hang around here all day, but he did want Carmichael closer to the portal so he had more complete data.

Oliver narrowed his eyes just a bit. "We could let Luis and Carmichael do it."

Oh no. If he thought Oliver had suggested that because he wanted to take Brandon back to the apartment and fuck him stupid, Brandon would—probably—throw the job to the werewolves and go back to hump like bunnies. But he suspected he was still in protection mode.

"I'm staying. I'm not completely incompetent."

Oliver opened his mouth, and Brandon glared. If Oliver said a damned thing after he promised not to tell anyone his secret, Brandon wouldn't be responsible for his actions.

"Fine." No mistaking that grudging tone. "You and I will take the west side, Luis and Carmichael will go east, and we'll meet up at the back. If the exterior's clear, we'll head inside."

Better. Some of his tension bled away. No matter how defective he felt most of the time, he didn't want anyone to treat him as though he was. Now he just had to prove that Oliver's tentative faith wasn't misplaced.

# NINE

Oliver stepped into the building, and the eye-watering stench inside confirmed vagrants had undoubtedly been using it for shelter. Luis, who'd proven talented with a set of lock picks, reassured them most homeless would depart during the day, only to return to the roost at night. Odds were good they were alone, which meant Brandon was that much safer.

"Brandon and I will check out this floor and the basement." Oliver directed the other two men to check out the upper floors. Unlike the other three apartment buildings, which had twenty floors apiece, this much smaller edifice had only six. "We'll meet out front in two hours, no longer."

If MIA could take horror stories as gospel, the portal would be located in the basement, probably the furnace room. The Umbrae certainly created horrors when they infected humans, but folklore and fiction were guidelines, not instruction manuals. The portal *could* be anywhere in the building, and Oliver suspected the most structurally sound architecture would be on the lower floors.

He trusted both Carmichael and Luis to have enough sense to avoid problem areas, but he wasn't as sure about Brandon. As smart as Brandon was, wandering around a condemned building in the projects wasn't an academic exercise, with or without a portal present. His privileged upbringing kept him out of areas like this, and even MIA fieldwork had taken them into urban areas exactly once, and the area hadn't been a slum. If Oliver had anything to say about it, Brandon wouldn't be going out on any more fieldwork, even if he had to shout Brandon's secrets from the main hall at MIA headquarters. Even if Brandon hated him for doing so.

At the stairs heading to the basement, Oliver flicked out a tiny flashlight and turned it on, pleased to note Brandon had done the same. Oliver preceded him, gun out and ready. He glanced back to tell Brandon to get his own weapon out, only to find Brandon already gripping one, poised and ready. He wasn't sure if that made him nervous or not; Oliver hadn't thought to ask if he'd kept up his training. Not wise to ask now, in case Brandon got angry and decided to demonstrate. Truly, though, if anything made him nervous, it was the glee and eagerness in Brandon's expression. Apparently his willingness to dive into a situation headfirst hadn't abated much.

"Watch where you're going," Brandon whispered. "Condemned building, remember?"

The dark was enough to hide Oliver's flush as he turned his attention back to the staircase. Even if Brandon did everything right, he was a distraction for Oliver and made it hard to focus. But convincing Brandon to leave was a lost cause so completing the mission as quickly as possible was the only solution.

Oliver rushed downstairs, avoiding the gaps and cracks in the staircase with ease. Once in the basement, he paused, the dark so intense it almost pressed on the eyeballs. Behind him, Brandon's light moved fast and erratically, as though he was hoping to illuminate the whole area at once. Oliver swept his light in a rhythmic circle, getting a sense of his immediate area before taking a step and doing it again.

After they'd gone a few feet, the pass of Oliver's light illuminated a network of cracks in the cinderblocks on the wall.

How had this place not collapsed already, all on its own?

Brandon's light followed, and he stepped closer to the wall. He tucked his weapon into the back of his pants and traced the larger cracks with his fingers.

"No wonder this place was condemned." Brandon's whispered words were filled with concern.

A concern Oliver shared... or exceeded. Oliver had visited the Mammoth Caves in Kentucky on a family trip, back in his late teens. Before he'd gone down into the caves, he'd been excited, fascinated. But as soon as they'd gone down deep, with the cavernous ceiling above, stalactites and stalagmites dotting the alien landscape, he'd become painfully aware of the sheer weight of the rock and earth above their domed protection.

All he could think about was how could this empty air surrounded by a shell of rock possibly keep the weight of the mountains above from collapsing? He'd been shaky and nauseated when the two-hour tour finally ended, and he stayed in the hotel room the next day when his mother and sister went on the longer tour. For the first time in a man-made structure, that same sensation hit, an awareness of the weight of concrete and girders holding up the floors above them.

Brandon turned back to him. "Are you okay? This isn't a cave, but..."

Oliver should have known Brandon would remember how much he hated dark, dank confines. His stomach rolled, and he took a few deep breaths and realized he hadn't answered Brandon's question.

"I'm fine. But we should keep moving."

Brandon nodded but stepped closer and squeezed Oliver's shoulder. The gentle gesture shouldn't have meant much, but the comforting weight of Brandon's hand eased the constriction in Oliver's chest.

They moved through a passageway that resembled a tunnel from a slasher flick, Oliver sticking close to Brandon's back. Several yards along, Brandon skidded, arms wind-milling, and Oliver dropped his light to steady him.

"You okay?" Oliver's lips were so close to Brandon's ear, under all that blond hair, and Brandon relaxed into his arms.

"I'm good," Brandon whispered back, clearly in no hurry to move away. This time the questions and concern were reversed. Their proximity gave comfort, and Oliver wasn't the only one who needed it. But there was work to be done. The smell of whatever Brandon had slipped on completely overwhelmed the clean scent of Brandon's hair. Between the oppressive weight of the building above and the repulsive smell, Oliver wasn't even slightly turned on. He pulled away and retrieved his flashlight.

When he turned back, Brandon was already crouched down, a circle of light illuminating some sort of slimy chunk. With a sharp gasp, Brandon stood and backed away. He put a hand over his mouth and sucked air in through his nose. Oliver curled an arm around him and rubbed his back. When it became clear Brandon had gotten his stomach under control, Oliver stopped rubbing but didn't sever their contact.

"You okay?" Oliver asked again.

"Sorry," Brandon gasped out. "I forgot... what they could do. Or made myself forget."

"Forgot what?"

"What the Umbrae are capable of, what they're driven to."

That was another reason Luis was going to be an asset. Unlike the majority of them, whose previous professions hadn't dealt with the sordid underbelly of humanity, Luis wasn't going to have the acclimatization period of dealing with ugly death, on a semiregular basis. Brandon had at least had the advantage of having been in medical school, but blood and guts in a hospital setting were never the same as coming across a scene with those things splashed across concrete.

"Umbrae? Are you sure? I thought it was a dog or a cat." Or what was left of one. It had hardly been recognizable as anything other than a piece of meat. Umbrae didn't usually bother with nonhumans.

Brandon laughed, only a slight hysterical edge to it. He'd always recovered quickly. "Not unless someone decided to tattoo a dragon on their pet."

"What?" Oliver skimmed his light back over the chunk of flesh. "Holy shit. It's an arm."

"Part of one." Brandon took another deep breath, then brandished his light at Oliver. "Hold this for me, would you?" He fumbled in his bag and extricated a camera. After taking a few pictures, he pulled out a specimen bag and packed away the remains.

"You're bringing it with us?" Oliver shuddered. The partners he'd had since Brandon all had different specialties, none of them medical, so it had been a long time since they'd brought body parts back from a scouting mission. "Keeping it in the fridge?"

"Of course. Might be able to learn something." Brandon stuffed everything back into his messenger bag.

Oliver grinned. "Don't tell the other two." Carmichael was going to kill him, but he'd die laughing when either Carmichael or Luis discovered that little morsel.

Brandon stared at him for a minute, then laughed. "You're terrible. But I'll let it be your surprise. I—" He broke off and shifted his gaze away from Oliver's eyes.

A vibration thrummed the floor, getting louder and more forceful, shaking the foundations and showering dust and dirt. The tremor was too rhythmic to be an earthquake, and it seemed to go on forever, paralyzing Oliver as his mind tried to calculate exactly how many tons of brick and steel could bury them in this abandoned piece of shit.

Beside him Brandon looked around, but without the wildness that ramped Oliver's heart rate into palpitations even though he had no way to demonstrate it. If he could, he'd run, but as terrified as he was, there was no way he was leaving Brandon down there. Brandon knew, though, and wrapped a steadying hand around his forearm.

The vibration rose to a crescendo, then left, fading away at the same rate it had blown in. Gripping his flashlight murderously tight,

Oliver breathed in, slow and controlled, trying to ignore the noxious scent and the swirling dust.

Brandon chuckled nervously and swept his light over Oliver's face. "Better now?"

After wiping the sheen of sweat from his face, Oliver nodded, not trusting his voice.

"The subway must run under here. Can you imagine what it would have been like living here? I bet the whole building rumbled each time a train went by."

Oliver let out a wavering chuckle of his own. No wonder the building had been condemned. Whoever built the place must have fucked up. The constant vibrations likely had shaken the shit out of the building, eventually making it uninhabitable.

Brandon stepped closer to steady him or perhaps hug him.

A soft scuff had Oliver looking around, trying to identify the source. Didn't much sound like a rockfall.

"What?" Brandon asked.

A movement at the edge of their light caught Oliver's eye. The blur moved toward Brandon's exposed back, and Oliver snapped out of his paralysis. He yanked Brandon out of the way and curled his own body around to provide a human shield.

Fire lit up his back as the person—or creature—collided, and he howled, every bit as primal as one of the monsters they chased. He dropped his light, somehow still noticing Brandon's freaked-out expression. The attacker clung to his back, and all he could focus on was the pain. With a few stumbling steps, he maneuvered them close to a wall and then slammed backward with all his might, pinning his foe. His attacker cried out, angry and pained, and there was nothing human in that sound.

"Shit, Oliver, give me a shot," Brandon shouted, panicky, as he did his best to aim both flashlight and gun without completely blinding Oliver.

Bony fingers curled around his throat and squeezed. Oliver threw himself backward at the wall again, trying to break the creature's grip.

Spots whirled in front of his eyes, and he wondered idly if Brandon was going to shoot him. Brandon had been an excellent shot, once upon a time.

"Oliver, goddammit!"

Brandon lunged and slammed the flashlight down behind him. The wet thunk of metal hitting flesh told him Brandon had hit his mark. Oliver grabbed the wrist at his throat and twisted, turning in the creature's grip. Brandon hit it again, and it stumbled back, stunned for a moment before it shook its head. They both sprang away as Brandon fired between the creature's eyes, and it dropped to the floor, dead.

Brandon turned to him. "Are you okay?" His gaze roved over Oliver from head to toe.

"I'm fine. Just bruised." Wasn't a total lie. If that thing had broken the skin when it bit him, well, there wasn't a damn thing he could do, but most likely he'd only end up with a nasty bruise. Slightly worse was the suspicion he'd opened his partially healed wound. But his black suit jacket would hide a multitude of sins. Even if he'd ripped all his stitches, he wasn't going to bleed out. Better all round to tough it out.

Adrenaline making his hands shake, Oliver retrieved his flashlight and shone it over the creature.

"God, she's tiny," Brandon said. "How the hell didn't you break her with that first body slam?"

"She was fucking strong." Not that she looked it. Her frame was small, and she appeared almost emaciated. "Zombie, you think?"

"I don't know. She didn't go for your head. She could just be a junkie." Brandon knelt by the body and drew out a syringe. "I'll take a blood sample, but I'm not sure I brought anything to test for drugs."

Oliver almost asked him why the fuck not, but he remembered just in time that testing for street drugs wasn't standard procedure. Perhaps that needed to change.

Damn. He should have never brought Brandon to this building. Brandon hadn't heard the infected woman approach, and Oliver had been so caught up in having Brandon as his partner, he'd put Brandon in danger. Put both of them at risk. He was a fucking fool.

Before their eyes, the corpse seemed to gain flesh. Though it wasn't easy to be sure under the glare of the flashlights, she seemed to gain a little more color too. But she stayed just as dead.

Brandon grunted and turned her arms over. There was no trace of needle marks. "Probably not a junkie. It's been a while, but she really didn't seem like a zombie to me."

He drew blood, but Oliver knew it might not tell them anything. Once the physiological changes reversed in death, there was little information to be found in the body.

"Should we call in a cleanup team?" Brandon asked.

"No. It's better if we don't draw any attention. Not yet." He took a deep breath. "Ready to finish our search?"

Brandon nodded tightly and gestured with his flashlight for Oliver to precede him.

---

BRANDON FOLLOWED Oliver out of the building and breathed a sigh of relief to be standing in the watery autumn sunshine after the depressing chill of the abandoned building. The remnants of adrenaline had disappeared while they completed the search of the basement. It had been years since he'd fired a gun to kill, and seeing Oliver under siege had freaked him out. Completely and utterly. He just thanked all the stars above that neither incident had triggered a panic attack or an LSA. Otherwise Oliver would box him up and ship him back to headquarters, no matter what arguments he gave or the help he could still provide.

Aside from a number of gruesome finds that supported their conclusion that the derelict building was a dumping ground—and the attack, couldn't forget that—he and Oliver hadn't discovered anything. No portal and no assurance regarding what type of creature they were after. Maybe he'd know more after he had a chance to examine his specimens. No matter what Oliver thought of his abilities as a man in the field, this was one way he knew he could contribute.

But he hadn't heard the creature approach. Brandon pressed a fist to his aching stomach. Yes, he'd shot her, but that didn't change the fact that his limitations had been a liability. Oliver probably wouldn't have been attacked at all if Brandon hadn't been there. Or more to the point, he would have been able to kill the Umbrae before she'd had a chance to lay hands on him. He wasn't a field agent, and there was no going back in time. But he couldn't leave yet. Not until he'd at least had a chance to discuss the sabotage with Oliver.

They stood in silence, the weight of his failure hanging over him like a cloud. Not the best way to gain Oliver's trust, dammit. He owed Oliver an apology, but admitting he was wrong was so fucking hard. He was going to have sack up, though, and do it.

Oliver rolled his shoulders, first one, then the other. Brandon frowned as Oliver twisted again. The altercation with the Umbrae had ripped up his suit jacket. Was Oliver hurt? Apologies could wait until later.

"Are you sure you're okay?"

Tossing a dark look over his shoulder, Oliver straightened. "Just stiff."

"We've got thirty minutes before we have to meet Goodson and Carmichael. We can check out your back, make sure you're okay, and be back before they're finished searching."

"Brandon." The warning in Oliver's tone wasn't going to work. Not a chance. He'd already shown up unannounced to keep Oliver safe—bit of a fail already, and he damn well wasn't going to risk him when simple actions could prevent a nasty infection.

"That basement was filthy. Please, can we go back and check you out?" Brandon stepped close and stared into Oliver's warm brown eyes, pleading. He stretched out a hand, laid it on Oliver's forearm, stroked slightly. Wasn't the first time he'd talked Oliver out of his "can't show weakness as the senior agent" mindset, and if Goodson or

Carmichael had been there to witness it, Brandon wouldn't have had a shot.

Oliver's lips thinned, but he nodded almost imperceptibly and let Brandon lead him back to the apartment.

---

THE SECOND THE apartment door closed behind them, Oliver's adrenaline rush faded, making the aches sharper, his muscles weak. Brandon had already seen him at his worst; there was no point in hiding a few scrapes now. He trudged into his bedroom and slipped off his jacket and shirt before sitting on the corner of the mattress. The air thickened when Brandon arrived a few moments later after dropping off his specimens in the fridge.

"Holy shit. Oliver."

A black pit of fear lodged in his gut. "What?" The word almost didn't make it past his suddenly dry throat.

"She bit you."

"No. No way." He'd told himself there wasn't a chance. Biting clear through layers of fabric and skin didn't seem possible. He twisted to get a look in the mirror over the dresser. There it was, right beside the slightly puffy, razor-straight wound on his back. Teeth marks. Fucking teeth marks. He licked his lips and told himself to reconsider the next time Kyle offered him a promotion that would take him out of the field. How much longer could he go on like this?

He turned back around to see Brandon staring at him, eyes wide in a white face.

"It'll be okay."

"Oliver..."

"There's four of us searching for this portal, and we've got a better fix on its location than usual. I'll be fine." Oliver didn't let himself think of the alternative.

Sure, being previously bitten conferred immunity... sometimes. Both he and Brandon were well aware that most agents were saved from possession by closing down the portal within three days—because they were already in the vicinity and searching for it. The Umbrae infection required three days to make the required physiological changes, and if the portal was shut down within that time frame, the person recovered with no ill effects aside from the occasional mundane infection. Which Oliver already had antibiotics to combat.

Brandon's eyes glimmered, but Oliver shook his head slightly. He didn't want either of them to dwell on this development. They were going to find the portal in plenty of time.

"Can you help me clean and patch it up?" There wasn't much else to be done. But now they had a time limit on finding the damned portal. "And the other one too. It bled a bit last night."

"What? Shit. I knew you'd been injured, but I didn't realize I was making you bleed. You should have said something."

Having been reminded of the discomfort, Oliver gave him a one-shouldered shrug. Like a little blood was going to keep him from fucking Brandon.

"It's getting better." He chuckled. "I was going to tease you this morning, tell you that you'd taken my virginity."

Brandon frowned for a second. "You've got to take better care of yourself. Let me look." Without waiting for an answer or permission, Brandon moved behind him and pressed his fingers gently alongside the older wound. "This is infected."

"I know. I've got antibiotics. I was going to ask Carmichael to help me this morning, but I forgot."

"I'll help you. You don't have to ask Carmichael." Brandon's words were fierce. He smoothed a hand along Oliver's shoulders for no other reason than to offer comfort.

Oliver pulled the necessary items out of the first-aid kit on the dresser and handed them to Brandon.

# TEN

With two minutes to spare before their designated meeting time, Brandon stood next to Oliver outside the abandoned building. Oliver had had more dark suit jackets to choose from, and he didn't appear any worse for wear as they watched Carmichael and Goodson emerge, dusty and grimy but intact.

The bite changed things. Until he'd seen that, he'd been ready to admit his culpability and apologize, pack his stuff up and go home. No matter how sorry he was, he was still an extra person who was determined to find the portal and shut it down before Oliver became possessed. He'd been a fool, but he wasn't admitting a damn thing before this mission was completed. Oliver's life was at stake and there was no fucking way Brandon was leaving now.

"Let's go back to the apartment," Oliver said.

"What did you guys find?" Goodson asked.

"We can't talk about it here," Brandon said. Whatever any of them found, they didn't want to alert the Umbrae any sooner than they needed to. The four of them hanging around outside a dumping ground could spook the resident Umbrae.

Goodson glared at him and opened his mouth, undoubtedly to

lay down a scathing rebuke, but Oliver interrupted. "Brandon is right. We'll discuss this back at the apartment."

Brandon led the procession; he knew Oliver would feel more comfortable if he could see them all in front of him instead of having to glance over his shoulder to check on them—on Brandon. He wondered if Oliver would still appreciate it if he played the prank on Goodson and Carmichael. His jealousy was more on a professional level than a personal one this time, but he was jealous nonetheless. Spending time with Oliver, in and out of bed, was always enjoyable, and Oliver's desire to trick the other two men reminded Brandon so much of the fun, sarcastic man he'd fallen in love with all those years ago.

He bit his lip. There'd been a moment in that awful basement where he'd nearly blurted out that he still loved Oliver. No way did he want to deal with Oliver's pity. The overprotectiveness was bad enough, but if he knew Brandon—pathetically—hadn't moved on... No, Brandon didn't have the stomach to deal with that. He wasn't the same man he'd been when they'd gotten together; he was good enough to fuck, but that would have to be the end of it. Oliver's resistance to sleeping with him only underscored that this was temporary.

As soon as this mission was done, they were done. They'd go back to living their lives without seeing each other. Eventually Brandon would have to come to terms with Oliver getting involved with someone else. And as usual, Brandon would throw himself into his job. Assuming Oliver survived the Umbrae bite. Brandon's breath hitched, the prelude to a sob, and he furtively glanced around, making sure the other guys hadn't heard him. He couldn't concentrate on the worst-case scenario, or he'd be no help at all finding the portal in time to keep Oliver safe. He took a deep breath and shoved that concern way down in his psyche, where he'd kept his feelings for Oliver all this time.

Blinking, he looked up and realized they were at the elevator already. He'd been so wrapped up in his thoughts, he didn't recall the walk.

The doors rattled open, and they got in. Brandon, having gotten in last, stood in front of the other three. Even though he could probably hear whatever was said in this enclosed area, he shifted into the corner, just in case.

In truth it was merely a convenient excuse to watch Oliver. But after only a moment, Oliver met his eyes before he tilted his head at the carpeted floor and lifted an eyebrow. Brandon looked down, and sure enough, between Carmichael and Goodson was a damp patch.

He coughed to cover his laugh. Oliver's cheeks were pink, and mirth danced in his eyes. So like his Oliver, to try and break the tension for him.

How Brandon wished it were just the two of them. Like old times. He wanted to return the favor, make sure Oliver wasn't going to brood about the bite.

When they stepped out of the elevator, Brandon allowed the other men to precede him as they walked down the hall, giving him the freedom to stare at Oliver's spectacular backside—getting caught ogling wasn't on his agenda. All too soon they were inside the apartment, where Brandon reluctantly raised his gaze to eye level.

Amazing how a couple of orgasms could change one's perception. It would be foolish to think there was a way to salvage any kind of relationship with Oliver, but during this mission? He'd take what he could get. The adversarial vibe had completely disappeared, to be replaced with horniness, for sure, but also a sense of comfort Brandon never felt with anyone else since the accident. A whisper of the camaraderie they'd had when they were partners.

Brandon shifted his weight. He didn't know what Oliver's plans for this evening were, but Brandon was going to try to convince him that they needed more mutual orgasms, and hopefully they could both put the ticking clock out of their minds. Too bad it was only lunchtime.

He grabbed a couple bottles of water before joining the others.

"Did you find a portal?" He settled down into the same chair he'd had last night and tossed the other bottle to Oliver.

"Thanks for bringing us some water too, Brain Trust."

Brandon just stared at Luis. Normally he would have, but having one of them get their own water would spring Oliver's prank.

"He's not your servant," Oliver admonished Goodson, who rolled his eyes.

Oliver defending him sent a tiny spurt of warmth curling through Brandon. "Back to my question—did you find the portal? Oliver and I didn't."

Carmichael shook his head. "No, it's not there. It's close—I'm sure of it—but not where we looked. We did find some human remains."

"As did we," Oliver interjected. "It might be a dumping ground, but there's no portal there. Is there a field or park nearby?"

Brandon nearly inhaled his water. "A park? Wouldn't we have seen more concrete evidence of an infection? The disappearances would hardly be limited to this apartment complex."

"Actually, we don't know for sure it is limited. It could have a wider spread, but differences in reporting might have some effect on the pattern we're seeing." Luis's tone held no recrimination or condescension.

Oliver shrugged. "A park is a long shot. I would have thought the abandoned building ideal, especially if the Umbrae are capable of choosing their portal locations. Now, though, I'm starting to wonder if there's any truth to that theory."

"And we still have no idea what sort of creature we're after," Carmichael said.

Brandon glanced at Oliver. One of them was going to have to broach the subject.

A crease appeared between Oliver's brows, and his shoulders dropped. Yeah, he knew it too. "It might be zombies."

"Zombies?" Carmichael's tone indicated the last thing on earth it could be was zombies.

Brandon scrunched up his nose. "We were sort of attacked—"

Carmichael flushed a deep, angry red as he sprang to his feet and loomed over Oliver. "What the fuck? You were attacked? What happened? Are you okay?"

Neither of them paid Brandon any attention at all.

"Sit down, Carmichael. If I wasn't fine, you'd know about it." Oliver's tone of command had Carmichael obeying with a sullen sneer. Brandon didn't fail to notice how cleverly Oliver had skirted the question.

Oliver and Brandon explained what had happened and why they weren't sure if the woman had been a zombie.

"And you're sure you're not hurt?" Carmichael was now as suspicious as Brandon would have been after that explanation. It was hard not to like someone who clearly cared for Oliver almost as much as Brandon did.

Oliver's nostrils flared. "Can we get on with this?"

Carmichael paused for a moment, then shrugged. Brandon relaxed a bit. Oliver tended to pretend he was superhuman, but with Brandon backing him up, they managed to fool Carmichael. He hadn't agreed with Oliver's decision to keep them in the dark about the bite, but neither was he ready to throw his authority around, considering he was responsible for Oliver getting attacked in the first place.

"Could she have had... an incomplete transformation?" Carmichael asked.

"It's possible. I took some samples from the building. Maybe that will help, assuming it is a dumping ground." Brandon's stomach punctuated his words with a loud rumble. He'd had an orgasm and been attacked by a possible zombie since his last proper meal. He was starving. This morning's half-eaten toast didn't count.

"I ordered pizza while you were in the kitchen," Oliver said.

Goodson snorted. "Hope you like veggie."

"That's what I usually get." If it hadn't been for Oliver's convincing demonstration the previous night, Brandon might have been surprised Oliver remembered his pizza preferences.

"It is?" Goodson and Carmichael spoke in unison, both of them turning incredulous looks on Oliver.

Oliver appeared almost bored. "Does it matter?"

"Great," Brandon said. "After we eat, Carmichael, maybe you could go out again, walk around the neighborhood, get some more data for the monitor."

"Good idea," Oliver agreed. "Now that we know, or at least suspect, that the abandoned apartment is the dumping ground, there must be a good reason the Umbrae is using it. If it's a vampire we're dealing with, it could be a feeding ground. Assess the neighborhood with that in mind. Find out if vagrants are still using the building."

Goodson scowled. "What the hell is that supposed to mean? The place is way exposed. No killer in their right mind would transport bodies there, not if he hoped to get away unseen."

"Umbrae may not be in their right minds, but they're cunning. Secretive. And highly into self-preservation. That dumping ground is one they believe will not be discovered for a long time, or if they expect it to be found soon, there will be a good reason. It wouldn't be the first time they tried to throw suspicion on someone else to hide their crimes."

The reproachful look Oliver gave Goodson, followed by the slight flush in Goodson's cheeks, told Brandon that Goodson was familiar with this tactic in some way.

"Right, yes, sorry." Goodson spit out the apology with reluctance.

"I'd like you to accompany Carmichael again this afternoon."

"Again?" Goodson must have realized how cranky that one word sounded. "No offense, Carmichael."

Carmichael shrugged. "None taken."

"Yes. Put those investigative skills to work. Remember that you're hunting for a creature more like a predator than a human." Oliver's tiny nod of approval apparently was enough for Goodson. Was Oliver always so sparing of praise? Not that he'd been particularly effusive with praise when Brandon had been his partner, but he'd had a lot more enthusiasm and many more smiles than Brandon had seen thus far.

"And what will you be doing?" Carmichael split a suspicious look between him and Oliver.

"I'm going to work on the specimens I collected. And I have some files to catch up on from the office." Brandon took a sip of water and tried to look innocent.

He had no idea if he and Oliver were on the same page here, but so far, the afternoon was shaping up to the point that Brandon wasn't going to have to wait until tonight to get Oliver naked. Which he was going to do whether they had sex or not. He hadn't missed the fact that Oliver sat stiffly upright and hadn't relaxed against the back of the couch. Another look at Oliver's wounds was warranted.

Neither lust nor pain were visible in Oliver's disapproving expression. "And I will be taking a closer look at this apartment, in case the landlord missed a clue to the previous tenants' whereabouts."

Goodson slumped back into his chair, a hairsbreadth from sulking. Brandon couldn't really blame him, the man had been a police detective, after all. But Oliver had had a lot more experience investigating Umbrae, and sometimes Goodson's background might be more hindrance than help. The Umbrae weren't like human killers. The R&D department had sunk thousands upon thousands into profiling, but when an entity not of this world infected a human to create a mythological creature in ways that still weren't understood, profiling wasn't any more useful than Stoker or Shelley.

The knock on the door must have seemed like a reprieve for Oliver, since he leaped up to answer it while Carmichael and Goodson gave him sullen looks. Brandon did his best to appear unconcerned and took another swig of water.

Oliver returned and slung the pizzas on the coffee table in front of them. Goodson stood and turned to Carmichael with an exaggerated, deliberate movement. "Want a water, Carmichael?"

"Yeah, thanks." Carmichael's tone held a bite Brandon knew was directed at him.

Goodson glared at Brandon on the way to the kitchen. Brandon didn't think a hardened police detective truly had his boxers in a bunch over a perceived rudeness but was rather expressing a knee-jerk reaction to being out of his element. Hell, Goodson could throw a tantrum right now, and Brandon wouldn't care so long as it meant he was leaving the damned apartment with Carmichael after they ate.

Stomach rumbling, Brandon leaned over and flipped up the top of one of the pizza boxes.

"What the flying fuck is that?" Brandon didn't need lipreading to help him hear Goodson's angry cursing. Oliver had pushed himself partway out of the chair before he remembered exactly what Brandon had stored in the fridge.

Oliver laughed as Goodson continued to swear at the top of his lungs. Brandon couldn't help it; he joined in. Like all professions that dealt with death on a regular basis, their humor tended to be more ghoulish than most—sometimes it was the only way to cope.

"What the hell is going on?" Carmichael had gotten to his feet, and he shifted his weight back and forth as though he couldn't decide if he should stay or find out what had upset Goodson. The decision was taken out of his hands when Goodson returned—no water, but dark spots of color on his cheeks.

"He's got his samples in the fridge." Goodson pointed straight at Brandon, and tears began running down Oliver's face he was laughing so hard. Brandon couldn't control his own laughter enough to appease Goodson, who flexed his fingers in anticipation of throttling someone.

"What samples?" Carmichael asked, body poised for battle.

"I didn't look at them all, but there's a hunk of tattooed skin in the fucking vegetable crisper."

Carmichael's eyebrows scooted toward his hairline. "There's what where?"

"You fucking heard me."

Carmichael just stared at Oliver like he'd never seen the man before, until his laughter died down some. Then Carmichael turned that icy blue gaze on Brandon.

"What? They need to be preserved. They're in plastic bags." Brandon's argument was slightly undermined by Oliver's breathy chuckles.

With an exasperated sigh, Carmichael scrubbed his face with his hands and dropped back into his seat. "Sit down and eat, Goodson."

Then Goodson cracked a smile. "Okay, Brain Trust. You got me. I can see the guys in the precinct doing the same thing. But just remember, payback's a bitch."

"Uh-huh, sure. Whatever helps you sleep at night." Brandon grinned, pleased the man had a sense of humor. As long as Goodson didn't have any designs on Oliver—or vice versa—he could try to like the guy.

Brandon noticed his little trick didn't affect Goodson's appetite any. The pizza disappeared quickly, and in less than thirty minutes they were ready to get back on the job.

Like managers giving pep talks to their prospective fighters, Oliver pulled Goodson to one end of the room to give him instructions for the afternoon while Brandon pulled Carmichael to the other end to double-check his devices.

"I don't know what's going on between you two, but it had better not interfere in this investigation." Carmichael didn't speak loudly, but he did look directly into Brandon's face.

"There's nothing going on between us." *Deny, deny, deny.* Brandon wasn't going to lay the whole mess out for a virtual stranger.

Carmichael just stared at him, and Brandon scowled.

"Many times, I've wanted Oliver to loosen up."

Brandon's eyes widened involuntarily. Carmichael wanted Oliver to loosen up? He hadn't seen that coming.

Carmichael curled his lip into a sneer before he continued. "When he's not acting like a stereotypical stoic government agent, he's playing the part of someone's disapproving dad."

Disapproving dad? That didn't sound like the Oliver he knew.

Carmichael wasn't finished, though. "And I know damn well he was in on that prank. It was pretty obvious, the way he started laughing. But I've never known him to pull a prank or even laugh like that. I've also never heard your name before, but you and he obviously go way back. So, like I said, I don't know what's going on, but we've got a job to do, and as soon as it's done, you're going to send me back to fieldwork. Got it?"

Huh. Carmichael hadn't heard Oliver laugh? That couldn't be what Carmichael meant, could it? What had happened to Oliver that wasn't covered in the field reports Brandon had read over the years?

"Don't worry. We'll get the job done, and as long as I get my data, I'll see about getting you transferred back."

---

THE APARTMENT DOOR slammed shut behind Luis and Carmichael, leaving Oliver alone with Brandon as they stared at each other. The Umbrae attack, the blowjob in the elevator, rubbing off last night... none of it seemed quite real in the bright light of day, with the detritus of lunch on the coffee table between them. Silence hung thick and heavy in the air, charged with a sudden sexual awareness, masking the dull throb in Oliver's back. He darted a glance at Brandon's groin. Under the scrutiny, Brandon's cock filled and pushed against his fly. Oliver swallowed heavily, unsure where they went from here.

Brandon took a step forward, and Oliver lifted his gaze. God, he wanted this man, and the sight of that same desire reflected back in Brandon's eyes made Oliver's prick stand at immediate attention. Pretty good for an old man of forty-three. But then, Brandon had always stimulated his libido like no one else ever had. That surfer-boy look wrapped around a sharp wit and acerbic intelligence was an instant aphrodisiac.

He should tell Brandon having sex was, and would be, a mistake. He should ask why Brandon wanted him or if he wanted more than these moments stolen from the mission. But the truce between them was as fragile and delicate as a soap bubble, with all those loose ends

—for him, anyway—seething under the surface. Mistake or not, all Brandon had to do was crook a finger, or... Oliver swallowed heavily. Or unzip and pull out his gorgeous, fat, hard cock and give it a stroke or two, as he was doing now. A ding from the elevator, heralding the other men's departure, underscored how easily they could get caught. One forgotten wallet and they'd be back in the apartment to find Oliver erect and fixated on Brandon's sweet, naked dick.

One more time. He deserved one more reprieve from discussing this with Brandon. A reprieve from worrying if he was too old and broken-down for this job. Hell, a reprieve from worrying about his odds of dying on this mission. One more time to feel and taste and touch and pretend time had turned back.

"Bedroom, please."

"Naked, please," Brandon mimicked Oliver's choked-out request. He released his cock, licked his thumb, then stroked it over the flushed cap of his erection.

Oliver's mouth watered, and his own dick begged to be released from confinement. He vibrated in place, held captive by the almost predatory way Brandon stalked closer, sinuous and sensual. Brandon slicked precum over the head of his prick, making it shiny and even more tempting. The ease and amount of Brandon's precum had always fascinated Oliver, and he wanted to taste.

"Think there's any dry cleaners around here?"

Oliver frowned, but his thoughts were shattered by Brandon's cargo pants dropping to the floor, baring cock and balls for Oliver's perusal. He wanted to grab Brandon, but the man stood just out of reach. The reward for letting Brandon tease him had always been spectacular.

"You didn't answer me." Brandon's bottom lip pushed out in a fake pout before he stripped off his shirt.

God, what he'd missed in the dark the previous night. All of Brandon's muscles were more defined. He hadn't bulked up any—still had that sleek body—but it looked as though he'd lost a few pounds, tightening the skin over those firm muscles. No way should Oliver have remembered that, but as he'd told Brandon, he'd not forgotten a thing. What he hadn't mentioned was how completely the memories of sex with Brandon filled his fantasies, always with a pinch of guilt for added masochism.

Sunlight streamed in from the sliding door out to the rickety little balcony. The light made Brandon glow as it picked up the golden hair covering his body. Sixteen floors up, there was no way anyone could see, but the hint of getting caught smoldered in the room with them.

"Oliver?"

"Yes?"

"I asked about dry cleaners."

Right. He'd asked a question. Dry cleaners? "Yes, what? Why?"

Brandon gave him a devilish grin. "Too late." He sprang into Oliver's arms and wrapped his legs around Oliver's waist. Oliver clutched the peach-fuzz skin of Brandon's ass and moaned as Brandon rubbed against his erection.

"Why dry cleaners?" he panted in Brandon's ear.

Brandon pulled back a bit in Oliver's arms, careful not to separate their groins any. "Because if you didn't get naked, I'm going to mess up your nicely pressed suit pants." He glanced down between them. "And your starched shirt. But it's too late now."

Oh yeah, he'd forgotten that. Brandon's precum did tend to get messy when Oliver was still dressed. But back then he'd worn jeans all the time and never had to worry about dry cleaning.

Brandon nipped at his ear, and Oliver realized he didn't care about it now either. "I have other pants and shirts." The last word extended into a full-on groan as Brandon sucked on his earlobe.

"Good. Then let's get you out of these ones," Brandon whispered between licks.

Oliver carried Brandon to his bedroom, pausing periodically to press him against the wall and tongue fuck him.

By the time he tossed Brandon on the bed, they were both frantic. But this time Oliver wanted more. He didn't want the dim memory of Brandon's body opening to his; he wanted an immediate reminder. A new memory to keep him warm at night if Brandon cut him loose again.

Brandon spread his legs and cupped his balls, lifting them so Oliver could see the puckered flesh below. Groaning, he snagged some lube from his bedside table and slicked up two fingers. Tapping at the hole, he reveled in Brandon's attempts to coax his finger inside. But he was too far gone to attempt any payback for Brandon's teasing, and he slipped a finger inside the tight heat. Brandon let out a needy groan and pushed down. Oliver didn't know how many men Brandon had let into his bed since they'd broken up—seven years was a long fucking time, and he didn't want to think about it—but Brandon was tight and sweet.

"More," Brandon whispered. Like always, Oliver did what Brandon wanted, and he pushed another finger inside. Brandon winced slightly, but Oliver held his hand still, and within moments Brandon writhed on his fingers like he couldn't get enough. Oliver thrust gently, taking care to avoid Brandon's prostate. He was saving that because there wasn't anything sexier in the world than having Brandon whimpering and begging on the end of his dick. He pushed Brandon's hand away and took over stroking Brandon's cock. He didn't dare get close enough to let Brandon's skilled fingers near his own groin. He wasn't coming until he was fucking Brandon, and that was that.

The sexy man on his bed humped between Oliver's hands, a steady litany of expletives bleeding from his mouth in an undertone. God. Watching Brandon edge closer to orgasm was almost as good as the blowjob Brandon had bestowed in the elevator.

"So fucking hot," he whispered, interrupting the flow of Brandon's words.

Opening his eyes wide, Brandon stared at him, irises a mere ring around lust-blown pupils. "Fuck me."

Oliver paused, hands stilling, as he shivered in anticipation of that request...no, demand.

"Fuck me." Brandon's words got louder and more forceful. "Now, Oliver, now!"

Yes. Oh yes. Oliver pulled his hands away from Brandon, grabbed the slick, and stared down at his bare cock. "Oh goddamn."

"I need you." The words may have been a plea, but Brandon's tone was all demand. "Fuck me."

"I... I..."

Brandon snarled and tried to snatch the lube out of Oliver's hand. "Strip, put a fucking condom on, and fuck me with that big fucking cock."

Oliver growled. Brandon's blond innocence spewing those filthy words always turned him on, and there was no doubt in his mind Brandon did it on purpose.

"I didn't bring any with me."

"Didn't bring what?" Brandon pulled on his balls, a surefire signal he was getting close.

Oliver could fucking cry. "Rubbers."

Brandon's mouth opened as he stared at Oliver. Considering the man had initially assumed Oliver was sticking it to Luis or Carmichael or both, his surprise was understandable. But Oliver didn't fuck around on missions—not since Brandon had left him. There was no way he could even suggest going without protection. All those nameless, faceless fucks came back to haunt him. He'd always, always been careful and got tested regularly, but there was no way was he going to risk Brandon's health.

"Did you bring some?" Please, please, please.

Brandon shook his head. "No, I never expected..." He waved his free hand at their bodies, cocks still hard and straining for each other. No, Oliver hadn't expected this either.

Oliver licked his lips. Blowing Brandon was never a hardship, but he really, really wanted to fuck the man into a stupor.

"Shh," he soothed. "Move back a little." There was enough room for him to kneel on the bed between Brandon's legs, and he bent over to taste the precum wetting the head of Brandon's dick.

"No," Brandon whimpered. "Stop."

Oliver looked up. Who turned down a blowjob?

"I want fucking. I need you inside me. So bad. Would Carmichael have some?"

The discussion should have wilted their dicks, but it only backed them away from the precipice—slightly.

"Nope. The man never fucks around on Adam."

A funny little smile twitched Brandon's lips up. "And Goodson?"

"Uh... I don't know."

The funny little smile became a devilish grin as he grabbed Oliver's still-lubed fingers and thrust them back into his own body. "Go check."

Back on the edge of orgasm again, Oliver thrust gently once, twice, then dragged his fingers along Brandon's prostate. Brandon cried out and glared at him, but he deserved payback for making Oliver go look for fucking rubbers in a near-stranger's toiletry kit.

"You fucking save that for me," he warned as he stomped from the room.

"Hurry back, sailor," Brandon teased behind him.

The living room had never seemed so far away, and he skidded to a stop beside the table where Luis had piled his stuff. Oliver stared at his stained pants, shrugged, and wiped his slippery fingers on his thigh. A few minutes rooting around in the shaving kit found him what he was looking for, a whole strip of them, and he wanted to crow in triumph. He tore one off, reconsidered, then took another three. Might be a while before they got to a pharmacy, although he wasn't looking forward to explaining this little theft to his new partner. He considered trying to return everything to the way he'd found it, but his dick insisted he get back to the bedroom. Which he did with all possible speed.

Brandon didn't look like he'd moved, except to push a pillow under his hips. With his legs splayed, his hole was on display, glistening in invitation.

Oliver held up the foil wrappers.

"Thank God. And hurry the fuck up."

Oliver yanked his clothes off, uncaring that a couple of buttons went flying and he'd need a tailor as well as a dry cleaner for this suit.

A tiny bit of his urgency had faded as a result of his errand, and he licked his lips as he considered how much he could tease Brandon before the urgency returned. To be fully prepared, ready to slam into Brandon's body as soon as neither of them could wait a second longer, he rolled the condom on.

Brandon had anticipated an immediate thrust, and he yowled in frustration when Oliver stroked his flat belly. Holding Brandon's hips, Oliver licked around Brandon's navel, then nibbled his way to a well-defined hip bone. Brandon demanded and cajoled and pleaded, but Oliver sucked up a little mark on the soft skin beside Brandon's ruddy erection instead of sucking or fucking what Brandon wanted.

With light touches, Oliver teased Brandon's balls, fingers smoothing down to his pucker, tapping and rubbing but without penetration.

"Damn you. Fuck me already. Fuck me so hard I feel it until next week. I want your cock filling my ass, and I want it now."

Shit. Oliver squeezed the base of his dick, the words ramping up his need. He slicked up his cock and shifted back between Brandon's legs. "Did you—"

"Jesus fuck, Oliver, fucking fuck me already."

Oliver shuddered. He loved it when Brandon lost his academic veneer and became a completely sexual animal. For a brief second he rested his dick against Brandon's hole, savoring the anticipation. When Brandon lifted his head and glared, Oliver obeyed the previous demand and sank deep into Brandon's body with one thrust. Brandon's back arched clear off the bed, and he groaned in pained pleasure even as he spread his thighs wider to accept the invasion.

Brandon's ass gripped Oliver like a virgin's, and he closed his eyes, breathing deeply to give Brandon the chance to adjust to the invasion. Almost before Oliver was ready, Brandon rotated his hips, silently encouraging him to thrust. In, out, he moved harder and faster, Brandon meeting every movement, the slap of flesh on flesh echoing in the room. Sweat formed a sheen on their bodies, their skin gliding together smoothly. Brandon's slightly opened mouth and pink lips called to Oliver, but he couldn't bring himself to slow his thrusts enough to take a kiss.

"Harder, harder," Brandon whispered, one hand clutching at Oliver's back, the other stroking his cock.

Oliver shifted position, searching for Brandon's prostate. The effect was electric and immediate as Brandon's breath hitched before he spurted. The pulse of Brandon's orgasm yanked Oliver over the edge, and with a deep groan, he ground his cock into Brandon and filled the condom in long, hard pulses.

Careful not to rest all his weight on Brandon's smaller form, he nudged his nose into Brandon's neck and rested for a moment, trying to catch his breath.

The condom wouldn't wait forever, though. As soon as he thought he could move his post-orgasm rubber muscles, Oliver disposed of the condom while Brandon grabbed some tissue to wipe up. A twinge in his back made him pause, just enough to alert Brandon.

"How's the back?"

"It's fine. Just tender."

"I should clean and redress it."

Oliver considered that, but it had only been a few hours. "I think it's okay."

"You sure? A shower might be just the thing. I'll wash your back." Brandon winked, and Oliver's spent cock gave a valiant attempt to rise. Brandon might be able to coax a full recovery from him. All this sex was going to kill him, but he'd die a happy man.

Oliver grabbed Brandon's face with both hands and kissed that soft mouth. Brandon hadn't bothered shaving, and the day's stubble scraped against Oliver's chin, proclaiming loud and clear he was kissing a man. He thrust his tongue into Brandon's mouth and slid his hands up over Brandon's ears and into his hair.

Brandon stiffened like a cat that didn't want to be held and pulled away. He nervously adjusted his hair and picked up his shirt off the floor. "Maybe a shower isn't a good idea."

Where the hell had his brash, sexy Brandon gone? Had Oliver done something? They'd only been kissing and... *Oh.*

"A shower is an excellent idea." Oliver moved back into Brandon's personal space and tucked those shoulder-length blond locks behind Brandon's ears. He held Brandon's head gently, thumbs and index fingers bracketing his ears. From his almost terrified look, Brandon hadn't missed the deliberation with which Oliver touched his hearing aids, but Oliver didn't let that stop him from kissing Brandon thoroughly.

After Brandon had relaxed, Oliver lifted his head. "Shower?"

Brandon bit his lip, telegraphing his indecision. Oliver brought their bodies closer. Sure, only a few minutes ago he was thinking they needed to cool it, but he didn't want Brandon to think that was because of the hearing aids. It was all his fault Brandon was wearing them, and the only difficulty Oliver had with them was the reminder of his guilt. But making Brandon doubt himself was almost as unforgivable as the inattention that had caused the injury in the first place.

Oliver fought with Brandon for possession of his lower lip, and when he won, Brandon smiled as best he could without control over the lip trapped delicately between Oliver's teeth.

Releasing Brandon, Oliver asked again. "Shower?"

"I... can't wear these. And the sound of the shower running..."

Oliver kissed his temple. "I think we can manage this without talking. Decide now how you want it, and we'll be just fine."

"I want to fuck your mouth."

Oh-ho. Brandon was still in sex-monkey mode. "Blowjobs it is."

Oliver leaned in, mouth next to Brandon's ear, and spoke softly. "I can't wait to feel your dick in my mouth. Taste your cum again."

There was no more need to talk.

# ELEVEN

When Carmichael and Luis returned, Brandon was working studiously at the dining-room table, and Oliver was checking the apartment for blood. All innocent-like. He'd gotten Brandon's agreement to stay silent on the matter of his bite. If they weren't worrying about him, they could focus on their job—finding the portal. Hell, he wished Brandon didn't know about it or his earlier injury, but having another secret with Brandon reminded him of better times, even if the secret itself was as shitty as it got.

"Well?" Oliver assessed the two men, who appeared to be getting along better than they had that morning. Carmichael's gaze darted suspiciously between him and Brandon, but Oliver was confident there was nothing to give them away.

"The portal's here. I just can't find it." Carmichael threw his hoodie on the couch in frustration. "I'm taking this thing off now," he warned Brandon, running his fingers over the electrodes on his temple.

Yanking off a pair of grimy latex gloves, Brandon leaped to his feet. "Hold on, hold on. Let me get it off for you."

Carmichael whipped his shirt off, Brandon moved in close, and

Oliver took a step forward, biting back a growl. Watching his ex touching another man for work purposes shouldn't piss him off, especially when Brandon had worn him out so thoroughly that it would be hours before his dick woke up. He didn't know what Brandon's intentions were, but Oliver knew he had to be prepared for the day Brandon cut him off, cut him out of his life again. The fact that he'd already given in to Brandon more than once was the height of stupidity, and he was going to get his heart broken all over again. Or he was going to kill them both with his inattention.

Every gently removed electrode from Carmichael's defined chest made Oliver grit his teeth just a little bit harder.

"I'll take a look at the data later, see if we can pinpoint something." Brandon finally stepped away from the half-naked man, and Oliver's tension dialed down. His stomach grumbled; the pizza had been hours ago.

"I still can't figure out why anyone would store bodies at a condemned apartment building." Luis spoke from Oliver's left, and he suppressed his instinct to jump. Once more his focus had been so intent on Brandon, he'd lost track of what was going on around him. He couldn't go down this rabbit hole again. Not when Brandon was more vulnerable than ever to the dangers of fieldwork.

"Oh?" Oliver turned to him, striving for an emotionless expression.

"It's too damn exposed. And the thing could come crumbling down at any minute. We did find out that vagrants used to sleep there, but very few in the past months. In fact, I'm surprised there weren't full-on squatters there. We saw some evidence of it, and with winter coming, it's an ideal roost. But if they've been officially rousted by the cops, or even private security, no one we spoke to was aware of it."

Brandon had paused in packing up the monitoring equipment to face Luis while he gave his report.

Oliver waved a hand. "Let's have a seat and discuss what else we've found. Carmichael, put your shirt back on." *Please, please, put your fucking shirt on.*

"Give me a second." Brandon bent back toward the monitoring equipment. He placed it on the dining room table next to one of the disgusting samples he'd been testing.

"Are you done with that?" Oliver waved a finger at the gooey mess. The sample didn't smell any better than it looked. "I think we might want dinner soon, but that..."

"Fucking stinks." Carmichael's voice was slightly muffled through the shirt he pulled over his head.

Brandon looked surprised for a moment but put on a fresh pair of latex gloves, rolled the specimen back into its bag, and returned it to the kitchen. The sound of the fridge door opening and closing was closely followed by the sounds of hand washing—thankfully. When he returned to the room, everyone was seated. Brandon had told him being able to see everyone made it easier if there was any noise interference, and Oliver wanted to help him out as much as possible.

"So, no portal yet?" Brandon sank into the chair Oliver had already labeled Brandon's. Funny how all four of them had their allotted spots.

"No." Carmichael spat the word out. Over time, Carmichael's sensitivity to portal activity hadn't increased, exactly, but he was able to decipher it better. His ability to find new portals, once he got within range, was why the R&D department had insisted on having a piece of him. The portal's proximity had them all on edge, and for the first time, Oliver's frustration exceeded Carmichael's at their inability to locate it. Too many places to search, with only three days and counting down. But he did his best to prevent his fear from leaking out.

"After dinner we'll map out your route today and see if we can correlate any of it to the data on your monitor." Brandon's tone was conciliatory enough that Oliver almost expected him to lean over and pat Carmichael's knee. Even more surprising was that Carmichael actually appeared mollified.

Oliver cleared his throat. "The infected, whether there's one or several, must be familiar with this area. I found enough traces of human blood in here that I suspect the previous tenants didn't abandon this apartment. They might have been victims of another type of foul play, but I doubt it."

"And there were no police reports filed?" Carmichael sorted through the take-out menus on the coffee table, his mind already on dinner.

"No, hardly any. Most of the people who've gone missing didn't have anyone to file reports. A few employers did, but like the land-lords, most times they just assumed the people have moved on without notice. In fact, the biggest red flag came from the sheer number of forms filed to evict without contest in these buildings. Much higher than the surrounding areas, although it could have meant nothing at all." Oliver gave Luis a nod to acknowledge his part in picking up on that anomaly.

"What about the specimens?" Luis threw Brandon a dirty look, but Brandon smiled serenely.

"Actually, I found something weird. The bite marks look like they're made with human teeth."

Human teeth? Luis looked disgusted, but Oliver and Carmichael exchanged a look. Almost all of the Umbrae manifestations MIA had seen over the years triggered a physiological change in the infected's teeth. Werewolf teeth, vampire teeth, yeti teeth... all made distinctive bite marks when you knew what to look for. Even zombie teeth were modified to allow them to rip through the skull. And Brandon, with his medical training, sure as hell knew what to look for.

"Are you sure?" Oliver got a dirty look all for himself from Brandon.

"Yes, I'm sure. Teeth were maybe a bit sharper than normal, but that's the only difference I can see with this equipment."

"This is not like any zombie incursion I've ever heard of." Carmichael hadn't been with the agency nearly as long as Oliver, but the ex-military man had studied many of the archived reports to ensure he knew the best way to kill the monsters the portals created. Full-fledged zombie incursions were rare, mostly because zombies didn't have any subtlety.

Brandon frowned. "I have to agree. Zombies go for the brain, and they leave a lot more of the corpse than the scraps we found."

With a frown, Carmichael scratched at his head and neck. "What did you glue those electrodes on with? Itchy as hell. I'm going to take a shower. Give me a summary after." He hoisted himself out of the chair and started stripping as he headed to the bathroom.

"Look, I read the files they gave me, but I still don't understand why... Fuck, I still can't believe... Sometimes there are vampires, sometimes werewolves, sometimes other things." Luis's mouth twisted. He'd spent his professional life dealing with the worst humans could do to each other. Believing in fables and folklore did not easily fit into the standard policeman's consciousness, even one who'd had his throat almost ripped out by a vampire.

"Honestly, we don't much know why the portals sometimes make one thing and not another. Once the strain has been determined by the alpha victim, the possession is generally spread via bite," Oliver said.

"Yes. I'm sure they covered this in your training, but make sure you inform us if you get bitten." The word bitten made Brandon's voice falter, and he shot Oliver a worried look, but managed to keep silent about Oliver's bite.

Luis rolled his eyes. "Training? I'm assuming most of it's on the job, because it was pretty sparse aside from the weapons and self-defense, although I didn't much need that."

Brandon shrugged. "Regardless, it's important that we know. It gives a hard deadline for shutting down the portal."

Oliver appreciated Brandon emphasizing that fact for Luis, but their countdown had already begun. And if they didn't have the portal shut within... less than 72 hours, the physiological transformation would be complete, and he might well die. Sure, he had a chance of immunity based on his first interaction with the Umbrae, but

Brandon had been super pissed off when he'd found out that being bitten previously was not the ironclad protection the agency claimed it was.

"Fine, fine. Are we crossing zombies off the list?"

Brandon grabbed the transceiver that had been strapped to Carmichael's neck and fiddled with it. "I'm sure it's not zombies. Not ones we've seen before. Whatever it is, they leave normal human bite marks instead of some variation of fangs." There was a faint lilt of lecture in Brandon's words, enough for Oliver to flash on a naughty-professor-and-student game they might be able to play.

Shit. When had he suddenly turned into a horny teenager? If they had sex again tonight—it would be a miracle if he got it up again —his dick might fall off from overuse.

"Have you got *any* idea what we're after, then?" Oliver stared at Brandon, whose lips were still a bit puffy from sucking him off in the shower. If Oliver concentrated, he could still taste Brandon in his own mouth. So damned distracting.

Brandon wandered over to the table to grab his laptop. "Not sure. But if the creature is, well, eating its victims, the abandoned building might be a feeding ground, not a dumping ground."

"Feeding ground?" Luis's eyes widened, horrified.

"I think there's a Native American tradition..." As Brandon sat back in his chair, he bit his lip in thought, and Oliver almost leaned over to claim it as he had earlier that afternoon.

"Wait—a wendigo?" Much like the Asian hopping vampires, wendigos could be related to the culture of the alpha victim. Oliver didn't know if there had ever even been a wendigo nest in all the years he'd been at the agency, but their training included reading about various mythological creatures.

With vampire and werewolf movies abounding of late, the majority of the nests over the past few years had consisted almost entirely of those types of monsters. Popular culture pushed them into people's consciousness, making them the most likely creatures for Umbrae to change victims into. That particular argument would be proven without a shadow of a doubt if they ever got themselves a sparkly vampire nest.

"A wendigo? What the fuck's a wendigo?" Luis looked expectantly at Oliver, who shrugged.

"Well, if I recall, it's a cannibal. Or it's created from a cannibal. There's definitely eating of human flesh." Brandon spoke almost distractedly as he continued to set up wires from the transceiver to his laptop.

"Shouldn't Cardoso know?"

He was the senior agent, but that didn't necessarily explain Luis's certainty that Oliver knew all about wendigos.

"No. We've never had a wendigo infection that we know of. And anyway, he's Colombian."

Knowing Brandon remembered yet another thing from their time together eased a bit of Oliver's growing tension.

"So... no wendigos in Colombia?"

Oliver snorted. Over the years, he'd been mistaken for a native from every Spanish-speaking country and almost every Native American tribe aside from Inuit. "Not that I know of. But we left Colombia when I was six, and I believe the wendigo myth was confined to the Algonquin tribes, not widespread through the Americas. But my memory could well be faulty."

Luis whipped out his phone and tapped at the screen. Then frowned.

"Good luck with that." Brandon chuckled.

"Seriously? The portal can do that?"

"Yep. But it's usually random enough that it can't be tracked... and most people tend to naturally avoid portals anyway. Probably reminds their subconscious of nightmarish things in the dark."

With an irritated grunt, Luis slipped his phone back into his pocket. "How the fuck are we supposed to find out about wendigos, then?"

"Library?" Brandon shrugged, and Luis glared at him. "No, seriously, out in the field, we're mostly on our own. Wireless is sketchy and unreliable, and even if it weren't, it's not like there are definitive texts on the subject. Even if we found a treatise on the wendigo, written by the foremost expert in Algonquin folklore and mythology, it would only give us a broad idea of what to look for or how to kill it. We can't assume everything in the folklore will manifest itself in an Umbrae possession. And if we find out that we need to bury a lock of its hair under the light of a full moon with the toenail of wild cougar... Well, who the hell is going to go to that much trouble? Our first priority is the innocents who might be killed by the monster, and we haven't found a creature yet that can't be taken down by a shot to the head, although certain weapons or ammunition are more effective than others, depending on the species."

Oliver wanted to kiss the man. Brandon was so incredibly level-headed, despite the worry he clearly felt for Oliver. He wanted to help people, but he'd always been cold-bloodedly practical about the Umbrae. Despite the fact that the original victims were also innocents, he was adamant that they not be allowed to hurt others.

"I can do a shot to the head." Luis nodded and patted his sidearm.

"Do you remember anything else about wendigos, Brandon?" Oliver thought he'd seen a bad movie with them, but he could swear there was something about screeching, not cannibalism. Maybe he was getting wendigos mixed up with banshees.

"Not much. The cannibalism is a given, especially based on the specimens we found, but I can't remember if the wendigo is so starved it eats human flesh—or if it craves it. Possibly both."

Oliver suppressed a grimace. The Umbrae were responsible for a lot of atrocities, but eating other people was an abhorrent idea. Craving them was even worse.

"Are we looking for a Native American?" Luis asked.

Oliver considered. "Maybe. But it's equally likely the alpha victim saw a movie or read a book about wendigos right before his or her possession. Or it's someone obsessed with Native American culture. Or someone who has a natural psychological makeup that well suits a wendigo."

Luis jumped up and wandered to the sliding door, rubbing the back of his neck. "Well, that narrows it down. What kind of fucking psychological makeup is suited to cannibalism?"

The sarcasm was not lost on Oliver or Brandon, and they exchanged a look. From the data they'd gathered over the years, the Umbrae tended to exacerbate and amplify people's worst, basest, most animalistic traits while remaking human physiology to mimic creatures of fiction and folklore. Or the folklore arose because of past Umbrae possessions. The chicken-and-egg argument had never been fully settled to the satisfaction of anyone in the agency.

"I'm going to get a bottle of water. Want anything?" Brandon asked.

Luis, still staring out the window, shook his head.

"No, thanks," Oliver replied.

As Brandon passed by, he ran his fingers through Oliver's hair, almost reflexively, resurrecting a ghost of their former relationship. Closing his eyes, Oliver savored the moment. Little by little, the wall keeping them apart was crumbling, and he didn't know what to do about it. If this truce was temporary, extending only the length of their time in this shitty apartment, he wanted to wallow in it.

Problem was, he couldn't afford to be distracted. Not with three agents' lives depending on him, as well as the lives of countless innocents. The apartment complex was rife with potential meals for a hungry wendigo or two. He turned his neck, trying to ease some of the tension that had rebuilt after his last orgasm, and the movement caused the skin over his wound to pull painfully. Even without the all-consuming distraction of Brandon, he might be losing his touch. He was so fucked.

Once Brandon left the room, Luis turned to him, eyes wide.

"I don't know if I'm cut out for this. I've arrested some mean assholes. I've seen crime scenes that were much worse than what we found. God knows, I've wanted to kill—again and again—the fucker that did this to me." He touched the scar tissue at his throat. "He's dead, so I joined the agency to help prevent another one from doing the same to someone else. But I've never felt so edgy, like my skin wants to crawl off. What if I freeze up at the wrong moment and get someone killed?"

Oliver might not be a cop, but he'd learned a bit about them over his years with the agency. "You ever been hurt on the job before? Shot, stabbed?"

Luis nodded. "Not this bad, but yeah. Stabbed trying to break up a nasty domestic disturbance, before I became detective."

"What happened after? Any hesitation, fear of doing your job?"

"No, not really." Luis frowned, thinking. "I was quicker to draw on suspects that might be armed or dangerous, but not any quicker to fire."

"I think you'll be fine. The bit where your skin prickles and you can't quite get comfortable? You're sensing the portal energy, not getting the yips."

Oliver's words startled a chuckle out of the cranky man. "Fuck, that's portal energy? It feels like we're right on top of it. No wonder you're all being assholes."

A quick wink told Oliver the man was joking. Buried deep under his crusty exterior, he did have a sense of humor. As much as Oliver truly didn't want to break in a new partner, train yet another green agent, he could probably work with this man. After all, it wasn't like he'd had the greatest introduction to the agency, with Kyle Bennett springing him on Oliver, and all the confusion and tension with Brandon.

Thinking of that tension and how he and Brandon had worked it off... His cheeks heated, and Brandon calling his name was welcome interruption. He clapped Luis on the shoulder and turned back to his surfer boy.

"Can you two set up the map on the wall while I finish calibrating?"

BY THE TIME Carmichael returned from the shower, Brandon had a projection from his laptop overlaid on the map on the dining room wall. At his request, Goodson darkened the route he and Carmichael had taken with a black marker to make it easier to see. According to the GPS data, Carmichael had been wandering around parts of Tokyo, Dubai, and Cairo, so Brandon ignored the portal-glitched data. GPS relied on wireless signals and was often badly affected. He just hoped the self-contained nature of the transceiver had escaped the portal's electronic jinx.

Oliver sat on the couch, observing. And if he imagined Oliver observing his ass as much as the projection, well, no one had to know. Thinking about the sex was a lot easier than paying attention to the giant countdown clock in his brain that had lit up as soon as he realized Oliver had been bitten by an Umbrae. His equipment had to make finding the portal easier. It just had to. It had never been more important to him.

Brandon worked with the other two men to pinpoint times and areas where Carmichael had sensed the portal energy more strongly, and correlated that with data from the transceiver. He had to filter the data by strength of reaction, or blips of red would have stained the entire map. With Carmichael's range of sensitivity, his body might have reacted to the portal's presence while they were still in their descent on the plane.

Excitement zipped through Brandon's blood as he stood back to inspect the final result. Aside from the GPS fiasco, it might actually work. Assuming the portal was where the transceiver indicated.

Oliver stood and got closer to the wall. "Shit, how accurate is this thing?"

Brandon shrugged, not wanting to appear too agitated, but the possibility of success made him smile. The area outlined on the map was a far smaller search area than he'd expected. He'd have to give Greg some serious kudos when they returned. If it meant saving Oliver's life, he'd owe Greg forever.

"We won't know until we find the portal, but look at it." He waved a hand at the map.

In addition to the spots where Carmichael had reported sensing portal energy, the transceiver had picked up other environmental and physiological data, of which Carmichael was unaware, forming a distinct circular path around this very building. R&D hadn't any luck calibrating a sensor to pinpoint the location of a portal, but this new data held some promise for that very thing. If Oliver hadn't been bitten, Brandon would have tried to do some additional testing with someone besides Carmichael. And if Brandon wasn't mistaken, the real work could begin—creating a device that could read the external factors that were stronger when Carmichael sensed portal activity more strongly, rather than having to rely on the man as a drug-sniffing hound.

Someone who wasn't an agent at all would make the best control subject, but in a pinch he'd use someone like himself or Goodson. Brandon had never been particularly sensitive to portal energy, worse now that he'd been out of fieldwork for so long, and Goodson wouldn't have had time to build up any sensitivity to it. But field trials would have to wait for the next portal. No way was he letting academic questions or even the potential scientific breakthrough get in the way of saving Oliver. Besides, Oliver was right—they were going to find the portal. With his equipment and Carmichael's sensitivity, how could they not?

"The portal is in *this* building, somewhere. Good work, Brandon." Oliver enunciated carefully as he continued to peer at the map, and Brandon preened—just a little—under Oliver's praise while being warmed by his thoughtfulness.

A shiver ran down his spine at the unexpected and gentle hand on his lower back. He didn't think Oliver was aware he'd slipped back into an old habit, but the angle was wrong for Goodson or Carmichael to see anything, and Brandon had no intention of complaining.

His contentment cracked a bit under Goodson's derisive snort, especially since it prompted Oliver to snatch his hand back. "You know that's still twenty floors. And how big are these portals? It could be inside any one of the apartments, right?"

"It still confines the area we need to search." Oliver's tone held a hint of reproach.

"I could hook Carmichael up again, have him walk the floors. Maybe we can pinpoint where we need to focus our search."

"For fuck's sake," Carmichael huffed. "Can it wait until after dinner? I'm starving."

Brandon laughed. "Sure. Oliver, order up some dinner, please."

Oliver gave him a dark look promising retribution, making Brandon shiver.

Did their tentative truce provide enough of a base to rebuild? He'd never thought Oliver would accept him, hadn't wanted to suffer the rejection, and had fled before Oliver could offer rejection or pity or even revulsion. They'd been together only sporadically, most of their relationship played out on missions, and when it had become clear Brandon wouldn't be doing any more fieldwork, he... Well, he didn't know what he'd been thinking, but he should have known his Oliver wouldn't have hated him or pitied him or been disgusted by him. And here they were, fucking on mission again.

He reached up and almost tucked his hair behind his ears. The near miss had him clenching his fists at his sides, his relaxed mood gone in a second. Oliver might know, but Brandon didn't want anyone else to know if he could avoid it. He'd spent years trying to keep anyone from figuring out his secret, and he wasn't about to let a few good—spectacular—orgasms loosen him up enough to reveal it to people he'd met less than a week ago.


SETTLED into the couch cushions beside Oliver, Brandon munched on his popcorn. Although the original plan had been to walk Carmichael through the building floor by floor, they'd decided it might be too suspicious to have four large men roaming the hallways at a time when many people would likely be returning home from work. Trespassing on the Umbrae's feeding ground was plenty dangerous enough without wary neighbors calling in the cops. There wasn't anything else they could do today, and hunting Umbrae at night increased the threat level substantially. The monsters created by the Umbrae were almost all creatures of the night and, as such, had significant advantages over the less nocturnal humans.

Without any specific agency work to accomplish, the evening had become one of leisure. Over dinner—Greek food this time—Carmichael and Oliver had regaled Brandon and Goodson with tales of missions past. Missions that had gone well, missions where the shit had hit the fan, and missions that were surprisingly comedic. Listening to the stories had given Brandon some insight into the years he and Oliver had spent apart.

By unspoken consent, neither he nor Oliver offered up any stories from their partnership. Brandon was happy enough not to have to edit his stories, since most of them started with "I was blowing Oliver," or "We were rubbing off, and..." Embarrassing, really. For all that he and Oliver had never ended up in a truly compromising position, they sure had screwed around a lot. Not the best impression to give to men who were expected to follow their directives.

Brandon needed the downtime, if he was going to remain level-headed and optimistic. When sharing stories over dinner had morphed into popcorn and watching a movie on the shitty-ass TV, Brandon hadn't had a word of complaint. Fortunately, the movie was one he'd seen before, so he could follow along without insisting the volume be turned up, as there wasn't any closed-captioning available.

This time the four of them hadn't aligned in their typical seats. Oliver had tilted his head, indicating the seat on the couch next to him, and Brandon had dropped into it before either of the other guys could, leaving the single seats for Goodson and Carmichael. Carmichael had turned out the lights, leaving the room in darkness, lit only by the glow of the television. The warmth of Oliver's solid body beside him reminded Brandon of other times on other missions or occasionally at Oliver's house when they'd just hung out, enjoying each other's company.

"Have you seen this one before?" Oliver spoke over the opening credits, directing his question to Brandon.

"Yeah, not long after it came out." He watched an awful lot of movies—alone—to fill up his time. This one had been hard because the main love interest looked a little like Oliver and it had come out about six months after they'd broken up.

"Any good?"

"Not bad. Some funny bits." Carmichael gave his opinion before Brandon could, but he nodded his agreement.

Goodson huffed from his chair. "Why are we watching a romantic comedy, and why the hell have you guys already seen it?"

"There are only two decent stations we can pick up, and the other one's showing a werewolf movie." Carmichael waved the remote to emphasize his words.

"What's wrong with the werewolf movie?"

Brandon could barely contain his laughter, and even Carmichael chuckled.

Oliver shook his head. "We'll talk again in a year, see how interested you are in watching any sort of monster movies or even ones with too many explosions. Rom-coms are popular choices among the agents."

Goodson rolled his eyes and settled back into his seat. Oliver shuffled a tiny bit closer, his thigh flush against Brandon's but not near enough that their proximity should garner any commentary from the other two agents. Brandon placed the popcorn bowl atop their thighs, further obscuring how close they were sitting, and focused on following the movie as best he could, although the exaggerated, over-the-top arguments were the most clearly audible portions.

A few minutes into the movie, Oliver leaned in, placing his lips close to Brandon's ear. "The volume okay?"

Brandon smiled. He never wanted to make a big deal about his hearing, but it pleased him Oliver realized movies weren't always ideal for him. He kept his voice low when he replied. "It's fine. Like I said, I've seen it before, and the plot is rather simple."

They shifted again as Oliver drew his head back, and this time they ended up pressed together shoulder to thigh.

BY THE TIME the credits rolled and segued into the evening news, Carmichael had gone to bed in the den, and Goodson snored softly in his chair. Brandon snuggled closer to Oliver, enjoying the strong arm wrapped around him, as it had been for most of the movie, popcorn bowl long since emptied and pushed to the floor. He hadn't wanted to check to see if Oliver too had fallen asleep and pulled him close out of habit, because this evoked too many good memories, and not just of the smoking sex.

Desire simmered in his blood, but it wasn't a driving urge. Brandon didn't want to break this simple connection. Why hadn't he stayed at Oliver's house more often when they'd been a couple? He should have been storing up moments like this to savor in the empty, lonely years since.

Oliver sighed, and Brandon tensed, waiting for their inevitable separation. Instead Oliver stretched, then replaced his arm where it had been, tangling his fingers in Brandon's hair. Brandon let himself sink a little closer, trying to ignore the dismal news stories.

"The device you've been strapping on Carmichael, is that one of your projects?"

"No, not mine."

"Really? Seems rather clever, and you're one of the smartest guys I know."

A warm glow lit Brandon from within, accompanied by a blush, at the unsolicited compliment. He knew he was smart, but Oliver was the rare man who could admire someone's accomplishments without jealousy or envy. Problem was, he never quite knew how to respond to sincere compliments.

"They don't let me work on projects myself now that I'm director." Brandon couldn't keep the disgruntlement out of his tone, but as soon as the words were out of his mouth, he froze. Was that even too much of a reminder of their new circumstances? Perhaps he shouldn't admit that he'd more or less packed up Greg's research and sailed out the door with Carmichael while the man sputtered behind him.

Oliver laughed, dispersing Brandon's tension. "Yeah, I've been offered a more senior position a time or two over the years. But most times, I like having hands on, just like you. I bet the paperwork is hell."

Brandon shrugged as best he could in the shelter of Oliver's arm. "You saw the stacks of files I brought. It's only a portion, and most of them aren't even computerized!"

A snort ruffled his hair. "Oh, that must make you nuts."

"Well, I managed to hang on to one project." Brandon took a deep breath. There weren't too many people who would understand why this project was so important to him. "I think it could replace sonic charges."

Oliver squeezed him a little tighter. "If anyone can find another way to shut down the portals safely, it's you."

Discussing this calmly with Oliver was an enormous relief, like Brandon was floating at half gravity. He'd missed this so much. Talking to someone about work, someone who wasn't trying to claw his way over Brandon, who wasn't going to wring every scrap of conversation for an angle he could use to get ahead.

"Thanks. There's only one issue right now. Theoretically the device needs to be activated from within the portal."

"Within? What, like, toss it in?"

"No, I don't think so. I haven't had a chance to properly calibrate it, as we haven't had any success duplicating portal conditions in the lab, but the wavelengths need to harmonize first, so someone would have to go inside with it."

"Go inside? That's a suicide mission." Oliver's body tensed just a bit, but he still thought they were talking theory. Brandon was too, but he was ready to put theory into practice.

"Not necessarily. The device, properly calibrated, should protect the subject from the portal's effects."

"Really. You think you could convert it so teams could cross the portal?"

Oh, he did love talking with Oliver. So smart, just not suited to research. "Would take a hell of a lot more investigation, but it's a possibility."

They fell into silence for a few minutes. There were other ramifications, both moral and ethical, to crossing the portals. Since MIA had never discovered if the infection and possession of the Umbrae was a deliberate act of aggression or an unintended manifestation of an alternate universe, most agents disagreed on what the appropriate course of action would be should they ever have the capability of crossing over. Having come to MIA through field operations, Brandon had a similar outlook to Oliver's—prevent the Umbrae from infecting anyone. Once that was done, there was no need for retribution.

His breathing deepened, and his eyelids drooped. Moments later Oliver gave him a little shake. "C'mon. Let's go to bed."

# TWELVE

Brandon stretched as he slowly came awake, content and happy. He was rarely either these days, and the shock of it brought him to full wakefulness. The arm across his waist, warm body curled around him, the erection drilling into his lower back were unusual, and yet so familiar. He had to credit Oliver for his current mood, and he snuggled into the shelter of Oliver's larger frame, wondering if he could fall back asleep. Brandon had awoken in this manner plenty of times and knew Oliver was still asleep. Not deep enough that Brandon couldn't coax him awake, but he'd not felt this safe and comfortable since... the last time he'd woken up in Oliver's arms.

The countdown clock in his mind ticked, but he quashed it. Oliver might not be infected, and even if he was, they still had plenty of time, especially since they'd narrowed down the search area. For now, he wanted to savor the pleasure of being in Oliver's embrace.

He lightly stroked Oliver's arm, glad they'd had some downtime the previous evening—he could be as confident as Oliver that everything was going to work out. He had to believe it, or he'd be completely unable to function. After the movie, Oliver had ushered him into the bedroom as though there was no question about where

Brandon would be spending the night. He'd assumed they were just going to go to sleep, but it had been extremely gratifying to find Oliver naked, hard, and waiting when Brandon had returned from brushing his teeth.

The fucking had been quick, dirty, and oh so good. He would need to escape sometime today to get to a pharmacy. They only had one condom left, and with any luck they'd be using it before getting out of bed.

Brandon stretched again, sliding against Oliver's sleep-warmed skin. Thinking about fucking made him want to do it again. He wiggled his ass to get Oliver's erection between his cheeks and undulated, making Oliver's cock slide up and down the crack, rubbing ever so tantalizingly against his hole.

His own cock stood at attention—he needed to do something more drastic to wake Oliver. He was done waiting and snuggling. A good, solid orgasm would start the day out right, a million times better than a balanced breakfast.

After lifting Oliver's arm, he slid down the bed and sucked the head of Oliver's cock into his mouth. Oliver came awake with a pleased grunt and a little jerk of his hips.

Oliver dug his hands into Brandon's hair, coaxing more of his length down Brandon's throat. Even without his hearing aids, the silence of the early morning allowed him to hear Oliver's lusty groans.

After a few moments, Oliver grabbed Brandon's hand, pulled it up to his mouth, and began tracing patterns on Brandon's wrist with his tongue. Brandon groaned around the fat cock in his mouth and reached down to start jacking his own cock. How the fuck could this feel so damned good?

He needed a chance to fully reacquaint himself with Oliver's erogenous zones. He'd loved using them to persuade Oliver into giving him complete control over their pleasure while Brandon fucked him into incoherence. Sinking into Oliver's tight hole once last night hadn't been enough, would never be enough, but right now he just wanted to roll onto his back and spread his legs. Oliver filled him up so right, like his cock had been custom made to stuff Brandon to the gills.

Oliver pulled out of his mouth. "Come up here." The low, growly voice should have been difficult to hear, but it wasn't. Oliver accompanied the command with a gentle finger under Brandon's chin, exerting enough pressure upward to indicate what he wanted even if Brandon had been unable to hear him.

Instead of getting a blowjob, Oliver decided to drive Brandon crazy with rubbing and licking and biting and sucking. Just about everywhere. They both knew any sort of rimming would have to wait until they were alone; otherwise Brandon would wake the whole apartment. But aside from Oliver's tongue in his hole, nothing else was left untouched or untasted. It was a startling contrast to their fast fuck the night before—more like late-night sex, or even weekend spend-the-day-in-bed sex, rather than a morning wake-up call. Brandon was overwhelmed by Oliver's sensual onslaught. Slick fingers entered and stretched him while a hot mouth sucked on his nipples, his cock, and the balls tucked up close to his body.

When Brandon's body was humming, so ready to come he was swearing at Oliver, the man finally rolled on the condom.

The scent of coffee hit Brandon's nose, and he froze.

"Is that coffee?" He did his best to whisper, but without his hearing aids in, it was very difficult to judge his volume.

Oliver paused, cock a fraction of an inch from its goal, and sniffed. "The guys must be up."

Brandon stiffened, and not in a good way.

"Awake? What time is it? I need to get back into my room before they notice." He snatched his hearing aids off the bedside table and put them on, but that was all he had a chance to do before Oliver wrestled him back on the bed, legs wide.

His erection had no care for the predicament he was in, and flexed at Oliver even as he tried to wiggle away from Oliver's cock— the same cock that had led him into temptation over and over again.

A deep frown pulled Oliver's brows together, and he maneuvered Brandon into a more open position and pressed the tip of his cock against Brandon's hole. "What the hell was that all about?"

"What?" Brandon was still struggling, although whether he was struggling to be impaled or to get away was in serious question.

"The panic. What's wrong?"

"They'll hear. They'll know. We should go out there." They'd kept it quiet until now. Surely Oliver didn't want anyone to know.

"Then I guess you'll just have to be quiet, because we're not going out there yet." Oliver didn't make another move, though.

Brandon's limbs loosened in surrender at Oliver's growly words, and against his better judgment, he pushed his hips down, enough to indicate his permission to go ahead. Oliver wasted no time and slid inside. They both groaned at the sensation, the combined sound abnormally loud after having gone so long without his hearing aids.

Expecting another quick fuck, Brandon was taken by surprise when Oliver pulled out slowly before pressing in again and rolling his hips against Brandon's splayed legs. Within moments, he had Brandon writhing and begging—quietly.

"What's the matter? Afraid someone will hear you getting royally fucked?" Oliver had a determined look on his face, as though he intended to fuck like a machine until Brandon yelled loud enough to let everyone in the apartment know.

It gave Brandon a funny feeling in his gut, because Oliver just might succeed.

"It's getting late. We should stop." That was a laugh. If Oliver stopped now, he would scream—in frustration. Hell, he could barely get the words out, never mind remember why they shouldn't be doing this. There was a portal to be found and closed. With extreme prejudice.

"We're not stopping until you're wearing jizz. I don't care if they come in and watch."

So fierce. Brandon wasn't sure which sentence cranked him up more, but he was ready to blow. As he moved faster in response to

Oliver's thrusts, the fear of shouting out his pleasure got stronger. He couldn't stop either, and the fear made the pleasure more intense, sharper, the two emotions inexplicably entwined in a way that put Oliver firmly in control and pushed Brandon completely out of control.

Oliver moved his knees back and out, spreading him just that little bit more, making the cock driving into him feel just a little bit bigger.

"Are you going to come? Scream?" Sweat slicked Oliver's body, feral lust darkened his face.

"Uh." *Oh God. Yes.* Usually it was him using words to get Oliver wired. Usually it was him pushing Oliver for risky sex. Somehow, though, this felt riskier than any elevator blowjob he'd ever given Oliver. Riskier than any rub-off in a public bathroom.

"Are they going to come running in here? See if there's anything wrong? Maybe they'll stand by the bed, jacking off while I plow you."

Brandon's breath hitched. Oliver's little scenario was all too vivid in his mind. He'd never been so turned on in his life, but he was afraid—afraid of Oliver's words coming true even as the idea turned him way the fuck on, if only as a fantasy. His hand hovered over his dick, aching so badly to stroke. It wouldn't take much. One more bit of sensation and it wouldn't matter how scared he was.

Oliver smiled as though he'd made a fascinating discovery, then pushed himself as far inside as he could go. He paused there as Brandon wobbled on the brink, indecision preventing his hand from landing. The fat cock inside him throbbed, and in the stillness all his focus narrowed in on their cocks, ready to explode.

Deliberately Oliver pushed Brandon's arm out of the way and wrapped a hand around Brandon's cock. Fear blossomed inside. How could he feel both afraid to come and afraid he'd die if he didn't, all at the same time?

Leaning over him, Oliver said quietly, "It's okay. You can let go," before he kissed Brandon and stroked him firmly.

Brandon arched up and screamed into Oliver's mouth as the

white-hot pleasure ripped through him as though his entire being spurted out of him in forceful, almost painful pulses. Oliver didn't let up the kiss or the stroking until every tiny ounce of sweetness and spunk had been wrung out of Brandon's dick.

Somehow Brandon managed to keep his heavy eyelids open while Oliver reared back, his gaze on Brandon never wavering. Oliver brought his slick hand to his mouth and licked at Brandon's cum, then groaned as his dick pulsed inside Brandon's body, filling the condom.

Brandon smiled, the sight of Oliver getting off almost as good as getting off himself. No one had ever pushed him like Oliver did, no one had ever made it better—a fact he'd become all too familiar with in the intervening Oliver-free years.

When Oliver's breathing returned mostly to normal, he eased out of Brandon, and Brandon hissed at the tiny lick of discomfort. It had been a long time since he'd been fucked, never mind so many times, in two days. He'd be feeling it all day, and he couldn't be happier.

"You okay?" Oliver brushed the side of Brandon's face with his jizz-free hand. "I wasn't too rough, was I?"

Too rough? Dear God, no. "Nope. Perfect. It's just been a while."

A smile preceded a gentle kiss before Oliver rolled out of bed.

Pulling the covers securely over himself, Brandon shifted to his side, giving him a better view of Oliver's naked ass as he walked to the en suite bathroom to dispose of the condom. "You tired me out. Maybe you can take Carmichael for his walk while I take a nap."

Oliver came back to bed, yanked the covers away, and slapped him on the ass. "No way. You said you'd take care of Carmichael if I let you keep him."

Smothering a laugh, Brandon stood. Oliver always got him.

The sudden flush of the toilet in the shared bathroom beside Oliver's bedroom sobered Brandon, and he pinched the bridge of his nose. "Seriously, do you think they know? You think they heard anything?"

"Heard anything? Probably not. Do I think they know?" Oliver shrugged. "Luis is a detective. A detective from whom I've stolen four condoms. And Carmichael... well, Carmichael can be oblivious when he wants to be, but he's less deliberately obtuse when it doesn't involve his own relationship. Yes, it's possible they know."

Heat bloomed in Brandon's cheeks. He wasn't sure he wanted to face the other men, and yet he knew he'd be back in Oliver's bed tonight, begging for more, assuming they weren't winging their way home after closing the portal.

Oliver gave him another smile, this one tempered by something besides happiness. They both knew their time was running out. "I'll go out and grab some coffee, keep them occupied for a few minutes to give you a chance to go back to your room. In case they don't know yet."

"You're not going out there like that." Brandon couldn't bite back the words. If Oliver thought he was going to parade the goods Brandon had claimed for his own use—for the duration of this mission, at least—in front of two attractive gay men, he'd see Brandon really in a snit. What he really wanted was to claim Oliver for all time, and he would if he were sure Oliver felt the same way. He'd done a very stupid thing by pushing Oliver away, and he hoped he'd have a chance to make it up to him.

Oliver snorted. "No, I was going to wear sweatpants. Once I've had some coffee, I'll come back and grab a shower before getting dressed."

Sweatpants. Probably no T-shirt. Wasn't much better than being completely naked, in Brandon's opinion. Sweatpants were surprisingly sexy on Oliver. Perhaps because the casualness seemed out of character for the man he'd become.

Oliver dragged on the sweatpants he snagged from their resting place atop his suitcase, then gave Brandon a quick kiss before slipping out of the room.

Brandon should be happy Oliver had been willing to continue the charade that they'd slept in separate rooms and weren't fucking like bunnies every chance they got. Instead, he was unsettled, disappointed, like he hadn't gotten the toy he'd asked Santa for.

He pulled on his boxers and gathered the rest of his clothes before opening the door and peeking out. The coast was clear, and he snuck back to his own room.

---

LIKE DÉJÀ VU, the four of them stood in the living room, Luis mocking Carmichael's electrodes and Brandon appearing incredibly pleased at having created Frankenstein's monster. The expression was nothing on the satiated, fucked-out look Oliver had gotten that morning, but no matter how he'd teased and taunted Brandon while buried deep inside his tight, hot ass, that look was for him alone. He didn't want to share it, not if he could help it.

"Why don't you wear it, then?" Carmichael snapped. Luis smirked. Oliver hadn't been paying attention, but whatever Luis had said had pushed Carmichael too far. A faint frown creased Brandon's brow as he stared at the two men.

"Cut it out. We've got a job to do." Oliver was used to dealing with headstrong, cranky men. Being partnered with Carmichael had certainly refined that skill. Carmichael gave him an odd look that he couldn't quite interpret but Oliver wasn't in the mood to dig into it.

He checked to make sure his weapon was properly holstered, then straightened his suit jacket. As he checked the buttons, Brandon's gaze followed his hands. Undoubtedly, they were both remembering the last time Brandon had opened his jacket buttons, but he couldn't think about that now. It wasn't the first time his life had been in danger, but now he was working under the gun, and they had lingered in bed far too long. A naked Brandon had been a temptation too strong to ignore.

"Let's start at the fifth floor and work our way down," Brandon suggested.

"Why the fifth floor?" Luis asked.

"We've found portals on second or third floors before, but it's rare. They're usually close to the ground. Not to say it couldn't be on the twentieth floor, but it's less likely," Oliver answered for Brandon, but for all they knew, portals opened all the time a mile up in the sky and no one ever knew because no one was close enough to become infected.

BACK ON THE MAIN FLOOR, about to head into the basement, Brandon and Carmichael ended up several paces ahead, while Luis hung back with Oliver. They'd found nothing so far, despite the data from the monitor. Didn't mean there was nothing to find, only that evil could be hiding behind any one of the doors they'd passed. Made Oliver's skin crawl, trying to be prepared for possible ambush from both front and back. Would they have to search each individual apartment if Brandon's equipment didn't show them the way?

"So, you're boning Brain Trust?" Luis's words startled him, dropping suddenly into the silence. Oliver checked ahead, but he didn't see any sign that Brandon had heard. Not that he knew for sure, but Luis's soft words, several feet behind, were likely the sort of thing Brandon couldn't hear.

"Excuse me?"

"You're fucking him, aren't you?" Luis gave a sharp nod toward Brandon.

"What makes you think that?" Not exactly the best defense, but he'd held on to the ridiculous hope that no one knew. While he didn't care for himself, Brandon would shit kittens.

Luis rolled his eyes. "I'm a detective," he drawled, voice thick with condescension. "Aside from the protective thing you've got going on, I'm missing a few condoms—and, well, Brain Trust isn't exactly quiet in the sack."

Dammit. Brandon would shit kittens first, and then kill him, because he'd encouraged him to make noise.

"I don't think it's any of your business." Which was what he should have said first off, if he hadn't been taken aback by Luis's presumption.

"Don't get me wrong. The director is a hot number and smart to boot. I'd hit that if I had a chance, especially after hearing your little show this morning and last night."

Last night too? Oliver's hands fisted. Punching his partner would not bode well for their future working relationship, but he hated hearing Luis talk about Brandon like he was nothing more than the nameless fucks Oliver used to slake his lust. Brandon was better than that.

"I think you need to remember exactly who you're talking about. I'm sure you wouldn't have discussed your police chief in such terms."

Luis shuddered and pulled at Oliver's arm, yanking him to a halt. Oliver faced him. "What?"

"I'm new to this agency, and normally I wouldn't give a rat's ass who you fuck, but this situation is a liability. He's a liability."

"Brandon is not a liability." Oliver lowered his voice even more, although Brandon was farther away. The last thing he wanted was for Brandon to hear this assessment. Besides, if anyone was a liability here, it was Oliver.

"Yes, he is." Luis paced in a tight circle in front of Oliver. "He's the equivalent of a civilian, but a civilian with authority. I might not know which the fuck way is up, but this isn't like having the police chief along on a bust—this is like having the mayor along on a bust. Which means he thinks he's entitled to tell more experienced people what to do but will only put them in danger, because he don't know which way is up either. He's a scientist, for God's sake."

"There's something you need to understand. Very few of us in MIA are actually law enforcement of any description. Carmichael was with the MPs, but he's an exception. I was an accountant before being recruited. You've met Cooper, right? He was a behavioral scientist. His current agency partner, Adam—you remember Adam from the office?"

"Yeah, he's Carmichael's main squeeze."

"He's got a PhD in archeology."

Luis turned almost green. If this weren't so personal, Oliver would have laughed. Carmichael had had an almost identical reaction when he'd realized people he considered to be rank amateurs were wandering around with dangerous weapons, trying to kill dangerous creatures, while keeping it all secret from the general populace. They might not be natural investigators or protectors, but they all had plenty of training in combat.

"But... But..."

Yeah, the situation sucked, but Oliver had to squeeze all the enjoyment out of Luis's discomfiture that he could. "Actually, Brandon's background is useful. He was in med school before he was recruited. Unlike most of us, he'd actually seen the immediate aftermath of violence before joining the agency. We were partners."

"Oh, so he's your ex?"

"No. Well, yes, he is. But I meant, we were partnered at the agency for two years. Brandon's got experience doing fieldwork. He's not only a scientist."

Luis rubbed at his temples as though Oliver had just given him a raging headache. "You know that's not Ellison's only liability, right?"

Closing his eyes, Oliver let his head fall back against the wall.

"I know. It's my fault. He was injured on our last assignment together. He wasn't able to go back into the field." He didn't want to ask—he'd probably get the same mocking "I'm a detective" answer again. Nevertheless... "How do you know?"

Somehow Luis had picked up on clues Oliver had missed, even though he knew about Brandon's hearing loss. Perhaps he'd willingly blinded himself, which made them a sad pair.

"I volunteer with a community outreach program."

Now it was Oliver's turn for incredulity. Lots of cops did volunteer work to benefit their communities, but Luis was decidedly not the warm, fuzzy type. He'd probably scare kids into fits with his growling and scowling.

In the wake of Oliver's stunned silence, Luis huffed. "Fine. My partner on the force, Sheila Ames, talked me into it. But your boy—"

Luis broke off and coughed at Oliver's narrow-eyed stare. Brandon wasn't that much younger, and the term really was far too disrespectful for a junior agent to be using for a director.

"Sorry. Anyway, I recognized some of the mannerisms."

What could Oliver say to that? He had noticed them too, but until Brandon had confirmed that he hadn't recovered completely, Oliver hadn't recognized what they'd meant.

"Don't let on that you know. He'd..." Brandon would be devastated and embarrassed, though he had nothing to be embarrassed about. He didn't have the same abilities he had seven years ago, but so what? It didn't change Oliver's feelings any.

A grimace passed over Luis's face. "Hiding it makes it harder to deal with it. And harder to interact with others."

"I know. But just leave it for now, please. It shouldn't be an issue, not even with the mission. I intend to keep him out of any confrontations." The complete and utter truth, although he had no flipping clue how he was going to manage it, short of tying Brandon to the bed. If he did tie Brandon to the bed, the likelihood he'd leave him there alone would be... almost zilch.

"Good luck with that. And seriously, nice going. Young, hot, and brainy. You hit the trifecta." Luis clapped Oliver on the shoulder.

He couldn't tell if Luis was being genuine or just trying to piss him off. "Well, if that's what you like, I might know someone."

"Oh yeah?"

Was Rob too young for Luis? Wasn't for Oliver to decide, but maybe he'd see if Frazer could arrange a meet after this was all over.

The clang of a heavy metal door shutting silenced their discussion and had them both looking down the hall. Carmichael and Brandon had disappeared. Great. How was he supposed to protect Brandon when he let him get out of sight?

He throttled down the urge to sprint after Brandon and walked quickly to the end of the hall.

Beyond the metal door lay the stairs to the basement. Oliver leaned over the rail, but Brandon had enough of a head start that he was no longer on the stairs. The coughs and groans of an old furnace piping heat throughout a building of this size covered any sounds Brandon and Carmichael might have made. The slumlord didn't expend much money to keep the basement in any kind of reasonable shape, and Oliver steeled himself for rats and roaches aplenty. He pulled his tiny but powerful flashlight out of his pocket to illuminate the way. Luis turned his on as well, and the two rounded beams reminded Oliver of the recent investigation in the abandoned building. When they were a few steps down, the metal door banged shut behind them, making it suddenly impossible to believe it was still full daylight above ground.

Oliver's pulse sped up. If they encountered the portal down here, in the dark, they could easily stumble onto—into—it without seeing it, and the damned things were deadly. One hundred percent, not like the dice throw when you got bit. He picked up his pace down the stairs and heard Luis clattering after him.

At the bottom of the stairs, he paused. "Please stay behind me."

The spillover from the flashlight cast long shadows upward to Luis's hairline, but that didn't hide the flare of his nostrils. "Why?"

"You haven't seen what a portal looks like for real. They're hard to see, and if you stumble into one by accident, it will kill you."

"Fair enough. Lead on."

Oliver clicked off his light for a moment to make sure he was heading in the right direction. The basement wasn't laid out nearly as neatly as the upper floors. A faint glow gave him a direction, and he clicked his light back on, determined to move as swiftly as possible. A return of the odd claustrophobia he'd felt the other day swamped him, but he couldn't let it get the best of him. Not while Brandon was down here and at least one cannibalistic Umbrae was on the loose.

# THIRTEEN

Moments later they turned through a doorway into a room full of storage cages. From the thick coating of dust, few people ventured down here, and Oliver didn't blame them one bit.

Through the chain-link-fence maze, Brandon and Carmichael were visible. They'd stopped moving and were tracing patterns, ceiling to floor, with their flashlights.

"Hey," Oliver called out. He didn't want to startle Brandon if he could avoid it.

Brandon and Carmichael turned. Brandon's eyes were wide, and Oliver thought he might be pale, but it was hard to tell.

"Oliver, take a look at this."

Taking his cue from Brandon, Oliver flicked his light back and forth, up and down. An oily sheen—the most reliable visible indicator of a portal—shimmered in the air in front of him. "Holy shit."

"That's what I said." Brandon took a step closer to Oliver as if trying to draw strength from his proximity.

Luis gasped behind him as he figured out exactly what they were looking at. And there was good reason for Brandon's pallor.

"What the hell are we going to do with this? We can't set off sonic charges here." Oliver had never seen a portal like this before.

Carmichael snorted and gave Brandon a dirty look. "Especially not if they're the ones we used last time."

"About those... we need to talk about them," Brandon said. "But no, we can't set off charges here."

"Okay, I know the sonic charges disrupt the wavelength in the portals. But why can't you set them off here? We've got them with us. We could have this thing taken care of by lunchtime." Luis stepped closer to peer at the shimmering portal, inspecting it from both sides.

"The charges have a backlash. It can be dangerous to set them off in a structure of any sort, but this portal intersects with the ceiling and a load-bearing wall. Dispersing the portal with normal sonic charges could easily topple the building. If this basement connects all three apartment buildings, as I suspect it does, and this building goes down, the other two could sustain significant structural damage as well," Oliver said.

The bite on his back gave a vicious throb, as though in recognition of the portal, claiming him. He gritted his teeth against the pain.

"You have got to be shitting me. Bring the whole building down? That's out of the question. So what other options do we have?"

"Not too fucking many." Carmichael growled and scratched at the electrode at his temple. "The portal will disperse on its own eventually, but we have no idea how long that will take, nor how many innocents will die in the meantime. Adam thinks the portals go through cycles, centuries apart and the portals started a new cycle shortly before MIA was initiated. But he also thinks the portals are staying open longer than they used to, possibly because of the increased amount of noise pollution in modern society. Just one of the many theories he's got."

Huh. That was a new theory. He'd have to follow up with Adam, maybe even accept one of the many dinner invites Adam and Carmichael had issued. And arcane theories wouldn't be the only reason. Oliver suspected he'd need the support of friends when

Brandon left him again. He wasn't strong enough to do it alone. Not this time. Assuming he survived the next two days, the odds of which had become incredibly slim.

"What about the alpha victim?" Brandon asked.

"The doors down to the basement aren't locked. Anyone could have encountered the portal," Oliver replied.

"Well, sure, anyone could have, but have you seen this place? How many people are willing to come down here, do you suppose? I'm just surprised we didn't interrupt a drug deal or three." Luis used his flashlight to trace the line where the portal entered the wall.

"Any drug dealers down here would be appetizer, dinner, and dessert as soon as the Umbrae transformed the alpha victim. Or they'd became infected as well. We don't really know how many of them there are, or how hungry they are, but I'd be willing to bet there's more than the girl you killed," Carmichael said.

Oliver shuddered. What if the prediction models were wrong? What if they were facing several Umbrae, not just one or two? It was one thing to chase down a nest of werewolves. Most times, they nested in remote areas. When the portal collapsed, the third of them who became crazed homicidal creatures didn't have the opportunity to hurt too many people. Here, an Umbrae could rampage through multiple apartments, killing indiscriminately before anyone even realized what was happening, regardless of the possible destruction of the building. His life wasn't worth more than the hundreds of innocents above.

"Come on, let's get out of here. There's nothing more we can do now." He didn't like the way Brandon was staring at the portal. The sooner he got Brandon out of its malevolent presence and tucked away in their safe apartment, the better he'd feel. Then he remembered the bloody traces he'd found—remnants of the previous tenants —and realized safety was an illusion. He'd have to make sure Brandon was armed at all times and remained super-vigilant, assuming Oliver couldn't convince him to take a flight home. He didn't want Brandon's last memory of him to be Carmichael taking him down like a rabid dog.

---

ON THE MAIN FLOOR, by the elevators, daylight streamed in through the windows, illuminating the faded carpet and making dust motes dance in the air. Brandon found it hard to believe how innocuous this floor seemed after the horror-movie set in the basement. Every step he took, he imagined the foundations creaking and shaking beneath him. As far as they knew, portals dissipating on their own didn't have anywhere near the concussive force as those closed with sonic charges—yet another reason to try and do away with sonic charges. But he'd never heard of a portal situated like this one, and even ones that disappeared on their own expelled kinetic energy.

No matter what, they were sitting on a possible time bomb and the building needed to be evacuated, assuming the agency could be convinced to force the hand of the local authorities to do so. Situated in a big city as they were, it would be much more difficult to push the bureaucracy in the right place, especially as the majority of the tenants likely had nowhere else to go. Evacuation was one thing, but relocating the affected families was quite another.

If Brandon hadn't been looking, he wouldn't have noticed the minuscule tremor in Oliver's finger as he stabbed at the elevator's up button. He must be more worried than he appeared. He'd never exactly been an open book, but the stoic mask he seemed to pull on along with his sedate suits prevented Brandon from discerning his thoughts. Not even a glance at the carpet that still had the ghost of Brandon's knee prints cracked the mask.

The four of them rode the elevator in silence, and if Brandon hadn't known better, he'd have thought a defeated air accompanied them to the apartment door. That couldn't be right. He couldn't imagine Oliver admitting defeat. Nor the other two men. If anything, he'd normally have classified them as having an excess of confidence.

Luis sat in his now customary seat on the couch while Oliver headed into the kitchen. Carmichael ripped off his hoodie and threw it across the room. When he moved to yank at the electrodes on his temples, Brandon leaped to intercept, uncaring if he took a punch for his troubles. Although smaller than the other three men, he was still tough enough to take a hit. He had plans for that equipment, and he wasn't going to let Carmichael's frustration ruin it.

Under his attention, Carmichael stood still, but barely. He was like a restrained tiger, ready to attack, and Brandon stripped off the electrodes as quickly as possible. He stashed the equipment in his messenger bag, not quite trusting Carmichael's restraint. Carmichael twitched as though he was going to pace—or perhaps run around the apartment to expend energy—but instead plunked down in his chair so forcefully that the thing rocked under his weight.

Giving him a wide berth, Brandon moved to his own chair. A few times, Goodson sat up, took in a breath. But each time, he slumped back into the couch without saying a word.

Oliver returned from the kitchen holding four opened beer bottles, lips pinched together as he offered a bottle to each of them. It wasn't even noon. Brandon frowned at him but accepted the bottle proffered.

"We're fucked." Carmichael's words exploded into the silence.

"I'm going to call in some backup," Oliver said. "See if I can get this place evacuated."

Brandon almost smiled. Good to know he and Oliver were still on the same wavelength, in some respects.

"You think it's gonna work?" Carmichael snarled. "No one was even sure this was a portal site."

Oliver raised a brow. "They will when we confirm it is. Once I explain the situation, we should have all the backup we need."

Hopefully soon. The flight itself was just over an hour. As long as there were enough agents in the vicinity of HQ, Director Bennett should be able to gather a small force to assist. Brandon checked his watch and quickly calculated how many hours Oliver had left before he'd start manifesting symptoms, if he was going to. Any delays could be disastrous.

"We saw a pay phone at the convenience store at the end of the street," Carmichael said. "Whether it's still functional or not is anyone's guess."

Brandon refrained from snorting. Good fucking luck with that. Better chance of finding a unicorn than a functional public pay phone. He hadn't seen one in the last five years or so that had been anything more than a graffitied urinal. Even in poverty-stricken places, mobile phones were the norm not the exception, and whoever had rented this apartment before they arrived hadn't bothered hooking up a landline.

Swallowing the last of the beer, Oliver set his empty bottle on the coffee table. "Right. I'll be back. With any luck, Kyle will be able to marshal some assistance and have them here before nightfall."

"A pay phone? What for?" Luis clearly hadn't taken to heart the warnings about how the portals affected electronics.

"Landlines are the most reliable this close to a portal." Carmichael flipped on the TV while Oliver slipped out of the apartment. The resulting shit picture and sound were probably portal related, although it could just as easily have had something to do with the management of the building. No one in the place was likely to get much result from complaining.

Brandon wanted to go with Oliver, but he had data to compile from Carmichael's monitor, and he'd need all the information he could get, in case MIA decided to wait out the portal instead of evacuating and risking the building coming down. Oliver didn't have time to wait it out.

Sitting at the dining-room table, he let Carmichael and Goodson fight it out for whatever crap daytime show they were going to watch. Gave him the opportunity to make a few tweaks and adjustments to the equipment before tucking it back into his bag, where he could access it at a moment's notice.

Oliver opened the apartment door, and all of them looked up, waiting.

"A large team is heading in today. They'll be here this afternoon."

"Good. What's the plan?"

"Don't know. Kyle is bringing a few researchers along with the agents to inspect the portal. If he's going to evacuate and try to blow the portal, it will only be after the R&D drones have had a chance to study it until we're all old and gray."

Brandon couldn't even take exception to the bitterness in Oliver's tone or being lumped in with the R&D drones, as the field agents often called them. Oliver needed them to evacuate the building today, needed that portal to be dissolved today. Brandon would try to sway them, though he hadn't had enough interaction with Kyle Bennett in his new role to know how much counsel he would accept from other directors. They were technically peers, and both reported up to Senior Director Wong, but Brandon had spent his early years with MIA reporting to Director Bennett. He had a lot less experience in the role, but he'd make himself heard when Bennett and their back up arrived. He wasn't losing Oliver without a fight.

"Who's coming from R&D?" Brandon asked. It would have been nice to be consulted, since he was in charge of the department.

Oliver shrugged. "No idea. Let's grab something to eat while we can."

God. When had he learned to be so icy, so remote? If it were Brandon, he'd be screaming and cursing and shouting, bemoaning the fates. He knew because he'd done that exact same thing seven years ago, and then he was merely facing permanent hearing loss, not death. Then again, if Oliver lost his shit, morale would nose-dive. Sure, there were only the four of them, but they needed their wits about them.

Brandon couldn't help but admire Oliver's commitment to being a good leader. No matter what happened here, Brandon would change the way he operated. He could be an effective leader too, just not out in the field—and it was about time he accepted his life the way it was. But that didn't mean he wasn't going to try and square things away with Oliver. The man deserved a boatload of apologies, and they needed to talk in a way Brandon hadn't been ready to do back when he'd been in the hospital. Maybe, just maybe, they could figure out a way to make a new start, smooth away the antagonism. Friendship, if nothing else.

But there was another, more immediate and dangerous problem.

Who was coming with Kyle? Not that having a roster would matter. Brandon still hadn't figured out who was trustworthy at the agency, beside the people in this room. Right now, he'd trust any field agent over one of his fellow researchers. Impossibly, his stomach sank even more. Time to have a very difficult conversation, one that had been put off for far too long, and not about their relationship.

"Oliver, I need to talk to you. Now."

Oliver waved one of his strong brown hands in an invitation to speak.

He slid a glance at Carmichael and Goodson. No matter how much Oliver trusted them, what Brandon had to say wasn't for general consumption. Not yet. Oliver was working hard to keep their small team's morale out of the gutters and Brandon wasn't about to ruin that hard work unless he absolutely had to.

"Alone."

The brown eyes hardened, and he gave Brandon an impercep-tible shake of his head. What, he wasn't allowed to talk to the man alone?

The faint flush on Oliver's cheeks gave away his thoughts. Oliver thought he wanted sex. Brandon bit back a comment telling Oliver to get over himself. Most times, Oliver could make him hard just by being in the same room, but he wasn't completely ruled by his dick. He did understand the "time and place for everything" concept, even if he ignored it much of the time. This was not the time for sex. This was so fucking important, especially if his backup plan didn't work out as he expected.

Brandon stood and pointed at the bedrooms.

"No."

"Agent Cardoso, we need to talk."

Luis rolled his eyes and turned his attention back to the television, while Carmichael hadn't been disturbed by their discussion at all.

"Fine. After you, Director Ellison." Oliver gave him a half bow that no one could mistake as anything other than mocking.

He didn't miss the signs that Oliver was pissed that he'd pulled rank, but he wasn't going to come right out in front of the other two agents and explain he wasn't using "talking alone" as a euphemism for fuck like bunnies at a completely inappropriate time.

Brandon strode as confidently as he could into the bedroom and jumped when the door slammed behind. He turned, hating the angry set of Oliver's jaw and the flinty look in brown eyes Brandon had gotten used to being warm and sweet again. What he had to say wasn't going to improve things any.

"I'm a little worried about the R&D people Kyle is bringing."

A frown creased Oliver's forehead. "They're your people. Why are you worried?"

"I don't know any of them well. And I think at least one of them is trying to kill you. Or at least sabotage field missions." If only he had something concrete to give Oliver, something other than a hunch.

"Explain."

He was right—Oliver wasn't happy. But he didn't have a choice. Oliver needed to watch his back while the interlopers were here. The explanation about the potential sabotage and how someone had used his name to send the prototypes out into the field—with Oliver, specifically—well before they were ready didn't take long. Long enough to turn Oliver's face to stone, to make his eyes colder than they were before.

In fact, it looked like Oliver hated him for this fiasco, and that loss tore at his soul like his heart had been ripped from his body.

"Why the fuck didn't you tell me earlier? You should have told me, trusted me with this." Oliver had never, ever spoken to him with such venom.

"I didn't know enough to share. I still don't, but I'm worried about having R&D people here. And I didn't want to ruin our time here. I wanted to enjoy you while I could. I knew you'd be gone as soon as this mission was over."

Shock widened Oliver's eyes, made him look like he'd been hit with a two-by-four as he gaped at Brandon for a moment. Then his face flushed a dark red as his eyes narrowed. When he spoke again, the venom was still there, and the glacier had been replaced by the volatile volcano Brandon had seen once or twice, but never directed at him.

"I cannot fucking believe you're bringing our personal life into this. How can you possibly think the one has anything to do with the other?"

"I told you—I knew you'd go back to your normal life after this. I just wanted to keep this one reminder of how it used to b—" Brandon broke off and stepped back as Oliver swept a lamp off the dresser. It shattered on the floor.

"Shut the hell up. A reminder? Here's a reminder for you—you left me, remember?" Oliver was shouting now, and Brandon didn't know how to stem the flow of his words.

"You wouldn't talk to me about anything, you sent me away, and when I came back, you'd checked yourself out of the hospital. When I looked for you at your apartment, you'd already moved out and changed your phone number to an unlisted one. Your bitch of a mother wouldn't tell me where you'd gone. You moved to the other side of the fucking country to get away from me, which I only found out in a goddamned interoffice memo about your new job in Cali-fucking-fornia that had been sent to every-fucking-one. That sent a pretty clear message that you didn't want anything more to do with me. I would have apologized every damned day, and I understand why you couldn't forgive me, but chasing you across the country like some crazy stalker... I couldn't do that to you. Not after everything I'd put you through."

Every word hit Brandon like an arrow. He'd been so sunk in self-pity, wallowing in misery, he'd never really considered what his actions had meant to Oliver. When he realized he wasn't going to get better, was going to have to live with part of himself missing, was never going to be a field agent again, he'd broken off the relationship. Before Oliver could. But something Oliver said had confused him.

"Forgive you? For what?"

"For getting you hurt. For fucking up setting the charges. It's my fault. I... wasn't thinking straight. I never can when you're around." Oliver looked almost as confused as Brandon felt.

"There was a time, yes, that I blamed you. But that was a long time ago and I was so wrong. There were two of us fucking around on that hill. That afternoon is pretty fuzzy still, but I'm sure I made the first move. If there's anyone to blame, it's me."

Oliver's eyes got shiny. The wounds might be seven years old, but they'd clearly never healed for either of them. "Then why? Why did you leave?" The raw pain twisted Oliver's voice into something almost unrecognizable.

Brandon's eyes burned. What he'd done to this proud, strong man...

"I was broken. Defective. And there was no way they were going to let me out in the field again. I thought you'd be happy to be rid of me, once you realized."

Oliver's face turned an odd grayish color as a tear streaked down his cheek. "You thought fucking around on the job was all we had. For two years. I wanted you to move in with me... Never mind. It hardly matters now. You didn't trust me then, and you don't trust me now. I don't know why I was fooling myself."

Brandon took a step forward, arms out, ready to comfort Oliver. "Of course, I trust you."

The color rushed back into Oliver's face as he glared at Brandon. "No. Don't fucking touch me. You... You... I wanted everything with you, then and now. The only reason I cared about your hearing loss was that I felt responsible. But now... I see we had—we have —nothing."

"Don't say that." His vicious anger was tearing Brandon's heart into shreds. "Please, no." He took another step forward.

"No. Fucking no. I'm done." Another lamp flew to the floor before Oliver whirled around and ran out of the room, slamming the door behind him with enough force to knock one of the bland land-scaped prints off the wall. Brandon jumped as the glass shattered.

He walked to the closed door and placed a trembling hand on it before resting his forehead against it. How could he have been so stupid? How could he have twisted up his broken self-worth into imagining Oliver had hated him, or would hate him? Drops damp-ened his canvas shoes, and he wondered when he'd started crying. He wanted to sink to the floor, drop his knees onto the splintered glass. But injuring himself wasn't going to fix this. Blood wasn't going to bring back the years they could have had together if Brandon hadn't been so scared, so self-conscious, so fucked up.

Sobs shook him.

He'd been so afraid Oliver was going to push him away, he'd gone and done it first, convinced himself Oliver didn't want him. And his mother's version of comfort had only reinforced that stupid, erro-neous conclusion.

Oliver wasn't going to let him fix this. He'd fucked up, irrepara-bly, and his penance was to continue on in his lonely existence, hoping Oliver could find someone who'd make him happy. And he'd make sure Oliver was alive to do so.

A loud knock put his heart in his throat, and Brandon yanked open the door. The sight of Luis tore the last tiny shred of hope from his soul.

"Oh, good, you're still alive." Goodson scanned the room, assessing the wreckage. "What the hell was that all about? He hit you?"

Brandon stared at the tips of his shoes. Even if he'd had any experience talking about his feelings, he didn't want anyone to know what a pathetic coward he was.

"Nothing," Brandon mumbled. "He didn't hit me." Might have been better if he had. Brandon might have gotten some absolution from a punch.

"That was nothing, Brain Trust? Carmichael tensed way the fuck up when Cardoso started screaming. I guess he don't do that much. I thought he was going to flip out when Cardoso left, but right now he's mainlining beer like we're on a fucking vacation."

Brandon didn't know what to do with that information. "Oliver left?" His voice sounded small and pathetic, just like he was.

Goodson grunted and grabbed his chin.

"Oh," he said when he lifted Brandon's face to the light. "You and him... it was more than just fucking, wasn't it?"

Brandon gulped, and Goodson's craggy features softened into something like sympathy.

"I'm sorry," Goodson said gently.

If people were already offering condolences before the ashes of the relationship had even cooled, then the finality of Oliver leaving must have been painfully obvious to everyone. He didn't even care how Goodson knew about him and Oliver. Nothing mattered anymore.

"Look, I'll take Carmichael out, grab some grub. Give you a chance to get yourself together before the hordes descend."

Brandon pressed his lips together and nodded. He stood unmoving until long after he heard the apartment door close.

Every muscle ached in some sort of weird sympathetic response when he eventually hobbled to the bathroom to wash his face. He didn't bother trying to find a broom or dustpan, just wandered out into the living room. The TV was still on, and he sat in Oliver's spot on the couch. His suit jacket was draped over the arm, and Brandon scooped it up even as the sight of it tore at him. Oliver had clearly been too upset to grab it before he left. Apparently, all it had taken was Brandon being a total fuckup for Oliver to finally unbutton a little.

Another thought struck him, and he bit his lip until it bled. The suits... the stoic mask... the remote leader... He had done that to Oliver. He'd never realized how badly he'd hurt the man, when all he'd ever wanted to do was love him.

He glanced at his watch again. It had become a habit, calculating how long Oliver had before the Umbrae manifested, if it was going to.

Sirens blared from the television as a breaking news story about a fire interrupted the show in progress. Brandon sat up straight and stared unseeing at the screen. He had an idea that just might work. Running through the plan in his mind, he couldn't see any flaws. He checked his watch again, this time to figure out how long it would be before Kyle arrived with the others from MIA.

Yes. He had enough time.

# FOURTEEN

Oliver walked the neighborhood for three hours. Despite his nearly mindless state, he'd been given wide berth. For the first hour, he'd just wanted to throw up. The second hour, he had to clench his fists to keep from shaking. He had no idea how things between him and Brandon had gotten so twisted. He'd left because he'd been afraid of the rising tide of his anger. Those words he'd spoke had been like a slap in the face, to both of them, awareness of them too late to stop before he'd done something he couldn't take back—like, oh, killing their rekindled relationship, burying it, and then sowing the grave with salt.

His perception, his feelings, his whole life had been turned upside down, and he wanted to throttle Brandon for doing that to him, for tearing through him like a werewolf slicing though his gut with one swipe. He'd thought he'd been hurt and angry when Brandon had tossed him out of his life, but discovering that everything he'd thought was wrong only made it all more painful.

Brandon had thrown their relationship away because he didn't trust Oliver to love him enough. He'd thought Oliver was only with him for the convenience of fucking while on a mission. Stupidly, instead of asking Brandon to move in with him, Oliver had been giving him the space and time he thought Brandon needed to complete his studies, never realizing what misconception Brandon had taken away from that oversight.

The third hour, he came to the realization that no matter how much he might want to do otherwise, he didn't think there was any way to salvage this. Brandon was right—ending it now, not seeing each other after this mission, was the wisest thing they could do. The only way to stop wasting their lives in recrimination, guilt, and regret. They needed to move on, apart, even if the thought of walking away from his surfer boy again poured lemon juice on the gaping, raw wreckage of his soul.

Then again, he might not have time to worry about any of it, not when he might die from an Umbrae possession. But Kyle and the larger team would be there soon. He could pretend to be a competent professional for a short while. He had plenty of practice hiding his feelings away from the world. Years' worth. A few more hours were nothing in comparison.

As he returned to and approached the cluster of apartment buildings, the first thing he noticed was the trademark pearly off-white SUVs MIA agents used. Rapidly on the heels of that, he became aware of a crowd milling about on the sidewalk, staring at their apartment building as smoke billowed from windows on several floors. Now that he was paying attention, sirens blared behind him. The sound hadn't filtered through his consciousness, not when he'd been hearing them almost nonstop since they'd rented the apartment.

Oliver broke into a run and wove through the crowd to find the additional MIA agents ushering residents away from the building. Carmichael and Luis approached from another side. Spinning around, he didn't see Brandon anywhere.

"What the hell is going on? Where's Brandon?" Oliver grabbed Carmichael's shoulder, maybe too hard.

"Hey, man." Luis separated them. "We left him in the apartment." His voice lowered. "He was pretty wrecked."

Carmichael tilted his head. "Everything okay?"

Okay? Not fucking likely. But his emotional state was the least of their concerns. "I don't know. Where's Brandon now? Why isn't he out here? And why the fuck did you leave him alone when there's an Umbrae on the loose?"

He stared up at the smoke, which had a faint bluish tinge to it. He sniffed. This close, he should be able to smell something burning. "Wait. I think that's a smoke bomb. One of ours."

"No," Carmichael said. "Too much smoke."

"How many did we have with us?"

Carmichael shrugged. "The director let me take what I wanted."

Oliver's eyes widened. He was always paring down what Carmichael wanted to bring. The man seemed to have an abnormal fascination with gadgets. "How many?"

"Dunno. A dozen, two dozen?"

Luis grunted. "That could be smoke from all of them. What's going on?"

Oliver tapped his fingers against his cheek as he considered. The Umbrae might have a reason to break into their apartment, but it would be to take or kill Brandon. No reason came to mind for them to steal smoke bombs from Carmichael's gear, much less set them off to mimic a fire.

"Shit, shit, shit." Oliver dashed to the front door, dimly aware of the two men following him.

"What the hell is going on?" Luis called after him.

He barreled past one of the agents preventing people from reentering. "Brandon. He's evacuating the building."

"He's... what?" Carmichael shouted as they sprinted down the hallway.

"If he set the charges, wouldn't Brandon have left the building? Like we should be doing?" Luis panted as he caught up to Oliver at the door to the basement.

Oliver turned to him, so fucking scared he didn't know if he had the strength to open the door. "He's got some damned device he thinks will let him close the portal from the inside. He told me about it last night."

Carmichael wrenched open the door for him. "From the inside? Okay, never mind. Why fuck around with the fake fire?"

"Because he's not sure if it will mess with the stability of the portal, and he doesn't want anyone else killed."

Oliver pulled out his flashlight and ran down the stairs, shouting Brandon's name. He was dimly aware of other people running down the hallway, calling his name, but nothing mattered besides getting to Brandon.

He skidded to a stop in front of the portal. Brandon stood there, held captive by the portal, the fine lines of his face softened and slightly blurred by the shimmer. "Brandon! Get out of there!"

He waved his light over the edges of the portal. The perimeter— the parts that weren't embedded in the ceiling and walls—undulated in a manner he'd never seen before. "Brandon!" he screamed again. Brandon gave him a sad, apologetic smile and waved a couple of fingers by his ear.

Luis tapped him on the shoulder and held his hand out in front of Oliver, a pair of hearing aids cradled in his palm.

Oliver dropped to his knees, hands hovering inches from the portal. He didn't care about the tons of steel and concrete above him. He wanted Brandon out of there. He dredged up a memory from years ago, a sign language class he'd taken when he'd still thought he could convince Brandon to give them a chance.

*Come back, please.*

"What the fuck?" Luis stood beside him, staring at Brandon. "What is he doing?"

*Come back, please. I love you.*

There was a murmur of voices behind him, but they were nothing more than the annoying buzz of mosquitoes.

Brandon's eyes widened, and his face crumpled like he was in pain. As his image started to shake, he signed something back.

"What?" Either Brandon's signing had been too quick, or Oliver's memory was too faulty.

"He said he can't. He's stuck," Luis said.

"Stuck?" Oliver took his glance off Brandon for a second to stare at Luis.

Luis shrugged. "Outreach program, remember?"

How had he believed letting Brandon go would be the hardest thing he'd ever have to do? Watching him shake apart, in agony, was a million times worse.

Brandon's fingers moved, and this was simple enough for Oliver to recognize.

*I love you too.*

"No, goddammit. No!" The force of his scream tore at his throat. Brandon reached out as though to touch Oliver, but the distortion of the portal had gotten so bad it was hard to tell.

Fuck, no. He couldn't let Brandon go like this. Oliver shot his hand into the portal, the screams and shouts behind him deadening his own groan. Underneath the vibrating shards of pain clawing into every inch of his skin was the solid weight of a forearm.

He yanked. Brandon flew out of the portal and knocked him to the ground. Over Brandon's shoulder, the portal wavered and popped closed with no more than a faint, anticlimactic tremor. Oliver gripped him and stared up into his eyes. Heedless of the people milling about behind, he kissed Brandon. He wasn't giving this up. The shit they'd gone through before, the mistakes they made... didn't matter. Not anymore. They could make this work.

Brandon cradled his head and plundered his mouth like he was claiming Oliver, and Oliver let him.

Luis shook them. "There are people who want to talk to you. And Cardoso, you're bleeding."

"Oliver, you're bleeding," Brandon said at the same time.

When Brandon sat up, he remained straddled across Oliver's hips, generating a completely inappropriate erection.

Extending his hand, Luis offered Brandon his hearing aids.

Smiling gratefully, Brandon slipped them on while Carmichael knelt beside them and wrapped Oliver's bleeding arm with his hoodie.

Everyone's phones started buzzing and dinging with incoming messages and emails, proof positive the portal had been fully dispelled.

Unable to help himself, Oliver rubbed at Brandon's hip with his good hand. "Brandon."

Brandon looked down at him.

"Don't ever do that again. What were you thinking?" His reprimand lost some of its force from his position, but it didn't change the sentiment any.

"The bite. We couldn't wait."

Although he couldn't help but be warmed by Brandon putting himself in danger to protect him, they were going to discuss this later. Because he didn't want Brandon putting himself in danger for any reason.

"What happened here?" The imperious voice of Kyle Bennett reminded Oliver they weren't alone.

Brandon frowned. "I don't know. In theory it should have worked. In the middle of the portal, the device should have protected me. The destructive interference should have closed down the portal within minutes, but something changed. The frequency was wrong, and I got trapped."

"You sure you didn't set it wrong?" Luis glanced at Kyle. "I mean, you were, uh, under some stress."

"No, I'm sure I didn't." Brandon sounded lost instead of arrogant, and Oliver hated it.

"What about the sabotage?" Oliver asked.

"Sabotage?" Three voices echoed his word, but Oliver ignored them while he waited for Brandon to answer.

"How could they expect to kill you that way?" Brandon frowned down at him.

"Kill you? What the fuck?" Carmichael pushed his face close to Brandon's in a menacing manner.

"Carmichael, lay off."

"I'd like to know the answer to that too," Kyle said, "if someone is trying to kill my operatives."

Brandon became more bewildered, and his fingers snuck up to his ears as though he wondered if he was hearing correctly.

Oliver dragged him to his feet. Lying on the floor wasn't going to help convince anyone of anything. He kept his arms around Brandon because he didn't want to let him go. "Brandon thinks someone signed off on some projects on his behalf, without his knowledge. Which is why Carmichael and I ended up with prototype sonic charges on our last mission."

"Prototypes?" Kyle paced. "Why wasn't I informed of this?"

Oliver shrugged. He didn't want to admit he'd been afraid Brandon had done it to teach him a lesson because of their past. That assumption didn't reflect well on him at all, and had come from a dark, terrified place in his soul.

"Why would anyone think you'd put that thing on?" Luis waved a hand at the equipment, which looked a lot like the contraption Carmichael had had to endure.

"They wouldn't. I don't understand. Anyone who could tamper with it wouldn't assume I'd have you test it out." Brandon dropped a light kiss on his cheek, making him smile despite the topic of conversation.

Oliver shook his head. Someone needed to take care of his sexy, smart scientist, because he could so damned naive sometimes. "Has it occurred to you that whoever it is might be trying to discredit or get rid of *you*? Not necessarily trying to murder field agents."

Brandon pulled away, shocked. "Me? Why would anyone do that?"

Carmichael coughed and looked at his feet while Luis spoke up. "Well, you are kind of an asshole, Brain Trust. Er, sorry, Director Ellison."

A laugh, quickly smothered, escaped Oliver's lips while Kyle stood aside and observed.

Brandon sputtered before he began to laugh.

"Can we get this discussion back on track?" Kyle asked, completely unamused. "Who would have had access to both projects?"

"Oh shit. I looked for anyone who'd been attached to all of the affected projects and there wasn't a single suspect. But Greg would have had access to everything, even if he wasn't officially attached to a project. But I can hardly believe Greg would do that. So many people could have been killed."

"What, that pip-squeak at R&D who kept calling himself my handler?" Carmichael sneered. "He's the type who doesn't see people as people. They're pawns."

Brandon rubbed his temples. "His monitoring device worked perfectly. That was probably part of it. Make himself look good while my research and leadership were called into question."

Kyle pursed his lips. "That would also explain the email I got today from Senior Director Wong. It seems someone informed him that you'd been monitoring field reports you shouldn't have access to."

A furious flush lit up Brandon's face, even in the basement's dim light.

Field reports, eh? "Been keeping track of me?" Oliver asked, pleased beyond measure when Brandon's face somehow got even redder.

"Bennett also informed me that you do not have physical clearance for field duty, Director." Kyle's tone was unamused.

"Physical clearance?" Carmichael inspected Brandon from head to toe.

Clearing his throat, Brandon tucked his hair behind his ears, exposing his hearing aids. Pride welled up in Oliver's chest. His man had to feel so naked and vulnerable doing that, more so than if he'd stripped naked in front of all of them.

"I had no fucking clue." Carmichael shook his head, and Brandon smiled at him.

"Cardoso, you were senior agent out in the field." Kyle pinned him with a look usually reserved for interrogating people. "What's your take on this?"

After a quick glance at Brandon, who'd risked his life to save him, Oliver replied. "Director Ellison thought something wasn't right and decided to investigate. He was one of us, once. I think you need to look into Greg's background. Director Ellison was a valuable asset on this mission."

"Make sure you put that in your report." Kyle's words were slightly distracted as he typed a message into his phone. "And, Director Ellison?"

"Yes?"

"No more fieldwork, got it? That's direct from Senior Director Wong."

Brandon didn't look happy, but he nodded and let Oliver lead him toward the door.

Kyle's phone buzzed, and he checked the message. "I'm glad you called us in. There were twelve Umbrae, three of whom went on a rampage when the portal closed. Without the extra agents here, there would have been a lot of unnecessary fatalities."

---

THEY EXITED the building into chaos. The cacophony was overwhelming, and to Brandon's complete embarrassment, he only felt safe while glued to Oliver's side.

Agents and first responders knotted in clumps around the injured, people were crying, and sirens were blasting. He glanced around, wondering if someone needed his help, although in his current state he might do more harm than good.

"No, you're not going anywhere. You're staying right where I can keep an eye on you." Oliver grabbed his wrist, and Brandon gladly obeyed. This time.

They stood for several minutes in the driveway, surveying the aftermath.

"We've got a plane leaving in three hours. There will be room for you all." Kyle spoke without raising his gaze from his phone.

Three hours. Brandon wasn't sure he could stay upright for three more *minutes*.

Oliver pulled him aside. "Let's get our stuff together. Kyle's got everything covered out here."

Brandon nodded, and they retreated back inside the building, pausing in the foyer, where Brandon breathed a sigh of relief. Before they reached the elevator, Oliver hugged him, and Brandon sagged into his embrace.

"Don't ever scare me like that again. I thought I'd lost you. Again." Oliver spoke into his hair, but Brandon had no trouble hearing him.

No, he had no intention of getting himself involved in another mission. His fieldwork days were done.

Oliver kissed his forehead, then drew back to stare into his eyes. "You're it for me, you know that?"

If Oliver felt the same way Brandon did, then yes, he did know that. Oliver was it for him too.

"I want us to try again. A real relationship, just you and me."

His breath hitched. He was afraid if he tried to answer, he'd start crying. He'd already embarrassed himself enough for one day.

Oliver looked heavenward. "I'm really sorry about earlier. I lost my temper, and I'm so sorry."

Brandon stretched his neck and dropped a light kiss on Oliver's lips. "It's okay. I understand. We both hurt each other, but starting again means communicating better than we did before. I need to open up to you, and I will. I want this to work."

"Really? You're going to be mine?" Oliver's gaze roved over his face as though looking for signs of lies.

"You're it for me too. Always have been."

Oliver smiled and cupped his neck in a prelude to a kiss. Something warm and sticky on his cheek distracted him, and he pulled away from Oliver's embrace. Blood had seeped through the rough field dressing Carmichael had fashioned around Oliver's forearm.

"And as my first job as your boyfriend, I'm ordering you to go out there and get an EMT to look at that arm."

"But—"

"No buts. I'm perfectly capable of packing up our stuff." Even if he was going to take a short rest on the couch. "Am I going to have to march you out there?"

He walked with Oliver to the entrance, and once Oliver was under the care of a medical professional, he turned back toward the elevators.

"Director Ellison!"

The shout made Brandon whip around. "Greg? What are you doing here?"

The normally placid scientist screwed his face up in a scowl as he pulled out a laser pistol.

Why the fuck hadn't Brandon thought to arm himself again? He was completely defenseless. And alone. With all the crowds of people outside, somehow, he and Greg were the only people in the foyer.

"You came out on top. Again. You've got some sort of fucking charmed life, and you took the job I've been working towards for years. Who the hell are you to take that away from me? You're a nobody." Greg's pistol waved erratically as his words got louder and wilder.

"You did all this because you didn't get promoted?" Brandon was incredulous.

Considering Greg's face got redder and he took a couple of steps closer, perhaps Brandon could have made his words a little more conciliatory. But he could barely believe the man had almost killed people over a *promotion*.

A cool breeze preceded the appearance of Carmichael, who'd slipped quietly through the front door to stand directly behind Greg, who didn't notice. He'd never have passed the field agent exams.

"Drop your weapon," Carmichael said in a scary cop voice.

Greg snarled and steadied his arm, aiming his pistol at Brandon's head.

Was it the few days he'd spent in the field with Carmichael? Brandon sensed the exact moment Carmichael intended to fire, and he dived to the side as both weapons discharged.

Greg screamed and writhed on the cracked linoleum floor, clutching his shoulder. Brandon scrambled to his feet and kicked the laser pistol away while Carmichael moved in, keeping his gun trained on Greg. Blood welled from a hole in Greg's shoulder.

Oliver, Luis, and Kyle sprinted into the building, white gauze dangling from Oliver's unfinished bandage. Brandon let Oliver grab him in an almost too-tight grip and tried not to wince. He'd landed poorly. Hopefully he hadn't broken any bones.

Kyle glowered over Greg. "There you are, Wilson. I was looking for you. Senior Director Wong would like a word with you when we get back to headquarters." Glaciers had nothing on the icy tone of Kyle's voice. He looked up. "Director Ellison, are you okay?"

Brandon nodded, a few tremors shaking his body as reaction set in.

Carmichael and Luis muscled Greg to his feet and hustled him out the door. Greg was not going to have a happy life from here on out.

"I thought I told you not to scare me again." The scolding might have carried more weight if Oliver hadn't been dropping kisses on every bit of Brandon within reach.

"Should we try that again?" He didn't want Oliver to think he couldn't function on his own. "After all, you still need someone to finish up your bandage."

"No fucking way. You're coming with me, and then we'll both go up to pack. Bad things happen when you're not near me."

He wasn't going to argue. Because near Oliver? Good things happened.

# FIFTEEN

"Okay, get some sleep." Luis pulled up in front of Brandon's apartment and threw the car into park.

The building had never looked less inviting. But then, Brandon hadn't cared about appearances when he'd signed the lease. It had been clean, safe, and close to work. That had been the sum of his requirements.

He clambered gingerly out of the car's backseat, trying not to jostle his arm. He hadn't broken any bones, but he'd sprained his wrist and had far more bruises and cuts than he'd realized until the EMTs had started working on him.

Moving even slower than Brandon, Oliver got out of the passenger seat. He'd been injured worse, but thankfully nothing serious enough to require a hospital stay. But neither of them had been in any shape to drive themselves anywhere. There'd be time enough later to pick up their cars. No rush, since Director Kyle had instructed them to take a few days off to recuperate.

Tying up all the loose ends had taken hours upon excruciating hours, and then the flight home had been filled with so many MIA agents, there hadn't been opportunity to either sleep or talk about how they were going to go forward. Brandon was almost certain they'd plunged back into a relationship, but they needed to communicate more clearly this time than the last time they'd been together.

"Are you sure about this?" Brandon stared at the apartment building. Part of him wanted to go right to Oliver's cozy little bungalow. But if they weren't on the same page, weren't planning to be together, he didn't want to taint the few sweet memories he'd had there. If Oliver broke his heart here, and the memories became too much, Brandon would just up and move again.

"Oh, for fuck's sake. Get the hell up there and work your shit out before you come back to work." Luis reached across the car's interior to pull shut the passenger door, then squealed out of the parking lot.

Brandon's lip twitched. "I guess he told us."

Oliver smiled back. "He sure did. I'm going to have to grovel later, because wow, that might the worst mission I've ever taken a newbie on."

Heat flared in Brandon's cheeks, because he also owed both Luis and Carmichael apologies for his erratic and unprofessional behavior.

"But seriously, are you sure?"

"I'm sure I don't want to let you out of my sight." Oliver looked slightly abashed at stating his feelings so clearly. "I know we need to talk some more, and I want you to be comfortable while we do that. And if you're still okay with me crashing here tonight, we can head to my place tomorrow."

Although he wasn't sure how comfortable his apartment was, he could absolutely relate to the rest of Oliver's statement. After the intense, emotionally fraught closure of the portal and subsequent near murder by a colleague, Brandon hadn't had a chance to process everything and he wasn't about to do so without being able to see and touch Oliver. The past hours where Brandon had had to pretend everything was normal, pretend that he hadn't experienced a life changing moment, had worn him thin and if he couldn't have some peace and quiet with Oliver he was going to lose his shit.

"That sounds perfect." Brandon coughed. "Uh, not sure I'm up for anything acrobatic tonight." He wanted Oliver in his bed badly, but the second he was vertical, he was going to pass the fuck out.

Oliver laughed. "I'm awake through sheer force of will alone. We need to talk. I want to talk. But I'm not up for anything more energetic than pulling you close and hiding under the covers."

Brandon didn't exactly sag with relief but it was close. Nothing sounded better right now. Oliver moved close and wrapped his good arm around Brandon's waist.

"C'mon. Lead the way inside before I decide to fall asleep in the parking lot."

Brandon smirked.

In the elevator, Oliver wiggled his eyebrows suggestively and glanced at the floor. Despite his exhaustion, a tiny thrum of desire sparked through his veins.

Laughing, arms entwined, they stumbled out of the elevator. Joy fizzed in Brandon's veins like champagne, making him tipsy and happier than he could remember. For the first time, Brandon had a sense of the future. A good future with the man he never wanted to let go.

At his door, Brandon kept missing the lock because Oliver kept poking him in the side, just shy of tickling him. His attempt at a glare was ruined by a giggle, because he'd never seen Oliver look so relaxed and content, despite the bruises, bandages, and scrapes.

Finally, Oliver let him concentrate long enough to fit key to lock and he opened the door. They walked in, letting the door slam behind them and Brandon led Oliver to his living room. Where he stopped dead, and rocked back on his heels.

"Mother. What are you doing here?" Behind him, Oliver stiffened—and not in the good way—and took a step back. Although he was only imagining it, an Arctic chill swept through the room, destroying any remnant of Oliver's cozy warmth. His mother might be the absolute last person he wanted to see at this moment. He'd rather find a vicious werewolf or a slavering zombie lounging on his sofa. Not that his mother ever unbent enough to *lounge*.

"Your mother has a key to your apartment?" Oliver asked, with barely concealed horror.

"No, she does not. And so, I repeat, Mother, *what* are you doing here? And how did you get in?"

"Well, I certainly wasn't about to wait in the hallway and you weren't answering your phone."

A headache began to form, like a thousand burning needles in his brain. So many, many things wrong with that sentence, not the least of which was she hadn't answered his most pressing question.

"And you thought that justified, what, breaking into my apartment?"

"Don't be ridiculous, Brandon. I paid your landlord to let me in."

Oliver let out a strangled sound that was part cough, part gasp. Brandon knew exactly how he felt, but he'd have to take that particular outrage up with his landlord later. If he tried to remonstrate with his mother about it, she'd only stare at him like he was an idiot, because of course nothing mattered to her but her own wishes and desires.

"I've been working in an area with poor reception, so no, I haven't answered any personal calls, but I'm sure I didn't receive any from you." Unless the portal's energy had for once done a good thing and filtered all his mother's calls, instead of simply fritzing the signal.

"My assistant tried several times over the past couple of days. You really ought to answer your phone. How do you know it wasn't an emergency?"

The effort to suppress his eyeroll only aggravated his burgeoning headache. "When an unknown number calls multiple times without leaving a message, I'm going to assume it's a telemarketer, not an emergency."

The only reasonable assumption for anyone except his mother and, apparently, her assistant. Who must be new, since he definitely had Simon's number programmed in his phone and he hadn't bothered calling back whomever had tried calling him a dozen times. Because no one would.

Oliver cleared his throat, and Brandon shook himself. Again, his mother was dragging him into the weeds.

"Mother, what was so important you had to bribe my landlord, when you've not once come to my apartment?" In no small part because he'd never invited her, but then, that wouldn't stop her if she'd wanted to visit.

"You've got a date tonight and it's important for your father's campaign that you make a good impression on the woman. Her father is an important contributor."

"No, Mother. Absolutely not. I told you before I wouldn't be pimped out for the family." Brandon had to speak over Oliver's imitation of a fish suffocating out of water.

"Don't use such vulgar language. And you haven't got much time to get ready, so you'd best cleaned up." His mother stood up, her lip curling as she swept her gaze over his furniture, as though Brandon had plucked it directly from the garbage dump to install in his place.

Brandon sucked in a deep breath in an attempt to calm himself but in addition to the looming headache, the muscles in his jaw were as tight as suspension cables.

"I'm not doing it. Ever."

There was no point in reminding his mother he was gay. His mother had doggedly ignored that significant piece of information, but Brandon had no doubt she'd change her tune if this donor had had a gay son. The end justified whatever unpleasant means might be required.

She slipped her glasses on and frowned as she looked at Brandon's face.

"What have you been doing? You're a mess." Then her gaze slipped over to Oliver, as though she were seeing him for the first time and her frown morphed into a scowl and the tension thickened.

"What are you doing here? Is this your fault? Did you beat him up?"

Brandon was so surprised by the venom in his mother's voice, he had no idea how to respond. Especially since it was visibly obvious that Oliver was the more injured of the two of them.

"No, Mrs. Ellison, I did no such thing." Oliver's tone was so wintry it gave Brandon a chill but it broke his temporary silence.

"Mother, why would say such a thing?" But she didn't even glance at him.

"I see the threat of a restraining order wasn't enough. Do I need to call the police and follow through with an actual restraining order for you to leave him alone? Isn't it enough his previous association with you has made him defective?"

Oliver growled. "He's not defective."

Brandon stepped in front of him. He couldn't allow himself to enjoy Oliver's defense of him, not just yet. "What do you mean, you threatened him with a restraining order?" Brandon's own voice was cold enough to freeze lava. His mother was way the fuck out of line. Being overbearing and bitchy to him was one thing, but attacking Oliver was a whole different thing.

"It was obvious when you ended up in the hospital that associating with such riff raff was only going lead you down the wrong path. And when he came to pester me about where you had gone, well, that was outside of enough. I told him you didn't want to see him and I'd take out a restraining order if he didn't leave you alone." She shrugged with a nonchalant indifference that set Brandon's blood on fire.

"You. Did. What?"

Oliver had said something similar while they'd been fighting... was it only yesterday? The day before? Brandon hadn't clued in to what he'd meant, not completely, but it made sense now. Oliver had tried. Had kept trying to see him. Until it no longer made sense. And Oliver was nothing if not sensible. If a person said things like "no" and "I don't want to see/date/have sex with you" Oliver would accept without it becoming awkward or threatening. Anything else would have made him a creep or a stalker. Between Brandon and his mother, his decision had been clear, however much Brandon regretted his actions now, and his mother's questionable assistance.

Nevertheless, that still didn't give his mother the right to decide on his behalf. Especially not with threats.

"Oh, stop wasting time. You need to get cleaned up and dressed if you're going to make your date in time. She's from a very suitable family, like I said." His mother wrinkled her nose with the clear subtext that Oliver did not live up to her standards.

"No. I'm not going, and you're going to promise not to interfere in my life again. Who I associate with, who I date, is none of your concern."

"Of course, it's my concern. And your father's. Whomever you date will influence your father's campaign prospects."

Oliver sputtered behind him.

"In case you haven't noticed, Mother, I don't give a shit about Dad's campaign prospects. It has less than nothing to do with me. And I have a boyfriend, so there will be no dates with anyone but him."

At his words, Oliver stepped up beside him, presenting a united front. Brandon gently grabbed Oliver's hand, getting a smile in return.

"Oh, I don't think so," Brandon's mom sneered. "I'm serious about the restraining order. And I am definitely calling the police. It's obvious you've assaulted my son, and you have a history of abusing him."

Brandon wanted to throw up. His mother was twisting everything, all because she'd taken one look at Oliver and hated him on sight. It certainly had nothing to do with any sort of love or protective instincts. His parents didn't know what love was, and the only thing they were interested in protecting was their reputation and status. But he'd let her call the shots long enough. It was time to take control of his life. He was already on his way to doing so professionally, and now it was time to do the same with his personal life.

"You will do no such thing." He was almost certain MIA could straighten out any potential legal entanglement, but he wasn't going to let his mother drag Oliver into his family's dysfunction.

His mother pulled out her phone and Brandon snatched it away from her.

"I'm serious, Mother. You will apologize, and accept Oliver in my life, or you and Dad can stay the hell away from us. There are no other options I'm willing to entertain."

"Don't be ridiculous. I can make Oliver's life very difficult."

Brandon snorted. "You can, but you won't. Because otherwise I will, in return, make Dad's life very difficult."

"How could you possibly do that? We've already endured the embarrassment of your *situation*, and come out stronger than ever."

His cheeks heated. He had no idea if his mother referred to his hearing loss or his sexual orientation when she said "situation" but either way, he despised her attitude.

"Mrs. Ellison, you son has nothing to be ashamed of, and he's not an embarrassment." Oliver's tone was flinty and annoyed, and his mother acted as though he hadn't even spoken.

"Mother, I think you forget that I haven't been hard of hearing my whole life. I heard plenty of things I shouldn't have while growing up in your house. And I have absolutely no concerns about airing your dirty laundry nationwide if I have to. Because I don't give a shit about your money, your political ambitions, or your country club membership. And if you ever even think about threatening Oliver again, you'll find out just how much I know about Dad's past deals."

His mother paled as she snatched up her purse. Brandon handed her phone back, which she tossed into the designer bag with much less finesse than her norm. He'd rattled her, probably because she sensed every word he'd said was unvarnished truth.

"I hardly think threats are necessary, Brandon. We'll talk later, when you've calmed down."

Brandon let her go, but if the first words out of her mouth the next time they spoke wasn't a sincere apology, he was blocking her number and cutting ties. Something he should have done a long time ago.

As soon as she left, it was like an evil wind had departed, leaving only a trace of Chanel to mark its passage. Brandon sagged against Oliver in sheer relief.

"Did you just *blackmail* your mother? For me?"

"Yeah, I guess I did. But she definitely had it coming."

"I'm sorry you had to force the issue like this. I don't want to be responsible for coming between you and your family." Oliver hugged him gently.

"You don't understand. My family is nothing like yours. And my old therapist told me for years I needed to stand up to her. Probably wouldn't have recommended the blackmail bit, but my mother can be a steamroller, and I needed something to stop her in her tracks. Fortunately, my dad hasn't done anything illegal that I'm aware of, or I would have turned him in ages ago. But morally and ethically questionable? You bet. Even as a teen, I knew I might need leverage someday, and I've got proof stashed away if I ever need it. We've never been close. Narcissists don't tend to form close ties, even with their own children."

"Just know I'll do my best to get along with them. As long as they don't insult you, that is. Or try to make you date other people."

"Thank you, but I have a feeling we're going to be polite and distant from here on out."

Brandon glanced around his utilitarian apartment. He didn't want to stay here another minute.

"Think we can just grab some of my clothes and head over to your place? I know we were planning to crash here, but I'd really like to not be here right now."

Oliver kissed his nose. "I'd like that. I know we said we needed to talk, but the only thing I want to say is that I want to be with you. I think we can make this work. I want to make this work."

Brandon's eyes burned. So much time lost, but he'd learned some valuable, yet hard lessons. "I want that, too. More than anything in this world. And between the two of us, I think we can do anything we set our minds to."

Brandon pressed their lips together in a passionate kiss that sealed their promise.

After a few moments, Oliver lifted his head, eyes dark, skin flushed. "I really, really hate to say it, but I need some sleep before I call follow through on this."

"Oh, god, me too." Brandon's cock had started to stiffen, despite his exhaustion, but unfortunately, every other muscle in his body was also stiffening, but in a bad, bad way.

"Then let's grab what you need and get going. I'll arrange a car."

They couldn't get there fast enough for Brandon. Oliver's little bungalow was the definition of cozy and comfortable and he was going to sleep for a week. In between sex and eating.

# EPILOGUE

Oliver placed his hand on Brandon's lower back. A noisy bar made it difficult for Brandon to follow conversations, but Oliver wanted to show him off a bit. He intended to keep his promise to socialize more. Keeping to himself was a mistake. He truly liked the men he worked with, and he wanted them to like Brandon.

"It's okay. We'll stay for a drink or two, then leave."

"It's fine. I'll be fine." Brandon smiled, without much hesitation.

All his friends were already at the table except for Frazer. Oliver had Brandon sit between him and Luis. He still hadn't recovered from the scare of Brandon's near-death experience and he didn't want Brandon out of reach.

They introduced Brandon to Cooper and found out Frazer was going to be a little late. Oliver wanted Frazer to meet Brandon because his discussion with Frazer had opened his eyes. Frazer wanted him to be happy, and Oliver was—happier than he could ever remember.

The first thing Brandon did was tell everyone he might not be able to hear everything that was said. His friends were careful to make sure Brandon was fully included, and they both slowly relaxed. Oliver kicked himself for not opening up to them earlier.

"So, Brandon, I heard you released Carmichael from R&D so he could go back to being Oliver's partner." Adam gave Brandon a boyish smile and switched to a heat-filled one when he glanced at Carmichael. Cooper chuckled as Carmichael blushed.

"Congratulations, Carmichael," Luis said.

"Who's got Luis, then?" Adam asked.

Oliver leaned around Brandon to see Luis. "I never got a chance to tell you. The agency finally agreed that having two agents train newbies would be more effective. So, you're still with us."

Luis's grin was relieved. "Thanks, man."

"Well, that deserves a toast," Brandon said.

Frazer slipped into a seat. "Hello, boys. What did I miss?" He stiffened as he saw Luis.

"Hello, Frazer," Luis said.

"Goodson." Frazer puffed up like a porcupine. "I didn't know…" He trailed off, clearly unsure what to say. Under normal circumstances, Frazer would never have encountered the man who'd suspected him of being a serial killer and almost arrested him.

Oliver clapped Frazer on his shoulder. "Luis is a good guy. Give him a chance, will you?"

Frazer nodded. "Only because you're asking, and— Are you wearing jeans?" Oliver didn't think the shock in Frazer's voice was all that flattering, but he'd endured an unending stream of comments all day at the office. Perhaps his surprise was warranted.

Frazer craned his head around to stare at the only stranger at the table.

"This is Brandon. Um… I told you about him last time we went out."

"Last time… Oh, Brandon, I'm pleased to meet you, but judging from Oliver's smile and his new relaxed wardrobe, Rob will not be pleased."

"Rob? Who is Rob?" Brandon turned a glare on Oliver before

giving him a smile. "Actually, I don't care. I can live with Rob's disappointment."

Oliver held up his hands in surrender. "Frazer tried to set me up with a friend. Nice guy, but he's not you."

Frazer aww'd at him, and Brandon smiled before pushing his chair back.

"I'm just going to the bathroom. No trying to set up my man while I'm gone." He pointed a finger at Frazer, who laughed delightedly.

Oliver watched Brandon's ass, completely losing track of the conversation. He'd been waiting for just this moment. "I'll be back in a bit."

Frazer winked at Oliver as he stood to follow, but he ignored the tiny gesture and threaded his way through the crowd like Brandon had him on a leash. He stood outside the bathroom door and tapped out a quick message on his phone. Readjusting himself in his pants, he leaned against the wall, each second taking forever until Brandon reemerged.

"Oh, hey there, sailor." Brandon sidled up to him. "You want to..." He tilted his head toward the bathroom.

Yes, he did, but he had something a little different in mind.

"Come on, I have a surprise for you." Oliver grabbed his hand.

Brandon's eyebrows rose, but he allowed Oliver to lead him out the back door and past the trash cans.

"Dumpster diving? That's your big surprise?"

Oliver shook his head. A few tidbits Cooper had dropped about his first meeting with Frazer had given him an idea he hoped Brandon would like. Night had fully fallen, but it was still early enough that the lot at Bar None was half empty, making it perfect. As was the weather, which had cooperated with an evening better suited to September than early December.

He steered Brandon toward the SUV. "Are we leaving?" Brandon asked.

"Not exactly." Oliver leaned him up against the passenger door.

The windows were tinted, but not enough to completely obscure the sight of the parking lot on the other side of the car. Or other potential people, although none were currently visible. He placed his lips next to Brandon's ear and one hand on Brandon's groin.

Brandon's cock filled quickly, and Oliver licked his neck as a reward. "Can you hear me?"

He didn't want to shout, didn't want to draw too much attention, but he needed Brandon to hear him.

"Yes." A breathy gasp followed as Oliver squeezed Brandon's straining erection.

"Good. I know you think you're going to miss being a field agent. I think you're wrong." While he spoke, he unzipped Brandon's pants, pulling his erection out into the chill night air.

Brandon made a strangled sound as Oliver stroked his dick with cool hands. "What do you mean?"

"I don't think it's the fieldwork you miss." He eased Brandon's pants down, although his spread legs meant they stalled at midthigh.

"What are you doing?"

The question had to be rhetorical. Oliver nibbled at Brandon's earlobe, but there was no distress in his voice, and he made no move to either pull his pants up or move away.

"I know you like helping people, but your work in R&D helps many people, even if it's not immediate."

"Uh-huh." Brandon shifted his hips, pushing his erection through Oliver's fists.

Oliver needed to get this said because he didn't want to talk much longer. His own erection pressed against his fly, desperate to sink into Brandon's tight ass.

"I think what you miss most is the adrenaline rush. And I can give that to you."

"You can?" Brandon's voice faltered.

Oliver reluctantly let go of Brandon's dick but sucked on his neck to keep him occupied while Oliver prepared. He reached into his pocket for a condom and a pillow pack of lube. Within seconds he'd unzipped, rolled on the condom, and lubed up his fingers. He placed the partially empty pack on top of the SUV and placed his dry hand back on Brandon's dick. Precum slicked his fingers, and he gave Brandon a couple of strokes before he eased a lubed finger inside Brandon.

"I'm going to fuck you." He slid his finger in and out while Brandon grunted. "Out here in the open. I'm going to fuck you, and then you're going to come all over the side of my work vehicle."

Brandon sucked in a breath. "I wondered why you drove this tonight."

Oliver slid another finger inside, and Brandon moaned.

"That's it. Let anyone passing by know how good it is."

"You trying to get on the director's good side?"

"Why, will fucking you get me a promotion?" Oliver teased.

"You know," Brandon gasped out, "they have court-mandated sessions for people like you."

Oliver didn't have time to laugh as Brandon shoved his ass back. Oliver moaned a little himself. Without any other words, he prepared Brandon with single-minded intensity, then slicked his cock and pushed against Brandon's hole.

"Ready, love? People can look through the windows, you know, and see you getting fucked." A lie. He'd chosen his work vehicle on purpose for the dark tinting, but reality wasn't going to intrude on the fantasy. "They'll see how much you love it. You want it?"

Brandon didn't answer, just thrust himself on Oliver's cock.

"Fuck me," he demanded, moving his hips.

"That's it. Fuck yourself on my cock." Oliver slid all the way home and grasped Brandon's cock firmly.

Brandon spread his legs as far as he could and pressed his chest against the car.

"Can you see anyone? Anyone who might see you getting fucked?"

The moaning was almost nonstop. The illusion was spectacular.

The odds of anyone actually seeing what they were doing were slim. And yet they were fucking out in the open.

"You know, someone could get worried about us. Come out and check on us. They'd come out and see you getting reamed. If they come around this side, they'll see your bare ass. Your hard cock in my hand."

Brandon's breath sped up, and he moved with Oliver's thrusts.

"They're not even going to have to see you," Oliver said, panting between words. "Because there's no mistaking this sound."

Oliver moved even faster. The slap of flesh on flesh was the unmistakable sound of fucking.

"We've been gone a long time. When we go back in there, everyone's going to guess what we were doing."

Faster. Faster. Oliver's balls pulled up, and he wanted to come so bad. But he wanted to make Brandon lose his mind. He wanted Brandon to be happy, and if he was pining for fieldwork, he'd never be truly happy.

Brandon's moans were getting louder, precum slicking his cock.

"Every time you shift on those hard chairs inside, you'll be reminded of this."

So damn close. Brandon was almost whimpering, and Oliver didn't know how much longer he could hold out. Brandon enjoyed the thrill that came with the chance of getting caught, and Oliver loved how thoroughly he fell apart.

"Hey, Carmichael," Oliver called out to the completely empty parking lot. Brandon's ass squeezed tight as he spurted, and Oliver ground into him, his grasping heat pulling Oliver's orgasm out of him.

"Oh my God, Oliver." Brandon dropped his forehead against the car as Oliver pulled out. He tied off the condom with shaking fingers, chucked it into the bushes, and tucked himself away.

As Brandon pulled up his pants, he looked wildly around. "Oh my God, how am I going to face Carmichael now? He probably went back in to tell everyone." Brandon's blush was vivid even in the partial shadows they stood in.

Oliver laughed. "Carmichael wasn't out here."

Brandon's eyes narrowed. "Oh really."

Oliver couldn't stop grinning. The fear of getting caught really got Brandon off, and he was going to keep that little trick up his sleeve.

Brandon opened his mouth to say something, but was interrupted by his phone vibrating loudly.

"You should probably get that," Oliver said.

Brandon frowned. "What if it's work?"

"Hey, it's part of the job and always will be, even if you're not doing fieldwork."

Reluctantly Brandon pulled out his phone. He stared at it as though he couldn't quite understand what it said, then flicked a confused glance at Oliver. "We've only been back together a week."

Oliver shrugged. "Don't care. It's what I want, and I've wanted it for a very long time." After those first couple of nights with Brandon in his house, he never wanted Brandon to leave. When Brandon had returned to his own place, it had sucked more than Oliver could have imagined.

Brandon walked away, lost in thought, before he bent over his phone and tapped out a short message.

Oliver's own phone buzzed.

> To: Ellison, Brandon <B_Ellison@autopartsandpas-
> tries.com>
> From: Cardoso, Oliver <O_Cardoso@autopartsand-
> pastries.com>
> Subject: Question
> Director Ellison,
> I believe we should consider immediate cohabitation.
> I have a position in my bed that requires your
> presence on a nightly basis.
> Cardoso

*To: Cardoso, Oliver <O_Cardoso@autopartsandpas-*
  *tries.com>*
*From: Ellison, Brandon <B_Ellison@autopartsand-*
  *pastries.com>*
*Re: Question*
*Agent Cardoso,*
*Yes. But we're going to your mother's for Christmas.*
  *And then we're going on vacation somewhere*
  *warm where we can learn how to surf.*
*Sincerely,*
*Director Ellison*

OLIVER LAUGHED, and Brandon flew back into his arms. He'd never met anyone who suited him as well.

"Love you," Brandon whispered.

"I love you too." Oliver tucked a key into Brandon's pocket. "C'mon, let's go inside and recruit help to move your things to my place as soon as possible."

"Are we really going back in there?"

It was too dark to tell for sure, but he suspected Brandon was blushing.

"Of course, we are. I'm the oldest guy there. I want everyone to know I can still get a hottie to go out back with me."

Brandon laughed and kissed him. "Come on, then. Show me off for a bit, and then we'll go back home."

*Go back home.* Besides *I love you,* they were his new favorite words.

# ABOUT THE AUTHOR

KC Burn is a Canadian transplanted to California who writes happy-ever-afters about men loving men, whether they're psychics, space travelers, aliens, professors, construction workers, cops, amateur sleuths... you name it, she'll probably write it. She's got a pair of black cats, aka muses/nuisances, and a supportive, understanding hubby.

# ALSO BY KC BURN

**Contemporary**

Cop Out (Toronto Tales #1)

Cover Up (Toronto Tales #2)

Cast Off (Toronto Tales #3)

Tartan Candy (Fabric Hearts #1)

Plaid versus Paisley (Fabric Hearts #2)

Just Add Argyle (Fabric Hearts #3)

Banded Together

Tea or Consequences

Rainbow Blues

Pen Name - Doctor Chicken

First Time, Forever

Set Ablaze

**Sci-Fi**

Spice 'n' Solace (Galactic Alliance #1)

Alien 'n' Outlaw (Galactic Alliance #2)

Voodoo 'n' Vice (Galactic Alliance #3)

Union of the Snake

The Tithe

**Paranormal**

Wolfsbane (MIA Case Files #1)

Blood Relations (MIA Case Files #2)

Craving (MIA Case Files #3)

www.ingramcontent.com/pod-product-compliance
Lightning Source LLC
Chambersburg PA
CBHW031724170626
46808CB00005B/1883